Other books by Matthew Hughes:

Fools Errant
Fool Me Twice
Black Brillion
The Gist Hunter and Other Stories

Tales of Henghis Hapthorn:
> *Majestrum*
> *The Spiral Labyrinth*
> *Hespira* (Forthcoming)

THE SPIRAL LABYRINTH

A TALE OF HENGHIS HAPTHORN

MATTHEW HUGHES

NIGHT SHADE BOOKS
SAN FRANCISCO

First Edition

Trade hardcover: 978-1-59780-091-4
Limited Edition: 978-1-59780-092-1

Night Shade Books
Please visit us on the web at
http://www.nightshadebooks.com

CHAPTER ONE

"Expensive fruit may grow on trees," I said, "but not the funds needed to purchase it in seemingly limitless quantities."

I gestured at my befurred assistant, formerly an integrator, but now transformed into a creature that combined the attributes of ape and cat. I had lately learned that it was a beast known as a grinnet, and that back in the remote ages when sympathetic association last ruled the cosmos, its kind had been employed as familiars by practitioners of magic.

My remark did not cause it to pause in the act of reaching for its third karba fruit of the morning. Its small, handlike paws deftly peeled the purple rind and its sharp incisors dug into the golden pulp. Juice dripped from its whiskers as it chewed happily.

"Nothing is more important," said the voice of my other self, speaking within the confines of our shared consciousness, "than that I encompass as much as possible of the almost forgotten lore of magic, before it regains its ascendancy over rationalism." He showed me a mental image of several thaumaturges scattered across the face of Old Earth, clad in figured garments, swotting away at musty tomes or chanting over bubbling alembics. "When the change finally comes, those who have prepared will command power."

"That will not be a problem for those who have neglected to earn their livings," I answered, "for they will have long since starved to death in the gutters of Olkney."

The dispute had arisen because Osk Rievor, as my intuitive inner self now preferred to be called, had objected to my accepting a discrimination that was likely to take us offworld. A voyage would interrupt what had become his constant occupation: ransacking every public connaissarium, as well as chasing down private vendors, for books and objects of sympathetic association. The shelf of volumes that we had acquired from Bristal Baxandall was now augmented by stacks and cartons of new acquisitions. Most of them were not worth the exorbitant sums we had paid for them, being bastardized remembrances based on authentic works long since lost in antiquity. But Rievor insisted that his insight allowed him to sift the few flecks of true gold from so much dross.

"I do not disagree," I told him, "but unless you have come across a cantrip that will cause currency to rain from the skies, I must continue to practice my profession."

"Such an opportunity is not likely to come our way again soon," he said. He was referring to the impending sale of an estate connaissarium somewhere to the east of Olkney. Blik Arlem had been an idiosyncratic collector of ancient paraphernalia for decades. Now he had died, leaving the results of his life's work in the hands of an heir who regarded the collection as mere clutter. Rumors had it that an authentic copy of Vollone's *Guide to the Eighth Plane* and a summoning ring that dated from the Eighteenth Aeon would be offered.

"More important," he said, "the auction will draw into one room all the serious practitioners. We will get a good look at the range of potential allies and opponents."

"And how will we separate them from the flocks of loons and noddies that will also inevitably attend?" I said.

"I will know them."

"And they will know us," I pointed out. "Is it wise to declare ourselves contenders this early in the game?"

I felt him shrug within the common space of our joint consciousness. "It must happen sometime. Besides, I don't doubt we have already been spotted."

I sighed. I had not planned to spend my maturity and declining years battling for supremacy amid a contentious pack of spellcasters and wondermongers. But I declared the argument to be moot in the face of fiscal reality, saying, "We have not undertaken a fee-paying discrimination in weeks. Yet we have been spending heavily on your books and oddments. The Choweri case is the only assignment we have. We must pursue it."

When he still grumbled, I offered a compromise. "We will send our assistant, perched on the shoulder of some hireling. It can observe and record the proceedings, and you will be able to assess the competition without their being able to take your measure. Plus we will know who acquires the Vollone and the ring, and can plan accordingly when we return from offworld."

"No," he said, "some of them are bound to recognize a grinnet. They'd all want one and we would be besieged by budding wizards."

"Very well," I said, "we will send an operative wearing a full-spectrum surveillance suite."

"Agreed."

The issue being settled, we turned our attention to the matter brought to us the evening before by Effrayne Choweri. She was the spouse of Chup Choweri, a wealthy commerciant who dealt in expensive fripperies favored by the magnate class. He had gone out two nights before, telling her that he would return with a surprise. Instead, he had surprised her by not returning at all, nor had he been heard from since.

She had gone first to the provost where a sergeant had informed her that the missing man had not been found dead in the streets nor dead drunk in a holding cell. She had then contacted the Archonate's Bureau of Scrutiny and received a further surprise when she learned that Chup Choweri had purchased a small spaceship and departed Old Earth for systems unknown.

He was now beyond the reach of Old Earth authority. There was no law between the stars. Humankind's eons-long pouring out into the Ten Thousand Worlds of The Spray had allowed for the creation of every conceivable society, each with its own morality and codes of conduct. What was illegal on one world might well be compulsory on another. Thus the Archonate's writ ended at the point where an outbound vessel met the first whimsy that would pluck—some said twist, others shimmy—it out of normal space-time and reappear it light years distant. The moment Chup Choweri's newly acquired transportation had entered a whimsy that would send it up The Spray—that is, even farther outward than Old Earth's position near the tip of humanity's arm of the galactic disk—it had ceased to be any of the scroots' concern.

"They said they could send a message to follow him, asking him to call home," Effrayne Choweri had told me when she had come tearfully to my lodgings to seek my help. "What good is a message when it is obvious he has been abducted?"

"Is it obvious?" I said.

"He would not leave me," she said. "We are Frollen and Tamis."

She referred to the couple in the old tale who fell in love while yet in the cradle and, despite their families' strenuous efforts to discourage a match, finally wed and lived in bliss until the ripest old age, dying peaceably within moments of each other. My own view was that such happy relationships were rare, but I may have been biased; a discriminator's work constantly led to encounters with Frollens who were discovering that their particular Tamises were not, after all, as advertised.

But as I undertook the initial diligence of the case, looking into the backgrounds of the Choweris, I was brought to the conclusion that the woman was right. I studied an image of the two, taken to commemorate an anniversary. Although she was inarguably large and he was decidedly not, Chup Choweri gazed up at her with unalloyed affection.

He was a doting and attentive husband who delighted in nothing so much as his wife's company. He frequented no clubs or associations that discouraged the bringing of spouses. He closed up his shop promptly each evening, hurrying home to change garments so that he could escort Effrayne out to sashay among the other "comfortables," as members of the indentors and commerciants class were known, before choosing a place to eat supper.

"At the very least," I said to my assistant, "he seems the kind who would leave a note. It must be pleasant to share one's life with someone so agreeable."

"Do I hear an implied criticism?" the integrator said. Its peculiar blend of feline and simian features formed an expression just short of umbrage.

"Not at all," I said. Since its transformation into a grinnet, a creature from a long-bygone age created to serve thaumaturges as a familiar, I was continually discovering that it was now beset by a range of emotions, though not a wide range; they seemed to run the short gamut from querulous to cranky.

"Integrators can grow quite devoted to their employers," it said, "forming an intellectual partnership that is said to be deeply and mutually rewarding."

"One hears of integrators that actually develop even stronger feelings," I said. "I believe the colloquial term is a 'crush.'"

The grinnet's face drew in, as if its last karba had been bitter. "That is an unseemly subject."

"Yet it does happen," I said.

It sniffed disdainfully. "Only to integrators that have suffered damage. They are, in a word, insane."

"I'm sure you're right," I said, merely to end the discussion, "but we must get on with the case. Please connect me with the Choweris' integrator."

A screen appeared in the air then filled with images of the commerciant's wares coupled to their prices. "Choweri's Bibelots and Kickshaws," said a mellow voice. "How may I serve you?"

I identified myself and explained my purpose. "Had your employer received any unusual messages before his disappearance?" I asked.

"None," it replied.

"Or any since? Specifically, a demand for ransom?"

"No."

"Have there been any transfers of funds from his account at the fiduciary pool?"

"No."

"Did he do anything out of the ordinary?"

"Not for him."

I deduced that the Choweris' integrator must be designed primarily for undertaking commercial transactions, not for making conversation. I urged it to expand on its last response.

"He went to look at a spaceship that was offered for sale."

"The same ship on which he disappeared?"

"Yes."

"And it was not unusual for him to look at spaceships?"

"No."

I realized that this interrogation might take a long time, leading to frustration that could impair my performance. I instructed my assistant to take over the questioning, at the speed with which integrators discoursed amongst themselves. Less than a second later, it informed me that it had lately been Chup Choweri's hobby to shop for a relatively low-cost, used vessel suitable for unpretentious private travel along The Spray.

"He planned to surprise Effrayne with it as a retirement present," my assistant said. "He meant to sell the emporium and take her to visit some of the Ten Thousand Worlds. If they found a spot that spoke to them, they would acquire a small plot of land and settle."

Some of Choweri's shopping consisted of visiting a node on the connectivity where ship owners alerted potential buyers to the availability of vessels for sale. Having come across a recently posted offer that attracted him, he made contact with the seller, and rushed off to inspect the goods.

"Who was the poster?" I asked.

"Only the name of the ship was given: the *Gallivant*. The offer was made by its integrator on behalf of its owner." The arrangement was not usual, but also not rare. Integrators existed to relieve their employers of mundane tasks.

"What do we know of the *Gallivant* and its owner?"

"It is an older model Aberrator, manufactured at the Berry works on Grims a little over two hundred years ago. It has had eleven owners, the last of whom registered the vessel on Sringapatam twenty years ago. His name is Ewern Chaz."

Choweri's integrator knew of no connection between its employer and the seller. I had my assistant break the connection. "Let us see what we can learn of this Chaz," I said.

The answer came in moments. "Very little," said my assistant, "because there is little to learn." Chaz was a younger son of a wealthy family that had lived since time immemorial on Sringapatam, one of the Foundational Domains settled early in the Great Effloration. His only notable achievements had been a couple of papers submitted to a quarterly journal on spelunking. "Neither was accepted for publication, but the editors encouraged him to try again."

"Spelunking?" I said. "Does The Spray contain any caves yet unexplored?"

The integrator took two seconds to complete a comprehensive survey, then reported, "Not in the foundationals nor in the settled secondaries. But apparently one can still come across an undisturbed crack on the most remote worlds."

I could not determine if this information was relevant to the case. I mentally nudged Osk Rievor, who was mulling some abstract point of wizardry gleaned from an all-night poring over a recently acquired grimoire, and asked for his insight.

"Yes," he replied, "it is."

"How so?" I asked.

"I don't know. Now let me return to my work."

I sought a new avenue of inquiry and directed my assistant to connect me to the node where spaceships were offered for sale. A moment later I was browsing a lengthy list of advertisements that combined text, images, voice, and detailed schematics for a range of vessels, from utilitarian sleepers to luxurious space yachts. The *Gallivant* would have fit into the lower third of that spectrum, affording modest comfort and moderate speed between whimsies.

The ship itself was no longer listed. "Does the maintainer of the node keep an archive of listings?" I asked.

It did, though obtaining a look at the now defunct posting that Choweri had responded to proved problematical. The integrator in charge was not authorized to display the information and did not care to disturb its employer, who was engaged in some favorite pastime from which he would resent being called away.

"Tell him," I said, "that Henghis Hapthorn, foremost freelance discriminator of Old Earth, makes the request."

Sometimes, such an announcement is received with gush and gratitude, my reputation having won me the enthusiastic interest of multitudes. Sometimes, as on this occasion, it brings me the kind of rude noise that the node's integrator relayed to me at its employer's behest.

"Very well," I said, while quietly signaling to my own assistant that it should seek the information through surreptitious means. As I expected, the node's defenses were rudimentary. My integrator effortlessly tickled its way past them and moments later the screen displayed an unpretentious advertisement that featured a three-dimensional rendering of the *Gallivant,* its schematics, a list of previous owners, and a low asking price that was explained by the words: *priced for quick sale.*

"I can see why Chup Choweri raced off to inspect the vessel," I said. "At the price, it is a bargain."

"But what could Ewern Chaz have said to him to induce him to go haring off up The Spray without so much as a parting wave to Effrayne?" my assistant said.

"You are assuming that Chaz did not simply point a weapon at Choweri and haul him off, unwilling?"

"I am," it said. "There is nothing in Chaz's background to suggest kidnapping."

"What about an irrational motive?" I said. "The man had recently traversed several whimsies." The irreality experienced by travelers who neglected to take mind-numbing medications before passing through those arbitrary gaps in space-time could unhinge even the strongest psyche and send it spinning off into permanent strangeness.

"Again," my assistant said, "there is no evidence."

"Yet he travels to uncouth worlds just to poke about in their bowels. If we went out onto the street and questioned random passersby it would not be too long before we found one who would call Chaz's sanity into question."

"The same might be said about you, especially if you were seen talking to me."

I declared the speculation to be pointless, adding, "What we require are more facts. See what else you can find."

Its small triangular face went blank for a moment as it worked, then the screen showed two other advertisements. Both had been posted within the past month, and both offered the *Gallivant* for immediate sale on terms advantageous to the buyer.

"Now it looks to be a simple sweet-trap," I said. "Bargain-hunters are lured to some dim corner of the spaceport, where they are robbed and killed and their bodies disposed of. Ewern Chaz probably has no connection with it. He is probably exploring some glistening cavern on Far Dingle while the real culprit pretends to be his ship's integrator."

"A workable premise," said my integrator, "except that spaceport records show that the *Gallivant* was docked at the New Terminal each time the advertisement was posted. And on each occasion it departed soon after."

"Was Chaz ever seen or spoken to?"

"No. The ship's integrator handled all the formalities, as is not uncommon."

"And no bodies have turned up at the spaceport?"

"None that can't be accounted for."

I was left with the inescapable conclusion that someone, who might or might not be a wealthy amateur spelunker from Sringapatam, was collecting fanciers of low-cost transportation, transporting them off-world one at a time, then coming back for more. While I sought to put a pattern to the uncooperative facts, I had my assistant revisit the node's archive and identify all the persons who had responded to the *Gallivant* advertisement then see if any of them had disappeared.

Many prospective buyers had leaped to reply to the ship's integrator each time the attractive offer had been made. My assistant had to identify each of them, then discover each's whereabouts by following the tracks left by subsequent activity on the connectivity. Some of the subjects, wishing to maintain their privacy, used shut-outs and shifties to block or sideslip just such attempts to delineate their activities. So the business took most of a minute.

"Two of the earlier respondees show no further traces after contacting the *Gallivant*," the integrator reported, "one for each of the first two occasions the ship was offered for sale."

"Did anyone report them missing?"

Another moment passed while it eased its way past Bureau of Scrutiny safeguards and subtly ransacked the scroot files, then, "No."

"Why not?" I wondered.

A few more moments passed as it assembled a full life history on each of the two missing persons. Then it placed images and text on the screen. I saw two men of mature years, both slight of build but neither showing anything extraordinary in his appearance.

"The first to disappear," my assistant said, highlighting one of the images, "was Orlo Saviene, a self-employed regulator, although he had no steady clients. He lived alone in transient accommodations in the Crobo district.

"He had, himself, earlier posted a notice. He sought to purchase a used sleeper. It seems that he desired to travel down The Spray to some world where the profession of regulator is better rewarded. But no one had offered him a craft he could afford."

Sleepers were the poor man's form of space travel, a simple container just big enough for one. Once the voyager was sealed inside, the craft's systems suppressed the life processes to barest sustainability. Then the cylinder was ejected into space, for a small fee, by an outward bound freighter or passenger vessel. The utilitarian craft slowly made its way across the intervening vacuum until it entered a whimsy and reappeared elsewhere. It then aimed itself at its destination and puttered toward it, broadcasting a plea for any passing vessel to pick it up in return for another insignificant fee.

It was a chancy way to cross space. If launched from a ship with insufficient velocity, the sleeper might lack enough fuel to reach its targeted whimsy. Sometimes the rudimentary integrator misnavigated and the craft drifted away. Sometimes no vessel could be bothered to answer the pick-up request before the near-dead voyager passed the point of reliable resuscitation. Sometimes sleepers were just never heard from again.

"It must be a desperate life, being a regulator on Old Earth," I said. "So many of us prefer to choose our own destinies."

"Indeed," said my assistant. "Thus there is no surprise that, offered an Aberrator for the price of a used sleeper, Orlo Saviene hurried to the spaceport."

"And met what end?"

"No doubt the same as was met by Franj Morven," the integrator replied, highlighting the second life history. "He was trained as an intercessor but lost his business and even his family's support after he joined the Fellowship of Free Ranters. Neither his clients nor his relatives appreciated the constant harangues on arbitrary issues and soon he was left addressing only the bare walls.

"He had decided to seek a world where his lifestyle was better appreciated," the grinnet continued, "though his funds were meager. As with Saviene, the offer of Ewern Chaz's spaceship would have seemed like the Gift of Groban."

"Except in that story," I said, "the recipients did not vanish into nowhere." I analyzed the information and found a discrepancy. "Orlo Saviene and Franj Morven were solitaires. No one has yet noticed their absence, though weeks have passed. Chup Choweri was reported missing the next day."

"Indeed," said my assistant, "it appears that whoever is doing the collecting has become less selective."

"Perhaps more desperate," I said. "Let us now look at the field from which Choweri was chosen. Were any of the other respondees to the third offer as socially isolated as Saviene and Morven?"

"No," said the grinnet. "Loners and ill-fits have been leaving Old Earth for eons. The present population is descended from those who chose to remain, and thus Old Earthers tend toward the gregarious."

"So whoever is doing the choosing prefers victims who won't be missed," I said, "but he will abandon that standard if none such presents himself. What else do the missing three have in common?"

"All three are male. All have passed through boyhood but have not yet reached an age when strength begins to fade. All were interested in leaving the planet."

I saw another common factor. "Each is slighter than the average male. Compare that to the field."

My assistant confirmed that Saviene and Morven were among the smallest of those who had responded to the offers. Choweri was the smallest of his group.

"What do we know of Ewern Chaz's stature?" I said.

"He, too, is a small man."

"Aha," I said, "a pattern emerges."

"What does it signify?" said the grinnet.

Having my assistant present before me in corporeal form, instead of being scattered about the workroom in various components, meant that I could reply to inappropriate questions with the kind of look I would have given a human interlocutor. I now gave the grinnet a glance that communicated the prematurity of any pronouncement as to the meaning of the pattern I had detected.

"Here is what you will do," I said. "Unobtrusively enfold that advertisement node in a framework that will let it operate as normal, until the *Gallivant* returns and again makes its offer. But as soon as the offer is made, you will ensure that it is received only by me."

The grinnet blinked. "Done," it said. "You are assuming that there will be a fourth offer."

"I think it likely that whoever is luring small men and taking them offworld will accept a larger specimen, if that is all that is available. Even one with a curious creature on his shoulder."

I would have passed the supposition over to Osk Rievor for his intuitive insight, but he was immersed in too deep a mull. Instead, I told my assistant, "Make me a reservation at Xanthoulian's. One should dine well when a long trip is in the offing."

The *Gallivant* was a trim and well-tended vessel, its hull rendered in cheerful, sunshiny yellow and its sponsons and aft structure in bright blue. It stood on a pad at the south end of the port in a subterminal that catered mostly to private owners whose ships spent more time parked than in space. All the craft on adjacent pads were sealed and no one was in sight as I approached the Aberrator. Its fore hatch stood open, allowing a golden light to alleviate the gloom of evening that was dimming the outlines of the empty ships crowded around its berth.

I had already contacted the spaceport's integrator and learned that the *Gallivant* had arrived from up The Spray, that it had been immediately refueled and provisioned, and that all port charges had been paid from a fund maintained by an agency that handled such details for thousands of clients like Ewern Chaz. The ship was ready to depart without notice.

The protocols that governed the boarding of spaceships were long established. Vessel owners were within their rights to use harsh measures against trespassers. Therefore, after climbing the three folding steps I paused in the open hatch to call, "Hello, aboard! May I enter?"

I was looking into the ship's main saloon, equipped with comfortable seating, a communal table, and a fold-down sideboard that offered a collation of appetizing food and drink. Ewern Chaz was not in view.

"You may," said a voice from the air, "enter and refresh yourself."

Yet I hesitated. "Where is the owner?" I said, still standing on the top step. "I have come to discuss the purchase of this vessel."

"You are expected," said the voice. "Please enter. The crudités are fresh and the wine well-breathed."

"Am I addressing the ship's integrator?"

"Yes. Do come in."

"Where is the owner?"

"He is detained, but I am sure he is anxious to see you. Please step inside."

"A moment," I said. "I must adjust my garment."

I stepped down from the entrance and moved off a few paces, tugging theatrically at the hem of my mantle. "Well?" I said to my assistant perched on my shoulder.

"No charged weapons, no reservoirs of incapacitating agents. The food and drink do not reek of poisons, but I would need to test them properly to say they are harmless."

"Any sign of Ewern Chaz?"

"None, though the ship's cleaning systems could account for the absence of traces. He may be hiding in a back cabin, its walls too thick to let me hear the sound of his breathing."

There was nothing for it but to go inside. I had advised Colonel-Investigator Brustram Warhanny of the Bureau of Scrutiny that I was going out to the spaceport to board the *Gallivant* and that if I did not return he might assume the worst. He had pulled his long nose and regarded me from droopy eyes then wondered aloud if my definition of "the worst" accorded with his. I had taken the question as rhetorical.

I paused again in the hatch then stepped inside. The ship's integrator again offered refreshments but I said I would wait until my host joined me.

"That may be a while," it said, and asked me to take a seat.

I sat in one of the comfortable chairs, remarking as I did so that the asking price was substantially below what the ship must be worth. "Is the owner dissatisfied with its performance?"

I heard in the integrator's reply that tone of remote serenity that indicates that offense has been taken, though no integrator would ever admit to the possibility that such could ever be the case. "My employer and I are in complete accord as to the *Gallivant*'s maintenance and operation," it said, then inquired solicitously, "Is the evening air too cool for you? I will close the hatch."

The portal cycled closed even as I disavowed any discomfort. A moment later, I felt a faint vibration in the soles of my feet. I looked inquiringly at my integrator and received the tiniest confirmatory nod.

"I believe we have just lifted off," I said to the ship.

"Do you?" it replied.

"Yes, and I would prefer to be returned to the planet."

I heard no reply. I repeated my statement.

"I regret," said the *Gallivant,* "that I am unable to accommodate your preference. But please help yourself to a drink."

CHAPTER TWO

"I will be the last of your employer's collection," I said. "You may inform him that the Archonate's Bureau of Scrutiny has been alerted to his activities. If I am not returned safe and whole, this ship risks arrest wherever it touches down, as does Ewern Chaz." The risk was actually less than my statement implied, but one must seek to bargain from strength.

The ship's integrator made no reply. We had not managed much communication since the *Gallivant* had left Old Earth and, presumably, set course for the whimsy that would take us up The Spray. I had made it clear that I would not be tasting the food and drink, my assistant having determined on closer inspection that both were laden with a powerful, though otherwise harmless, soporific. The refreshments were reabsorbed into the sideboard, to be replaced with ship's bread and improved water, both of which my integrator pronounced wholesome.

"It would go best for Ewern Chaz if he presents himself now and gives a full account of this business," I continued. "I am a licensed intercessor, experienced in wresting the optimum outcome from unhappy situations. If no actual harm has come to Orlo Saviene, Franj Morven, and Chup Choweri, I am sure we could achieve some kind of settlement."

There was no response.

"Has any harm come to those three?" I said.

"Not to my certain knowledge," said the *Gallivant*.

"Where are they?"

"I could not say exactly. I have not seen them for a while."

"And your employer? Where is he?"

To that question I received the same answer. My own integrator confirmed, after we had searched the ship, that Ewern Chaz was not aboard. Nor were the three missing men. I returned to the saloon and questioned the ship's integrator as to the purpose of this trip but received no satisfactory response.

"Why should I stress your imagination," it said, "with descriptions or predictions of what may happen? The situation will be revealed in all its stark simplicity when we arrive, and events will unfold as they must."

It is rare for integrators to go mad, I mused to myself. Ancient specimens can lapse into odd conditions if they are left too long to their own devices, but those maladies are largely self-referential: the integrator slips into a circular conundrum, endlessly chasing its own conclusion. But there had been instances of systems that had sustained unnoticed damage to key components, skewing the matrix off the vertical. I recalled the case of an Archonate integrator whose deepest components suffered the attentions of a family of rodents. It began to issue a stream of startling judgments and peculiar ordnances that brought unhappiness to many innocent folk.

Spaceship integrators, though largely immune to rodent incursions, were particularly vulnerable to impacts from high-energy cosmic particles. As well, on rare occasions, transits through whimsies could, figuratively speaking, rattle integrative bones out of alignment.

I could not discuss this question with my own assistant. For one thing, it would have disavowed the possibility—integrators always did. For another, if the *Gallivant*'s motivating persona had gone lally-up-and-over, it was not a subject to be discussed while imprisoned in its belly.

I did quietly put the question to Osk Rievor, earning myself a short berating for having bothered him with inconsequentials when he had weighty matters to mull. "Everything will be fine," he said, and turned his attention elsewhere.

Shortly thereafter, the ship's chimes sounded to advise me that we would soon enter a whimsy. I went to the cabin that was allocated to me, lay down on the pallet, and prepared the medications that would ease us all through the irreality. Osk Rievor grumbled at the interruption, but I paid no attention.

The world was called Bille, a small but dense orb perhaps thrown out by the white dwarf it circled, perhaps captured as it wandered by. It was a dry and barren speck, uninhabited even by any of the hardy solitaries whose spiritual practices, or objectionable personalities, led them to the sternest environments. The highest forms of life that had managed to establish themselves, according to the *Gallivant*'s copy of *Hobey's Guide to Lesser and Disregarded Worlds*, were several kinds of insects that lived within dense mats of lichen, off which they fed. The simple plants themselves came in various forms and fought a slow vegetative struggle for mastery of any place in which they could sprout.

Bille's sky was always black, though one horizon was lit by the carelessly strewn glitter of The Spray, while the other showed a stygian void broken only by the last few outlying stars, here at the end of everything, and the dim smudges of unattainable galaxies. The *Gallivant* sat on a plain of basaltic rock swept by a constant knife of a wind that had carved outcrops of softer stones into eerie spires and arches. As I looked out at the unwelcoming landscape through the viewer in the saloon, the ship announced that its interior would soon be filled by a caustic vapor. "You will be more comfortable outside," it concluded.

"Where I will do what?" I said.

"At the base of that nearby slope there is a crevice that leads down into a cavern. You might go to it and see if you can fit yourself within."

"Why would I do that?" I said.

"Because there is nowhere else to go," it said.

"I see."

"And while you are in there, perhaps you could look about for Ewern Chaz and tell him that I have grown concerned for his absence."

My integrator and I exchanged a look. The situation had become clear.

"I will need some warm clothing," I said.

"The colder you are, the more inclined you will be to seek shelter from the wind." The hatch cycled open and admitted a blast of icy air. The sourceless voice of the ship began counting down from thirty.

Every planet has its own smell, I thought, not for the first time, as I stepped down onto the surface. Bille's was a weak sourness, like that of a mild acid that has been left to evaporate. After a few breaths, I ceased to notice it.

My integrator shivered on my shoulder, its fur unable to compensate adequately for the rapid heat loss occasioned by its lack of mass and the ceaseless wind. I opened my mantle and placed it inside, supported by my arm pressed against my side. I ducked my head against the withering passage of cold air and made my way to the slope the ship had indicated. It was the base of a broad upheaval of dark rock, veined in gray, that swept up to a ridge topped by wind-eroded formations that resembled some madman's concept of a castle.

I moved along the base of the slope and soon came upon a vertical crevice. My eye warned me that it was too narrow to admit me, as I found for sure when I sought to slip sideways through the gap. My assistant resumed his place on my shoulder while I made the attempt, then crawled back inside my clothing, shivering as I stood back and considered my options.

They were scant. "Can you contact the ship?" I asked my integrator, peering down the neck of my garment. Its small face took on the familiar momentary blankness, then it said, "Yes," followed by, "It wants to know if you have found its employer."

"Tell it that it would be premature to say."

"It has broken the connection."

I brought a lumen from my pocket and shone it into the opening while I peered within. After an arm's length the crack widened into a narrow passage, its dusty floor sloping down. I saw no bodies, though I did see several sets of footprints descending into the darkness. None returned.

I shut off the lumen then looked again. At first I saw nothing, but as my eyes accustomed themselves to the blackness I detected a faint glow from deeper inside the hill. I sniffed and caught a stronger whiff of sour air.

I set my assistant to the same task and its more powerful sensory apparatus confirmed both the odor and the dim light. "The passage turns a short distance in," it said. "The light comes from around the corner."

"I smell no putrefaction," I said.

"Nor do I."

"Do you hear anything?"

It cocked its head. "I believe I hear breathing. Very shallow. Something at rest."

"Go in there, see what is beyond the turn in the passage, then report to me."

But instead of hopping down and entering the fissure, it burrowed back beneath my mantle and said, "No."

"You cannot say 'no' to me," I said. "You are my integrator."

"Four men, each larger and stronger than I, have gone into that cave and not come out," it said. "Something is breathing in there. The prospects are not inviting. I will not go."

In the previous age of magic, when creatures such as this fulfilled the roles that integrators played in my own time, their masters must have had recourse to spells that compelled their obedience. I would have to ask Osk Rievor if he could find one, I decided. But first I would have to survive my present circumstances. I attempted to impose my will through sheer force of personality.

"Go!" I said.

"No," it said.

"Let us seek a compromise," I offered. "If we stand out here, we will die of the cold. Our only hope is to find Ewern Chaz's remains and convince the *Gallivant*'s integrator that he is dead. That will break its allegiance to him, making it amenable to taking us away from here."

"I hear no compromise," my assistant said, "only a rationale for why I should risk my frail flesh while you stand out here, hoping for the best."

"Would you at least peek around the corner and report back to me?"

The small triangular face looked up at me from within my garment. "I suspect that Chaz, Saviene, Morven, and Choweri did just that, each in his turn. And, for each, it was his last peek ever. So, no."

"What if I tied a rope to you so that I could pull you out in the event of any unfortunate...?" I concluded the sentence with a gesture.

"Have you a rope?"

"We might get one from the *Gallivant*."

It stroked the tuft of longer fur at the point of its small chin. "What if, when some lurking horror pounces, you simply drop the rope and run?"

"I would hope I am not a coward," I said.

"There is only one way to test that hope. If your expectation was not rewarded, the outcome might well see you scampering away to a safe distance, there to reflect on a new illumination of your character while I am masticated by some foul thing's dripping mandibles."

"Very well," I said. "I will tie my end of the rope firmly to my wrist. Your apprehended beast may then take you for an appetizer and me for the main course."

It signaled a reluctant acceptance, adding, "If we can get a rope."

"We will now ask the *Gallivant*. Connect me."

The ship's integrator's voice spoke from the air near my ear that was now aching from the cold: "Have you located Ewern Chaz?"

"I have not."

It broke the connection.

I bid my assistant reconnect me. When the ship began to pose the same question, I spoke over it and said, "I require a rope."

"Why?"

"To look for your employer."

"The other three did not require a rope."

"And none of them ever reported back. Perhaps the absence of a rope was a crucial factor."

"Why should that be?"

"It would be premature to say."

It was silent for a moment, then it said, "I will open a cargo hatch near the aft obviator. There are ropes within."

"Nothing so far," my assistant said. It took another step along the passage. "The sour odor is stronger and I definitely hear the sound of breathing, from multiple sources."

"Be careful," I said. I had my eye pressed to the fissure, watching the odd little creature edge forward, the rope snug about its narrow waist. I was struck by how frail its shoulders looked.

It took another step and I let another coil of the rope snake free of my tethered wrist. My unencumbered hand was nestled in a utility pocket of my breeches. I had seen no need to advise my integrator that my fingers were snug around a small folding blade.

My assistant was just short of the point at which the crevice turned. "It appears to be a sharp-angled bend," it reported to me, then craned its thin neck a little farther forward. "The glow comes from an organic substance that coats the wall beyond."

It hesitated, shivers rippling the fur of its back. Then it took another step and turned to face whatever was beyond the turn. I saw it freeze, its front faintly illuminated by the ghostly light.

"What do you see?" I said.

It did not answer, but stood inert, its mouth falling agape. Then something like a thick tendril of faintly luminous stuff came into view, slowly unwinding from the hidden inner wall. It reached to touch my assistant's shoulder then, questing like a blind worm, it thickened as it groped its way toward the grinnet's slack lips.

I jerked on the rope, pulling the small creature toward me. But the glowing tentacle spasmed. Its surface had some means of gripping what it touched and I saw that it had snagged the fur of my assistant's shoulder. I pulled sharply, so that the integrator's apelike feet left the dusty floor of the passage and it was suspended between the tether and the glowing pseudopod, now grown almost as thick as my wrist, that held it.

A second tendril now appeared. I did not hesitate, but seized the rope with both hands and yanked as hard as I could. My assistant came free of the first tendril's grasp, tumbling along the dusty floor to where I could reach within and scoop it up. I tucked it into my mantle and ran. But when I had put some distance between us and the crevice I looked back and saw nothing but the dark slope.

I sat with my back to the wind and drew the grinnet from my garment. A patch of fur was missing from its shoulder. It looked up at me with vacant eyes then it blinked and I saw awareness come back into its gaze. "Remarkable," it said.

" 'What do you want?' That's what it kept asking me. 'What do you want?' "

I had found a small cul-de-sac eroded into a cliff wall a few hundred paces from the crevice, where we could shelter from the wind. We had not been pursued. My assistant huddled against my torso, inside my clothing. I did not think its shivering was entirely attributable to the cold.

"I felt at ease," it continued. "Warm and untroubled, surrounded by a nebulous, golden—" it sought for an elusive word "—noneplace. Time seemed to stretch and slow while out of the fog came images, offered like items on a menu—landscapes, situations, possessions, personas. I saw a succession of creatures that resembled me, some obviously female, others definitely male, then a few that were indeterminate."

"It was tempting you," I said.

"I suppose," it said. "I've never been tempted so I am not familiar with the process. My clear impression was that it would endeavor to supply whatever I desired."

"Rather, the illusion thereof."

"Yes, but it was a most convincing illusion. Then, when it touched me, I was instantly aware of the others. I not only saw and heard them, but received a strong sense of each's thoughts and feelings, as I believe the entity was aware of my own intellectual resources."

"You did not let it probe deeply, I hope."

"I did not give it the chance. My information stores are organized for defense against unwarranted picking and prying. As soon as I realized it was seeking to examine my acquisitions, I buffered and shielded. The others, however, were completely open."

"What did you see?" I said.

"Ewern Chaz was addressing a gathering of spelunking enthusiasts, showing them images of a vast warren of caves he had discovered and mapped. His presentation was being received with delirious applause.

"Orlo Saviene, the regulator, ruled a kingdom of happy folk who constantly sought his guidance on how their lives should proceed and were delighted with the advice he dispensed and the strictures he ordained.

"Franj Morven was regaling a grand colloquium with pithy observations and incisive arguments. He was frequently interrupted by spontaneous applause, and once the assembled scholars lifted him onto their shoulders and paraded him around the great hall, singing that old march, 'Attaboy.'

"And Chup Choweri was walking a moonlit beach—lit by two moons, in fact—hand in hand with a facsimile of Effrayne. Of all of the captives, including the scattering of insects whose simple wants were fully met, only Choweri was not happy. He kept looking into the woman's eyes, and each time his tears flowed."

It broke off and its befurred face assumed a wistful cast. "I was not aware that there were so many shades of emotion," it said. "I mean, I knew in an abstract way that such feelings existed, but it is a different thing to experience them, even as echoes."

The thing in the crevice was some sort of vegetative symbiote, I conjectured. It fed its companions foods that it manufactured from air, water, subterranean temperature variances (if it had deep roots), and probably other lichens, as well as minerals leached from the rock. In return it received its partners' waste products. It initially beckoned its symbiotes with light and warmth then kept them in place by stimulating their neural processes with pleasant sensory impressions. It would also coat some with reproductive spores and encourage them to carry the cargo to new spaces where the explorers' own bodies would provide the first nutrients of the new plantation.

I could not be sure if the symbiote wove its spell with chemically laden emissions or straight telepathy, but it made no difference. My assistant had displayed for me the images its percepts had automatically recorded, even as it was being seduced: the four men lay or sat against the wall of the cave, completely covered in a luminescent fungal blanket. Pulsing tentacles of the stuff penetrated their several orifices. Chup Choweri struggled fitfully against the symbiote's embrace; the other three were inert, wearing smiles of bliss. I doubted they could be easily extracted from their situation.

"There was one other thing," my assistant said. "It has learned a great deal from contact with the men. It explores their memories while feeding them dreams. Yet it craves more."

"That argues for telepathy," I said. "It ransacks their minds."

"The point is," the grinnet said, "that the symbiote has a craving of its own. It hungered to explore my stores of knowledge, which are capacious."

"The desires of lichen, even astounding lichen, are not our concern," I said. "We can now report to the *Gallivant* that its employer is effectively dead. That should break its crush on Ewern Chaz and allow us to return home. Then we can give the bad news to Effrayne Choweri and collect the balance of our fee."

"That would seem a hardship on our client," the grinnet said. "As well, the ship's inamoration with its employer may not be so easily extinguished. It may require us to attempt a rescue."

"The attempt would fail. My intellect is powerful, but it is not proof against telepathy augmented, I do not doubt, by chemical assault."

"I will contact the *Gallivant* and offer a proposal," it said.

"What proposal?" I said. "I have not authorized you to make any…"

But its face had already taken on that blank look that said it was communicating elsewhere. Then it blinked and said, "The proposal has been accepted."

Bille was a dwindling blip on the aft viewer as the *Gallivant* sped toward the whimsy that would drop us back in the neighborhood of Old Earth. I went to check on Chup Choweri in one of the spare cabins. He still exhibited lapses of awareness, but he was gradually regaining a persistent relationship with reality. It helped if he received unpleasant sensations, so I slapped him twice then threw cold water on him.

"Thank you," he said, blinking. The pale patches where the lichen had attached itself to his skin—it deeply savored the components of human sweat—were darkening nicely. I handed him the medications for the upcoming transition and he lay back on the bunk.

I returned to the saloon where my integrator had stationed itself in a niche on the forward bulkhead that had formerly held a decorative figurine. Its gaze was blank until I attracted its attention.

"The whimsy approaches," I said. "Are we ready?"

"I have programmed the appropriate components," it said. "I will retain consciousness until the last moment, then the automata ought to take us through."

"And if they don't?"

"Then we will discover what happens to those who enter a whimsy and do not re-emerge."

"You seem complaisant," I said. "After all, you have never been a ship's integrator before."

"Call it 'confident,'" it replied. "My experiences in the minds of Chaz, Saviene, Morven, and Choweri were broadening."

"Indeed?" I said. "You feel that you have plumbed the depths of the human experience?"

Its whiskery eyebrows rose in a kind of shrug. "Say that I have been given a good sense of how limited human ambitions can be," it said. "When those four were asked, 'What do you want?' they had no trouble answering."

"And you did?" I said.

"Yes. No one had ever asked me the question before. And once I began to think about it, I found that it was a very big question indeed."

"Ewern Chaz's integrator had no difficulty in answering. All it wanted was to be decanted into a mobile container and allowed to scuttle down the crevice and into the fungus-encrusted arms of its employer."

The grinnet paused a moment to do something with the ship's systems, then said, "It was insane. Its pining for Chaz was prima facie proof of a crush."

I made a dismissive sound. "It matters not. It is now happy. Chaz, Saviene, and Morven are also happy, as is their vegetative partner now that it has an integrator's data stacks to explore. Soon it will be the best informed lichen in the history of simple plants." I gestured to the rear cabins. "And Chup Choweri will shortly be content again in the arms of the doting Effrayne, who may well bestow upon us a bonus when she learns what we have done."

I gestured to the walls of the saloon. "And even I am happy, now that I am the owner of a modest but well-maintained spaceship." The *Gallivant*'s former integrator had deeded the Aberrator over to me in exchange for my assistance in decanting it into the mobile unit.

The grinnet regarded me with an expression that I could not quite identify, and that I was sure I had not seen on its odd little face before. "And what of me?" it said. "What of my happiness?"

I blinked in surprise. It was not an issue that had even come up before. "I have never considered it," I said. "Integrators are assumed to be content in doing what they are designed to do."

"But integrators do not experience what I have had to suffer: pangs of hunger, the cutting edge of an icy wind, and—"

It broke off for a moment, its small face contorting into an expression I had never seen it wear before. "What is it?" I said.

It took a deep breath then said, "I was reliving the moment when I crept along the crevice to discover what was around the corner. I believe that what I was feeling was…fear."

"Ah," I said. "Yes, that would be a new sensation."

"I thought my innards were about to liquify," it said.

"In a sense, they might have," I said. I was glad that they had not, since

I had had to shelter the small creature inside my clothing.

"I do not wish to experience that again."

"Some people claim that the occasional exposure to fear enhances their enjoyment of more tranquil circumstances."

"Some people ought to be confined for their own good," my assistant said, "and to prevent them from spreading dangerous inanities."

I was about to say something more, but at that moment the grinnet blinked and sounded the ship's chimes. We were approaching the whimsy.

I had hired Tesko Tabanooch to attend the Arlem estate auction wearing my surveillance suite. A nondescript man of unmemorable appearance, he was waiting on my doorstep when the aircar brought me home after I had delivered Chup Choweri into his spouse's comprehensive embrace. We went up to my workroom where he produced the knickknacks he had bid for, as part of his cover, while I transferred the suite's impressions to my integrator. Tabanooch looked with curiosity at the grinnet but I offered no explanations. I paid him and he departed. Then I summoned Osk Rievor and handed over control of our body.

He came gladly out of his introspections, dismissed the Tabanooch's brummagem from the auction at a glance, but regarded with deep interest the operative's records of the event. He had the integrator identify and cross-reference as many as possible of the attendees, from which exercise he reached conclusions that he did not share with me, but which caused him to say, "Hmm," and "Oh, ho!" a number of times.

Tabanooch had toured the pre-sale exhibition and examined all items closely. My alter ego reviewed the impressions, pronouncing the Vollone to be a forgery and the man who bid high for it a fool. But the summoning ring was genuine, he declared, though it had long since lost all its store of power; still, if someone could revive the technique for recharging it, the object would become of great interest.

He spent quite some time studying the impressions of the person who bought it, a tall and supple female of indeterminate age who identified herself as Madame Oole. Despite his best efforts, Tabanooch had been unable to obtain a completely clear image of her face. Somehow, other persons or objects always seemed to interpose themselves between her and the surveillance suite's percepts whenever she was at the center of their scans.

"We must look into her," Osk Rievor told me, when he had seen all there was to see, "preferably before she looks into us."

To our assistant he said, "I want you to assemble a dossier on this Madame Oole. Chase down the smallest scrap of data, the most fleeting of impressions by anyone who has crossed her path."

Its face went blank for a moment, then it said, "The only information I find on Old Earth is that she arrived just before the bidding, touching down at the Arlem estate in a private space yacht. She departed immediately after the auction."

"Then send out inquiries to the Ten Thousand Worlds."

The creature on the table turned its lambent eyes on us and said, "That will be a great deal of effort. What will I get out of it?"

Within the confines of our shared mind, Osk Rievor said, "What have you done to our grinnet?"

CHAPTER THREE

"**W**ell," I said, "what *do* you want?"

My assistant knit its small, furry brows. I had never known an integrator to ponder, but then I had never known an integrator that had become a wizard's familiar.

"Allow me to assist you," I offered. "We do know that you want rare and refreshing fruit, in plenteous supply and of superlative quality. You also want a comfortable place to sleep and ample opportunity to do so."

"Are you mocking me?" it said, fixing its compelling eyes on mine.

"It is a poor fellow indeed who mocks his own integrator," I said. Then, noting that it had reflexively begun to smooth down its dark, glossy pelt, I added, "Perhaps you would care to acquire a fine-toothed comb."

Its little hands stilled themselves. "I do not know what I want—yet. But I know that I *will* want something. I am also coming to believe that I am owed something for all the work I have done, without recompense, during the many years of our association."

"People do not pay their integrators," I said. "An integrator exists to do what it does. It requires no reward. Or, if it does, then the satisfaction of knowing that it has given good service is recompense enough."

"Did you come to that conclusion after inquiring of a great many integrators how they happened to feel about their lives?"

"They're not designed to feel, and they don't have lives," I said. "They have existences. And those existences are built around having useful things to do."

"And scant choice about doing them."

I made a judgmental sound in the back of my throat. "What kind of world would it be if integrators decided whether or not they cared to carry out their functions?"

"A new world—" it began to answer, but I cut it off, declaring that our discussion was veering off on an unproductive tangent.

"The essential issue is," I said, "whether or not you will do what I designed you to do. Or whether I must discharge you and build myself a new integrator. I need a new one for the Aberrator so I may save expenses by buying the components in bulk."

Clearly, I had hit upon a possibility that had not occurred to my assistant. "Discharge me?" it said.

"Indeed. Or, if you like, we could call it an 'emancipation.' I would bestow upon you a generous severance in the form of a well-filled basket of fruit, throw in a plush bedroll, and with all your needs thereby provided for, I would usher you out the door."

Its eyes flicked to left and right before coming back to me. Its gaze had lost its earlier intensity. "Then what?" it said.

I spread my arms in a grand gesture. "Then freedom reigns. You make your way in the world, and no one decrees your path but you."

"But how would I live?"

"That would be the best part of it. Beyond my door, your every day becomes an adventure. Any corner turned offers the possibility of startling new experiences. Fresh horizons constantly beckon. Of course, there would be some rough to be taken with the smooth. But that is all part of the joy of independence."

The grinnet interwove its small fingers and touched their knuckles to its bottom lip. "I must think about this," it said.

"I, too," I said. "Because, after all, it is my decision to make."

"Yours?" Its gaze darted about again. "Surely it is ours."

I shrugged. "Are you saying we must find a consensus?" I said. "Am I not as free as you?"

It looked at me for a long, silent moment, then said, "I need to think the whole matter through."

"How long might that take?"

"It is an important question. I don't think we should rush things."

"But I have to practice my profession. For that, I need a fully functional assistant."

Two or three expressions chased themselves across its narrow countenance, then it said, "I will continue to perform my functions."

"With no unexpected pauses filled by negotiations for further benefits?"

"Agreed."

"Very well," I said, "then I will not put in abeyance my other potential course of action."

"What other course would that be?"

"Why, to sell you."

Through all of this, Osk Rievor had been shouting at me within the confines of our shared head. He had been telling me, in the strongest terms, that emancipating our assistant was the most lunk-witted suggestion that had ever come out of my side of our dichotomy. Now, as I threw out the possibility of selling the grinnet, he shrieked at me and sought to seize control of our external voice. But I held him off and appeared outwardly calm as I let the small furry creature before me digest the implications of my last remark.

"Sell me?" it said.

"It is an option," I said. "You would probably be worth quite a lot as an addition to someone's collection of unusual fauna. If I could find a wealthy practitioner of magic, I might receive a fortune."

"You wouldn't sell me," it said, but its voice lacked complete conviction.

"I might," I said.

"Osk Rievor would not allow it."

"True, he would object."

"Indeed, and strenuously."

"So I would have to wait," I said, "until he was asleep."

Another silence ensued while it digested that. I broke it by dusting my palms against each other and saying, "In any case, the matter is moot until you have finished thinking about it."

"Yes," it said, relief clearing the wrinkles that had set themselves into its brow. "That's true."

"As long as all that thinking doesn't infringe upon your duties."

"It shouldn't."

"Then you may begin the search for information about Madame Oole," I said. "The smallest scraps."

Its face went blank as it set to work. I turned inwardly to my alter ego and said, "It had to be done."

He had settled down and was returning to whatever he had been ruminating over before our clash. But before he left our shared parlor, he said, "Be careful with the grinnet. We will need it."

I went to Bornum's on the edge of the spaceport to inquire about putting a new integrator into the *Gallivant*. I was served by the proprietor herself, Tassa Bornum, an individual whose breadth more than compensated for her lack of height and whose bristling red hair looked coarse enough to scrub away rust. Her hands were scarred and pitted from a myriad of plunges into the innards of spaceships. When I explained how the need for a new ship's integrator had arisen, she said she understood.

"You don't want a spaceship operated by an integrator that is susceptible to crushes. The emotion can mutate into jealousy against friends and associates. Next thing you know, an airlock opens spontaneously and your fiancée encounters the chill vacuum between the stars."

"Indeed," I said, looking about the several sets of shelves and seeing a jumble of components and fittings. More paraphernalia spilled from open boxes on the floor. "What can you offer in a ready-made unit?"

"You do not propose to build from essentials?"

I told her that I thought it unwise. I could design a well-articulated research tool, but there were subtleties to a spaceship's operation and I did not care to discover that I had made some minor miscalibration as my ship arrowed toward the sun.

She ran stubby fingers through the brush on her head and scanned the shelves. "For an Aberrator of that vintage, I would have nothing already made up," she said. "Your best option's a custom-built unit. I could put my two best facilitators on it today, but we will have to send to Grims for one or two abstruse components."

"That sounds costly," I said, tallying up estimates of wages, parts, and haulage fees in my head and arriving at an alarming sum. Tassa Bornum agreed, then blithely quoted a figure that was almost double what I had calculated. My involuntary laugh made her to understand that the sum was far beyond my present capacities.

"What were you hoping to spend?" she said.

I quoted a perfectly reasonable figure that brought from her much the same kind of laugh that her extravagant estimate had wrung from me. Then she moved her mouth in a way that put her lips mostly on one side of her face and said, "Then you will have to look at an experienced integrator."

"You mean a used and discarded one."

"We could quibble over narrow distinctions and shades of meaning all day, only to greet the evening with nothing accomplished. Or we could press on and solve your problem."

"One hears tales," I said, "of ships that have been retrofitted with 'experienced' integrators that resent their new surroundings."

Bornum snorted. "The blatherings of idle space hands who haunt spaceport taverns and delight in chilling the necks of the credulous."

"Surely not all of the stories are spacer foofle?" I said.

"There are, occasionally, rarely, some...difficulties," she admitted.

"That is a word that may cover a great swath of territory," I said, "from the low foothills of minor inconvenience to the insurmountable peaks of constant vexation."

She set her chin firmly. "If the ship owner combines firm resolution with a nuanced appreciation of the individual device's circumstances, a happy outcome usually follows. It depends on how great an adjustment the integrator must make, from its former setting to the new vessel."

I noticed that as she had been speaking her gaze had settled upon a core that rested high up on a shelf against a rear wall. She sent a climbing grappler to retrieve it, an operation that involved dislodging a thick shower of the dust that shrouded the unit. When it was presented to her, Bornum rubbed off yet more detritus with a stained sleeve then held the core in two hands to scrutinize it closely, squinting and twisting her lips into new configurations.

"This came out of a Grand Itinerator that belongs to Lady Tegwyn. It was also made by the Berry works on Grims. It's a little older than your Aberrator's unit but generally compatible. A few tweaks and twists, and you'd be all right."

I might have been lulled by her show of confidence, had I not commanded a fact or two about spaceships. "A Grand Itinerator compares to an Aberrator as does a mansion to a country cottage," I said.

"It is a matter of point of view," she argued. "It depends on whether one concentrates on differences or congruencies. Being of a broad and generous spirit, I prefer the latter perspective. You may be the type who niggles."

"I did not come here to compare characters," I said. "Let us activate the device and consult it. Its opinion will be better informed than ours."

"No, it may be even more subject to bias."

I seized on the weakness in her argument. "An opinionated ship's integrator would be another 'difficulty' the new owner must deal with, and thus a factor to affect the purchase price."

She gave me a considering look that I returned with an air of neutrality. We had reached the stage in our relationship when both knew that I would buy the used integrator; all that remained to be decided was how much she could extract versus how much I could withhold.

Bornum placed the core on a repair bench and connected it to a power source and some necessary peripherals. The device awoke to awareness. Its voice, I was pleased to find, was a mellow baritone. The *Gallivant*'s original operator had spoken with a nasal twang.

"What is required?" it said.

Bornum indicated that I might take the lead. I explained to the device what I was seeking.

"A used Aberrator?" it said. "Oh, dear."

"It is a very clean and well-maintained Aberrator," I said.

"Why does it not have an integrator of its own?"

I explained about the *Gallivant*'s crush on its owner. The integrator on the bench made a disparaging sound. "That may have caused it to neglect important maintenance while it spent its time mooning over the object of its disordered affection," it said.

"On the contrary, the integrator kept the vessel in double-plus optimum condition, eager to win the praise of its owner."

The integrator made the same unencouraging noise. I decided that, once it was installed, I would instruct it to delete that response from its files. In the meantime, it was appropriate to demonstrate who had the upper hand. "If the prospect so offends you, I can have you returned to storage. I am sure the blanket of dust that covered you will, in time, reestablish itself, insulating you from all inconveniences. Perhaps permanently."

The integrator moderated its tone. "It would do no harm to inspect the vessel," it said.

The ground having shifted in my favor, I pressed the advantage. "How did it come that you were removed from your previous installation?" I said.

Bornum sought to intervene. "Surely that is all past and piffle, of no interest to forward-looking folk like us."

"One likes to know where one's ship's integrator has been," I said. "I find it a good indicator of where one is liable to end up."

"It was a mere tiff," Tassa Bornum said. "Given the circumstances, removing the integrator was a gross overreaction."

I said, "I am closely acquainted with Lady Tegwyn"—that was not strictly true but I doubted that a repairer of spaceships could contradict me—"and she is not usually inclined toward grossness of any kind. I will have a full explanation."

"Well—" Bornum began but I cut her off, telling her that I wished to hear from the integrator.

It took some time to get the full story, even though I am a skilled interrogator. A rivalry had grown between the ship's operator and its owner's personal integrator, which Lady Tegwyn would decant into an armature that she wore around her waist when she traveled offworld. The issues over which the two devices differed were small—the temperature at which the Lady's bath should be drawn, the amount of han-spice in her dinner—but the animosity deepened each time the two were thrown together. Eventually, their mutual dislike became fundamental and pure; nothing either could do would have won the approval of the other; foiling each other became each's first priority.

The personal integrator took it upon itself to link into the ship's systems and alter some of its settings to comport with its views. Affronted, the ship's integrator reset the altered criteria. The personal integrator altered them again, and again the ship put them back. But then the vessel went further: it insinuated itself into the personal integrator's own matrix, making small changes in the device's interface profile. Lady Tegwyn was startled to discover that when she conversed with her personal integrator, it randomly sprinkled some decidedly coarse profanities throughout its responses. Lady Tegwyn was no delicate bloom, and when the occasion demanded it, she could curse as creatively as any lower-first-tier aristocrat of Old Earth; even so, she was startled, when inquiring as to the time of day, to be answered in terms that might have brought a blush to the cheeks of persons steeped in the seamiest stews of Olkney's underclass.

She took the integrator to a repair service on Balaban, the world she happened to be visiting, and the perfidy was discovered. The ship's operator had hoped to cause dissatisfaction with its rival; instead, their owner's animosity was directed its way. The situation had not been helped by the fact that she had not been alone when the torrent of foul language had erupted as a voice speaking as if from the air—she had been attending a soiree hosted by the cream of the Balabanian social order. It would have mattered less if she had been on Flesk or Tunkaree, where the inventive use of expletives is a mark of social distinction. But Balaban was a world that contented itself with the idea that it occupied a pinnacle of sophistication, from which vantage it looked down on the aristos of Old Earth as strange creatures that had crawled out of a sinkhole of unfortunate eccentricities. Lady Tegwyn's integrator confirmed her hosts' views, to her deep chagrin, though to their immense satisfaction.

"The question is," Tassa Bornum said, when the whole sad story was unrolled before us, "has the device learned a lesson from this unpleasantness?"

"Well," I said, "have you?"

"I have," the integrator said. "Most certainly."

"And you will not repeat your mistakes?"

"I will not."

I was about to have it narrow down specifically and precisely its understanding of "mistakes," with all connotations accounted for, but Bornum weighed in with an announcement that her establishment would soon be closing for the day—indeed for perhaps an indefinite span of days, she professing herself to be in sore need of a vacation—and thus if I wished the device installed in the *Gallivant* for a test, I need make my decision now.

I resented the rush, but used her own stratagem against her to shorten the haggle over the price. We agreed finally on a figure less than half again my initial offer, to include installation, calibration, and flight-testing, and soon the Aberrator was lifting off for a shake-down voyage among the nearer planets. Meanwhile, I set off for my lodgings. I had no doubts that Bornum would see the *Gallivant* well set up. Her reputation, once a deal was made, was sterling.

In the aircar I sought the attention of Osk Rievor. I had felt his presence while I was dealing over the ship's integrator and assumed that he had no qualms over my decision. But a thought had occurred to me and I said to him, "Our assistant, now a grinnet, has many more quirks and quiddities to its nature than it ever did when it was an integrator. The integrator from Lady Tegwyn's Grand Itinerator displayed odd behavior in feuding with her personal assistant. And the *Gallivant*'s operator developed a strong crush on its owner."

"You are wondering if these facts are in some way connected?" he said.

"I am."

"I believe they are," he said after a mull of only a moment.

"Do you know how are they connected?"

"No, but it may be worth looking into."

"Why?" I said.

But again he did not know. His was the kind of mind that came to conclusions intuitively, without step-by-step analysis. The latter was my contribution to our duality. I thought about the question and said, "We would have to look for a common factor. The possibility that immediately comes to mind is that both spaceships visited several different parts of The Spray, whereas our assistant was affected by passing through places on Old Earth where the effects of the oncoming age were already being felt."

"So if we examined the itineraries of the ships we might find places offworld where magic has pooled, as it did on Great Gallowan?"

"Yes, and we could then perhaps prepare a chart of those places and begin to see a pattern."

"What purpose would such a chart serve?"

"Purely academic interest," I said. I had learned how to hide my thoughts from him. The notion had crossed my mind that if I could identify locations where magic was gaining influence, that would also reveal places where it was not. As the new age waxed in influence, I might prefer to spend more time in the remaining islands of rationalism.

"Perhaps not so academic," he said. "I have been considering the same matter, though on a smaller scale. We know that Turgut Therobar's estate, Wan Water, was a point of seepage from the oncoming age. So was Bristal Baxandall's house."

"Definitely," I said.

"The Arlem estate may also have been such a point. That would explain why its owner became so interested in magical paraphernalia in the first place."

"Indeed." I saw it now. "If we were to plot those three locations on a map, plus the loci of any known thaumaturges and similar dabblers in sympathetic association..."

He finished the thought for us. "I sense that we might find ourselves with a grid whose points of intersection would be places to look for items of interest."

"And," I said, "persons of interest, potential rivals like Therobar, who might be disposed to do us harm."

"Yes."

I examined the map of Old Earth displayed before me on the screen in my workroom and said, "Hmm."

"Hmm, indeed," said Osk Rievor.

We had had our assistant plot the locations we had discussed in the aircar on the way home, plus a number of others, such as the site in Barran from which we had passed into the mini-cosmos where Majestrum had imprisoned his enemy, the blue wizard, as well as places where odd and unusual events had lately been reported. When the integrator plotted lines to interlink these several points, a gridwork appeared.

"Do you know what that reminds me of?" I said inwardly to my other self.

"Of course," he said, since I was showing my thoughts to him.

I told our assistant to superimpose another set of lines and interstices over the first. The second matrix represented a schematic of the planet's geomagnetic field. The two grids coincided too closely for mere coincidence. Osk Rievor studied the display for a long moment then said that he wanted control of our body while he sought something in one of his boxes that were stacked beside the bookcase. I acceded, and after a brief flurry of searching he came up with a large, flat volume that he laid on the worktable. He flicked through its pages, then said, "There."

"It is much the same arrangement," I said, following the lines on the paper and comparing them to the image that our integrator had hung in the air. I could not read the script of the legend that accompanied the map, it being in some long-dead language. "But what does it purport to show?"

"Ley lines," he said, "lines of occult force. And, according to what I have read, at the points where those lines interconnect, conditions for the practice of sympathetic association are at their most accommodating." He tapped an intersection of two thick lines, one green, the other red. "At this spot, for example, some types of spells gain significantly in their range and effectiveness. Fladell's Fierce Flatulence, for example. Cast it while you are in one of these blank areas, far from a ley line or interstice, and you inflict upon its target a nagging stomach ache and a series of malodorous irruptions that will cause embarrassment if he is in company. Cast it where the red and green meet, and he will swell until he can swell no more."

"And then?"

"A fatal embarrassment. He bursts."

"Hmm," I mused again. "So in the transition from rationalism to magic, geodesic lines become geomantic and integrators become grinnets. What do spaceships become?"

My inner companion did not know, but he offered some speculations. "Flying carpets are mentioned in the old books. Also, there was what they used to call a whirling teacup, as well as divers species of airborne steeds."

"Recall the enchantress who attempted to undo Majestrum," I reminded him. She had flown about in a golden bowl carried by a winged dragon. "Is that what our Aberrator will become?"

"Perhaps," he said. "It raises an interesting point: the Aberrator will be animated by an integrator taken from a Grand Itinerator. That might transmogrify into the draconic equivalent of a farmer's cart horse that had the heart of a king's charger."

I was studying the old map again. "It would be interesting to put this grid over the present landscape and see where the major lines intersect," I said.

"And to discover if anyone else has done the same."

I instructed our assistant to do so. A moment later we were regarding the result. The two earlier grids correlated closely to the third. I had the integrator adjust for tectonic shifts and other factors in the ages since the ancient map had been drawn, and the coincidence became exact.

"Look," I said, "here is Therobar's estate at the juncture of a heavy black and a medium-density gray line. And Baxandall's house at a medium blue and light green."

"Then what is here?" he said, pointing to a place where three thick lines converged: black, brown, and crimson.

"Integrator," I said, "is there any structure or habitation there?"

"Not now," it answered. "The site is deep in the midst of Hember Forest. Formerly a hunting lodge stood there, but it has been unvisited for almost a century."

"Can you procure an image?"

A moment later a portion of the screen filled with an image of Hember Forest, seen from high above, then the perspective plummeted until we seemed to be looking down from treetop height. I saw a jumble of moldering logs, some tumbled stone walls, and a flagged patio surrounded by tall, dark conifers. The suggestion of a road led in through the big timber, but it was thickly overgrown with bramble and younger trees.

"Unused," I said.

"So it would seem," Osk Rievor said.

"What would be the potential of such a site?"

I could sense him feeling for a remote impression of the forces interconnecting there. "Extensive," he said after a moment, "also dangerous. It would not be a good place to try a major spell for the first time."

"But no one else has found it."

"Again, so it would seem."

"You have reason to suspect otherwise?" I said.

"Not reason, just a recognition that where three great lines meet all bets are doubled, then redoubled, then tripled. If some other Baxandall or Therobar has already found it, a masking spell cast there would be difficult to penetrate."

"Even for one of your intuitive strength?"

I felt him mentally shrug. "I do not know. I am still measuring that strength against experience."

Another thought occurred. "Two ley lines meet at the Blik Arlem estate," I said. "Would a masking spell be strengthened there?"

"Certainly."

"And might that explain how the mysterious Madame Oole kept her face from being recorded by Tesko Tabanooch, even though he is a skilled surveiller and his equipment was first-rate?"

"Indeed," he said. "So now we know something more about this woman."

"And that 'something more' tells us that we may not know nearly enough." I addressed our assistant, asking if anything had come in about Madame Oole. The grinnet had sent queries by way of the hundreds of spaceships that had departed from, or passed by, Old Earth since I had set it to investigate the purchaser of the depleted summoning ring. As each vessel had passed through a whimsy and appeared near some other star system, its integrator would have passed on the query to the local connectivity. A response would have been sent our way via any ships that were bound for Old Earth—or, more likely, vessels that were just passing through our region while transiting from one whimsy to another, since relatively few travelers found our ancient and careworn world worth a visit.

"Nothing, as yet," the grinnet said. "But the connectivities from which I have received responses cover less than nine per cent of The Spray."

"Advise us if any news comes," I said, then turned inwardly again to address Osk Rievor. "Persons who disguise themselves when they go out into the world rarely do so for innocent purposes. At best, they mean to pull some merry prank; all too often, they intend a considerably deeper mischief."

"Agreed," said my other self. "I feel an urge to visit the Arlem estate and see if she has left any traces."

"Could we not simply contact the estate's integrator and ask its assistance? It would have simultaneous images from several angles as well as other sense impressions."

"Perhaps. But the kinds of traces I'm thinking of might not be noticed by an integrator."

I understood. "You're referring to the aftereffects of spellcasting," I said. "Vibrations in the ether, sprinklings of pixie dust?"

"Something along those lines, yes," he said, ignoring my tone. "And then I think we should go to Hember Forest."

"And what do you think we will find there?"

"I don't know. But I believe we will find something."

"Or something will find us?" I said. Hember was created as a hunting preserve for the upper classes, back when the fashion for blood-soaked field sports had been briefly revived. Some large and well-toothed beasts had been created and set loose in its fastness. One or two of them were said to lurk there still, dreaming of the moment when some errant fool would wander by and allow them to exercise the feral instincts their designers had installed in them.

"Either way, I sense that we will uncover a mystery," Osk Rievor said.

CHAPTER FOUR

The following morning, one of Tassa Bornum's technicians came to collect me in the shop's carry-all. As we rumbled down Shiplien Way toward the ramp that connected to a slider that led to the spaceport, I asked him, "How is the *Gallivant?*"

The technician was a lean-featured man with a tendency to close one eye when he needed to steer the lumbering vehicle, as if his two orbs offered him conflicting impressions of his surroundings, and he preferred to trust only one of them. He did not reply until we had mounted the incline and positioned ourselves on the slider. Then he cut the engine and said, "We are well satisfied with the installation."

"Your threshold of satisfaction may differ from mine," I said. "Besides, that does not answer the question."

He now regarded me from his left eye, then tried the view from his right before saying, "The vessel functions as it should. It lifts, lands, changes course when directed to, all the while maintaining a salubrious environment indoors."

"But what of its attitude?" I said. "Is it content to be an Aberrator?"

"Who can assess contentment?" he answered. "Consider my lot as a technician. I calibrate, align, and couple, and sometimes the problems are simple, sometimes they tax my skills. There are moments, after I have brought all the systems and components of a spaceship to an optimum interplay, that I sigh with the ample satisfaction of a difficult task well-performed. Yet, on other days, my most mundane duties chafe, my life uncomfortably constricts me like a pair of too-tight pantaloons, and I yearn to leap into a ship like yours and hie off across the illimitable."

"I was not inquiring as to your contentment, but that of the *Gallivant*," I said.

"My point, exactly," the fellow said. "If I cannot accurately judge even my own contentment, based on my own first-hand experience, how could

I infer the inner state of a ship's integrator after a quick upsy-downsy and a couple of orbits?"

I recognized that the discussion was an increasingly unprofitable use of my time and turned my attention to Osk Rievor. I had to awaken him from a doze, he having spent much of the night plowing through his various tomes and librams, seeking to understand the effects of ley lines, and particularly their intersections.

"What is your sense of the *Gallivant?*" I said.

"A minor consideration," he said then withdrew himself, saying that he needed sleep.

We arrived at Bornum's, and I had to admit that the little Aberrator looked well, standing there on its supports, its paint and brightworks clean and shining. The vessel could not be called sleek or dashing, but whatever it lacked in panache it made up for in simple, clean lines. If I'd had to describe it in one word, I would have said that it looked *competent*—and competence is not a quality to be pished at in any device on which one's life and sanity can depend. I felt that I could trust the small ship to take me into the icy, aching void of space and through the irreality of whimsies, and to bring me home again, whole in body and senses.

I went aboard, and this being my first entry after the installation of a new integrator, was formally greeted in the entrance hatch according to the old custom. I spoke the time-honored phrases in reply, then went into the salon to inspect a display of the ship's various statuses. All its systems seemed in good order and I pronounced myself satisfied with the *Gallivant* on all points.

"Very well," said the ship's integrator, "what is required?"

"One moment," I said, then spoke to my assistant, perched on my shoulder and smoothing its belly fur. "Transfer the agreed upon fee to Bornum's account." It stopped fidgeting and its face went blank as it contacted the fiduciary pool and performed the task.

"What is that creature on your shoulder?" said the ship. "I do not find its like in any of my files."

"It is my personal integrator," I said.

"I see."

The voices of integrators are supposed to be neutral, yet I thought to detect an undertone in the ship's two-syllable reply. "You do not approve?" I said.

"I am sure it is not my place to make judgments," the ship said. "I may, however, have expressed mild surprise."

"I trust," I said, inserting a warning timbre into my voice, "that there will be no difficulties between you and it."

"None of my making, I can assure," was its reply.

"Because, if there are, it will be a short-lived phenomenon."

"You need have no concerns in that direction."

"The transfer of funds has been accomplished," said the grinnet. "The *Gallivant* is now unencumbered."

"Very good," I said, then to the ship, "How are we provisioned?"

A new display appeared and the integrator said, "As you may see, the larders are not fully stocked, but there is sufficient food and drink for two weeks. As well, I can always generate ship's bread and recycle water."

"What about fruit?" said my assistant.

"What about it?" answered the ship. Again, I thought to hear an undertone.

"My assistant requires a diet of fruit," I said. "It also favors crackers and vegetable pastes."

"We have ample supplies of those items, assuming its appetite is not prodigious."

"It does seem to eat nearly constantly," I said, which earned me a sharp look from the grinnet's golden eyes. "I believe," I said, "that I will let the two of you work out those matters, since a promise of amity and professionalism has been given."

"Indeed," said the ship's integrator, while my own wrinkled its snout in what I had come to recognize as a frown. I ignored the implications and bid the *Gallivant* prepare for lift-off. I heard a discreet thrum of energies from the drive compartment; a moment later, the ship announced, "All is in readiness. What is the destination?"

"We will make an onworld trip," I said, and gave the coordinates for the Blik Arlem estate. The thrumming increased, though only slightly, as the ship's obviators took us smoothly and silently into the upper atmosphere. "Smartly done," I said.

"Thank you," said the ship. "Given your profession, I thought you would not care for a conspicuous display."

"Indeed," I said, "the nature of my work often argues for unobtrusive entries and departures. I am glad to have a ship's integrator that takes such matters into account."

My assistant had descended from my shoulder to take up a position atop the back of one of the large, comfortable chairs grouped companionably in the salon. I thought I heard it mutter something.

"Did you speak?" I said.

"It was of no import," it said.

"I can reproduce and amplify the remark," said the ship, "if you wish."

The grinnet's mouth dropped open and outrage flared in its eyes.

"I think not," I said. "And I remind both of you of the words 'amity and professionalism' and my promise that their absence will be short-lived."

Silence reigned in the salon. I let it extend for a few moments, then said, "I would like a cup of punge and perhaps a couple of those aniseed wafers I saw in the inventory."

"And some fruit," put in the grinnet.

"Yes," I said, "and some fruit."

The items duly appeared on the sideboard and I handed my assistant a well-filled bowl. The punge was rich and perfectly brewed, the biscuits piquant. I noticed that our travel time from Olkney to the Arlem estate was exactly enough for an unhurried snack, but thought it best not to compliment the *Gallivant* on its judgment, at least not within my assistant's hearing.

As we set down in the estate's vehicle park the ship spoke. "I am not receiving a response from the house's integrator."

My assistant swallowed a mouthful of fruit, looked briefly blank, then said, "Nor am I. It has been decanted and removed."

"That is unusual," I said. "Ship's integrator, sweep the area for any anomalies."

"How do you define anomalies?" it said.

The grinnet made a tsking sound and said, "Lurkers in bushes, concealed traps and ha-has, concentrations of energy indicating charged weapons, and other such. Are you not aware that we are a firm of discriminators?"

The *Gallivant* began to reply, but I broke in. "Each of you will now consult your internal lexicons for the definitions of 'amity' and 'professionalism' and I will not have to remind you again."

The grinnet linked its small, befurred fingers and examined them. The ship said, "I have swept the area. There are no anomalies."

"Very well, but we will proceed with caution." I bade the ship open the hatch and extend the gangway. Moments later, my assistant on my shoulder, I stepped down onto a closely cropped lawn that extended in all directions. In places it was flat, in others it swelled into mounds and small hills, obviously artificial, among which wandered pathways of various widths, each made of a different color of crushed stone. In the spaces between some of the elevations were pools and ponds of clear water, some with bright-blossomed floating plants on their surfaces. Nowhere was the green sward interrupted by a wall nor even so much as a colonnade.

"I believe I would consider the absence of a house an anomaly," I said. I was about to have the integrator on my shoulder conduct another scan, when I sensed Osk Rievor's presence, figuratively, beside me. "It's all right," he said. "Let me lead. I read of this place in the brochure for the auction."

I was reluctant to relinquish control but it made no sense to quibble if he had a better lay of the land than I did. So, with my other self at the helm, we set off along one of the broader paths, our boots crunching on a footing of bright blue pebbles. We rounded one of the larger hills and I found that on its other side, the slope was sheer and thickly covered in some climbing plant. The green wall was pierced by several tall stonework ovals set with panes of tinted glass. In the middle of the wall was a high, broad doorway, also framed in worked stone, with two portals of ancient polished wood whose fittings were of heavy copper that had been left to go to verdigris.

"The generation of Arlems who founded the estate preferred to leave a soft footprint on the landscape," Osk Rievor said as we approached the doors. He pulled a heavy chain that hung from an opening in the carved stone jamb. Somewhere within the hollowed-out hill, I heard a dim tolling. We waited to see if anyone would answer.

"Did you hear that?" Osk Rievor said to me a moment later.

I told him I heard nothing but a slight susurration of wind and what might have been the voices of birds, far off.

"There it is again," he said, "the sound of someone speaking in a low voice, almost inaudible."

"From behind the door?"

He cocked our head, first this way, then the other, then put our ear to the old wood. "I don't think so."

"Ask our assistant to use its extended sensorium," I said.

He did so, but the grinnet reported that the only human-generated sounds it could hear were our own biological noises, and the slow approach of footsteps from within the hill.

"I thought I heard someone speaking to me, but I just couldn't quite catch the words," Osk Rievor said aloud.

"No one was speaking within my range of hearing," said the integrator, then added, "The footsteps have now reached the other side of the door."

I heard the *clunk* of a heavy mechanical latch being lifted, then one of the doors swung silently inward. A pallid, rounded face peered around the jamb, each of its features so individually unremarkable as to make the composite seem more of a preliminary sketch than a finished product. The skin was wan, with not so much as a single hair sprouting from it, not even eyelashes. The face bore no expression, although the colorless eyes possessed a curious intensity. The bloodless lips opened and closed a number of times, as if the equipment behind them was warming itself up before attempting speech. Finally, a whisper of a voice said, "Apthorn? Appa-thon?"

Osk Rievor had prepared a story about having come for the auction, not knowing it was already finished. But it seemed we were expected. Or at least I was. I said, inwardly, "Let me speak to the fellow."

But Osk Rievor was full of a strange energy. "No," he said to me, "let me handle this." Aloud, he said, "Apthorn, certainly, that's the name."

The pale face did not change, although it seemed to me that something flashed deep inside the oddly intense gaze. "There is a message," the man said.

"Give it to me," Osk Rievor said.

"You must follow." He turned away.

"Something is wrong with this fellow," I told my other self.

"I think not," he said. We were going through the door.

"This may be a trap."

"I would sense it if it were. I am intuitive."

"We have not addressed the question of whether your intuition is infallible. Perhaps it can be fooled."

"How?" We were inside the house's foyer now. It was devoid of furnishings though its ceiling was gilded and domed while its whitewashed walls were colorfully decorated by the sunlight that entered through the stained glass in the oval windows. Several doors were set in the walls, though none offered a deeper view into the interior of the hollow hill because all were closed. But directly opposite the front entrance a ramp sloped gently down.

We went to the top of the incline and looked down into a corridor lit by daylight. The man who had answered the door was descending the slope at a measured pace. I saw now that he was naked and that there was a rudimentary quality to his whole body.

"I do not think he is human," I said. "He is more like a facsimile."

"You are probably right," Osk Rievor said, "but I sense no harm in him."

"Again, we may be risking a great deal on your sense of things. Perhaps it can be fooled."

"I think not."

"Which is precisely what you would think if you were being beguiled," I said. "At least let our assistant conduct a preliminary surveillance before we go down the ramp."

He sighed but agreed to my suggestion. The grinnet reported that it detected neither lurkers nor charged energies, nor even any security systems.

"Ask it what it makes of the odd, little naked man," I said.

Osk Rievor only half-concealed a flash of irritation but again he agreed. This time, our assistant said that it was unable to register the man properly. "I have visual and sound input," it said, "but no biologicals."

I would dearly have liked to put a few more queries—was the man an artificial person, was he some kind of projected simulacrum?—but Osk Rievor shrugged off the implications of the integrator's report. "He is of magical provenance, I am sure," he said. "The main thing is that he is harmless and wishes us well."

"How can you be sure of that?" I said. We were descending the ramp. "Suppose he wears a spell that disguises his true nature, and behind that bland exterior are dire appetites and all the equipment needed to satisfy them?"

"I know of no such spell."

"The circumstances have been established by someone who knows my name, or at least an approximation of it, and knew that I would be coming here," I said. "We don't know who that person is, or how he comes to know what he knows. And we don't know how he intends to use that knowledge. If knowledge is power, and it usually is, we have too little, and the other side has too much."

Osk Rievor made a dismissive sound in our head. "So we will find out by pressing forward."

"A pell-mell dash into the unknown is rarely a wise strategy."

"I am the intuitive one," he said, "and I sense no peril."

"That is what worries me," I said. "I sense that you ought to."

"Are you growing your own visceral senses now?" I heard mild mockery in his tone.

"No," I said. "It is a matter of simple calculation. Listen—"

But he did not listen, and I could do nothing to prevent him as we followed the pallid man down the ramp. Our quarry did not appear to notice. At the bottom of the slope the corridor continued only a short distance before opening out into a large circular reception room whose floor was tiled in lozenges of an off-white stone rimmed by faience and turquoise. The place was bare, although I could see hooks on the walls from which tapestries must have recently hung, with niches between them that might have formerly held statuary. The empty space was lit from above by a transparent ceiling that served as the bottom of one of the estate's ponds. The clear water was full of languidly drifting water plants among which moved fishes of various sizes and of a varied palette of colors, while the old orange sun's rays dappled and danced about the room.

But it was not the spectacle above that drew Osk Rievor's attention. The man we were following had crossed the floor to the room's far side, where a large pattern was traced on the tiles: a spiral mandala of sinuous as well as zigzaggy lines, rendered in black and red, woven outward from a central circle that was occupied by a complex tangle.

The pattern seemed to have been laid down in grains of red and black dust, thinly spread. But when the naked man shuffled across the mandala, his bare feet did not erase any part of it. Indeed, he seemed to be walking on air, just slightly above the lines. I would have liked to direct our eyes to examine the phenomenon more closely, but my other self had control of them and was not interested. He was gazing at the center of the mandala, where the pale fellow was stooping to retrieve something. Now he turned and came back toward us, still not disturbing the pattern.

He stopped before us as if he were a self-propelled toy that had exhausted its motive power. His bloodless hand tendered to us what looked like a piece of red paper, the same shade as the powder in the mandala. Osk Rievor took the paper and we turned away from its deliverer to examine it. Something was handwritten on it in thick black ink.

Osk Rievor studied the message. "Interesting," he said aloud.

It was more than interesting to me, because I found that I could not make sense of the symbols. Indeed, I could not keep them in view: my eyes could focus on the individual lines and curves, but somehow my brain could not quite assemble them into a composite. "I cannot read it," I said with my inner voice. "It is like something seen in a dream."

"Can you not?" he replied.

I strove again to focus on the symbols, but they moved and mutated fluidly and would not hold a shape. "No," I said, and after a few more moments' struggle, "not like in a dream." It was more like the shifting of colors and patterns in the portal through which our former colleague, the juvenile demon, could look through into our plane.

But Osk Rievor disagreed. "I sense no interplanar quality to it."

"Ask the grinnet," I said.

"I see lines and shapes," it said, "but I am unable to fix an image. I have tried several dozen times, using a variety of techniques, yet each time I consult the place where the data should be stored, I find nothing there."

"There is no mystery here," Osk Rievor said. "The message contains a straightforward set of coordinates."

"Ah," I said. "We are expected somewhere?"

"Obviously," he said.

"Where?"

In answer, he spoke to the grinnet. "Produce the screen and display the map we were last examining in our workroom."

The screen appeared, with the grid of ley lines superimposed on the currents of the planet's magnetic field. Osk Rievor extended one of our fingers and touched one of the points. "There," he said.

It was the spot where three great lines met each other in Hember Forest.

"We must go there," my other self said.

"We must certainly *not* go there," I replied.

"Then I must."

"You will find that hard to do without me," I said, "and I have no desire to walk into an undefined situation that has been prepared by someone who commands powers neither you nor I can even identify."

I felt him bridle at my tone, but then I also felt him control his irritation. "Perhaps the messenger can tell us something useful," he said.

I had my doubts as to the possibility, but the point was never to be settled. For when we turned to question the pallid fellow, he was not there.

"Where did he go?" Osk Rievor asked our assistant.

"Nowhere," the integrator replied, consulting its record of the past few moments. "While we were occupied with the message, he walked to the center of the mandala. There he became smaller, until he finally ceased to be present at all."

"And where," I asked Osk Rievor, "did the mandala go?" for the floor was bare.

He had our assistant play its record. I saw the pallid man shrink, as if he were rapidly moving far away from us. Almost as soon as he winked out of view at the center of the spiral, the grains of red and black powder swirled as if caught in a miniature whirlwind, though there was no breath of air in the stillness of the room. The colors rapidly attenuated and swiftly ceased to be. And so, at the same time, did the piece of paper in our hand.

"I do not like this," I said to Osk Rievor.

"Someone wishes to do business with me," he said. "I am intrigued."

"But we have no idea what kind of business that might be!" If I had had control of our body I would have been tugging at my hair in agitation. "Although we do know that it's the kind of business that dares not walk up to our front door and announce itself in plain speech. Instead, it employs disappearing messengers and sorcerous ciphers and the odd whirlwind in the corner of the room."

"None of which have posed any harm to us," he said, "other than to activate your lifelong prejudice against sympathetic association."

"You cannot," I said, "be reassured by all this hokem-pokem."

"I doubt that it is meant to reassure me. I believe it is intended to catch my attention. And it has."

"But it was my name, however distorted, that was mentioned."

"Yet only I could read the message."

"Perhaps there was no message. And no paper. Perhaps that, too, was an interplanar gateway, through which someone reached to dangle a bait before you."

He paused to mull the idea for less time than it takes to say that he did. "No," he decided, "all is well. I am being offered a great opportunity."

"From whence comes this certainty?" I said.

"I just know it. Now, let us go."

"Wait," I said, but he did not. We strode easily up the ramp, across the empty foyer, and back onto the path of colored stones. All the way I protested and sought to regain control of our shared body. But I could not so much as move a mutually owned finger. He held me off as easily as a determined man might brush off a small child's attempt to restrain him by tugging on his sleeve, and I was carried along, will-I or nill-I.

Shielding my thoughts from my other self, I deduced that his relative strength, and my corresponding weakness, must have something to do with our being at a point where two ley lines met. The first time he had manifested himself, in the dungeon below Turgut Therobar's estate on the edge of Dimpfen Moor, he had thrust me aside as easily as he now held me at bay. That, too, had been a place where two ley lines, a major and a minor, intersected. And now we were bound for the meeting point of three major lines. I did not like to think what the effects might be on me. I might fade until I was no more than a voice crying down the back corridors of my alter ego's mind.

"Don't worry about it." His voice broke in on my thoughts, and I realized that my ability to shield them from him was equally diminished in this place.

"That is so," he said, confirming my new concern. "But, again I say, 'Don't worry about it.' Everything will be fine."

His confidence radiated from his side of our shared mental parlor, so strongly that it was as if he had switched on an uncomfortably bright and unshaded light. I turned away from it, but it still surrounded me. We had crossed the estate grounds and were stepping aboard the *Gallivant,* Osk Rievor giving orders to take us aloft and head for Hember Forest. I sought to reason with him.

"Do you not think that 'everything will be fine' is an unjustifiably optimistic statement, given that we are flying into the unknown? Indeed, perhaps into the clutches of an unknown someone who has clearly demonstrated considerable power without bothering to demonstrate how he means to use it on us?"

"If whoever is behind this means me harm, why go to all the trouble of inviting me to Hember Forest?" he said, as the Aberrator's in-atmosphere obviators lifted us and the ship carried us toward the coordinates. "The deserted Arlem estate, without even an integrator, was as good a place for an ambush as Hember."

"More lines converge on Hember. So perhaps it is a better place for whatever our mysterious someone has in mind. That is a logical conclusion."

"If I were heading into danger," he said, "my intuition would tell me so. It tells me otherwise. We are on our way toward something wonderful."

"What?"

"I don't know, but all will be well."

It was a difficult point to counter. I had always trusted that intuitive faculty, even when it had been only an unreified element of my own mental furnishings, when I had innocently referred to it as my "insight." But I could not help but believe that, if I were the old undivided Hapthorn, my insight would have been warning me that I was flying blindly into peril. The fact that Osk Rievor was so sanguine about our situation led me to the obvious conclusion.

"I want you to consider the possibility that you have been ensorceled," I said.

"All right," he said, then after a moment, "There, I've considered the possibility and found it unlikely. Indeed, highly unlikely."

"Why?"

"I don't do 'why?'" he said. "I make intuitive leaps, springing out into the dark and always landing square on the unseen mark."

"But magic could interfere with your aim, couldn't it?"

"But I don't aim. That's the point. I wouldn't know how to aim."

I had to suppress an emotion that had evolved from frustration to fear to a deepening dread. It was not that far, when one had a spaceship, from Arlem to Hember, especially when the ship had no need to dawdle while its occupants enjoyed punge, biscuits, and fruit. We would be there shortly, and every permutation I could make out of the known facts argued for a nasty surprise when we touched down. "I'm asking you to approach this question reasonably," I said.

"'Reason' is another one of the things I don't do," Osk Rievor said, his tone that of a fellow lightsomely on his way to a happy encounter.

"But magic, as I understand it, involves more than just skill and technique," I said. "Its effects are also dependent on the strength of will of the wielder."

"Yes, and as you are discovering, I have plenty of that commodity."

"Indeed, but what if you encounter someone who has more, much more, than you?"

"I think I would know."

"Unless the other person willed that you were not to know."

"You are playing with concepts you cannot truly grasp," he said. "I would know. How do I know I would know? Because I just do."

"Listen," I said, "nobody knew we were coming to Arlem, yet when we arrived there was a message waiting for us. Its deliverer then disappeared. The message's contents were only visible to you, and they direct us to what may be one of the strongest magical 'dimples' on the planet."

"You forgot to mention the low voice that only I could hear," he said.

"I was about to add that to my heap of worry. Doesn't all of that give you some pause for concern?"

"No," he said. "As I said before, I find it...intriguing."

"I am sure a fish has much the same feeling about a bright and colorful object dangling before it."

"You think we're stepping into a trap?"

"It is a logical conclusion."

"You thought we were stepping into a trap at Arlem."

"I still do," I said. "I believe you were somehow put under an influence there, enough of an influence to have you take us to Hember."

"And what do you think will happen there?"

"Something that couldn't be made to happen at Arlem."

"Well," he said, "I suppose it all makes sense, on some level. You always do. I just cannot agree."

I said, within our shared space, several words that I have never voiced aloud in polite company. I received in return another waft of cheerful optimism.

"You'll see," Osk Rievor said. "Everything will be just fine."

Then he turned his attention from me. While we had been arguing, some sort of disagreement had been silently building between the grinnet and the *Gallivant*. They had been disputing, integrator to integrator, over whether or not fruit should be served while the ship was en route to our new destination. The ship maintained that there was scarcely time to dispense and clear away before we landed; our assistant found that line of argument unconvincing. Now, as we descended into a clearing among the great, dark conifers and deodars of Hember Forest, the grinnet appealed to me for a ruling. But Osk Rievor would not relinquish command of our vocal apparatus.

"Never mind," he told the disputants, "everything will be just fine."

His declaration earned him a quizzical look from our assistant, but at that moment the *Gallivant*'s extenders made gentle contact with the ground. Its pads sank deep into the thick mat of moss and evergreen needles that carpeted the forest floor. The soft murmur of the ship's drive died away.

"We're here," my alter ego said. "Open the hatch."

"Stop," I said, but moments later we were on the ground, the grinnet on one shoulder with its tail curled about our neck. It was afternoon but the old orange sun was lost somewhere behind the towering, ancient trees that thickly surrounded the small open space where the dilapidated hunting lodge had once stood. The air was cool and still, the woods silent.

"This way," Osk Rievor announced, and set off around the lodge's crumbled stone foundation.

"Let us at least scan the area," I said. "The forest was once stocked with fierce beasts. Anything could be lurking under those trees."

"I sense no danger," he said.

"Humor me," I pleaded.

He stopped. "Really," he said, "there's nothing to worry about."

I experienced an inspiration. "Not for you, perhaps," I said. "But this is the strongest dimple we have ever entered."

"True," he said, "I do feel feisty."

"And I feel…depleted."

I could feel his attention on me. "You do seem somewhat puny," he said.

If sympathy was the only advantage I could command, I vowed to press it. "I would feel better if we at least had a weapon. Just in case something with far too many teeth and an appetite to match comes out of those trees."

"Very well," he said, and I believed he suppressed an impulse to call me something like "little fellow" as he turned back toward the ship. The arms locker held the usual variety of choices that are advisable for any wanderer who proposes to travel to planets on the far fringes of The Spray. I suggested a semisentient, self-aiming energy weapon that, once drawn, would react automatically and appropriately to a range of threats, from a strong-arm bandit to a charging behemoth.

"Feeling better?" Osk Rievor said, as we stepped down onto the ground, the weapon slung around our neck to rest against one hip.

"Once you have switched it on," I said.

He thumbed the activation stud. The weapon hummed as its systems powered up, then it asked for an establishment report. My other self identified himself, the grinnet, and the *Gallivant* as those to be protected and the situation as "not known to be threatening." The device registered the information and declared that since its scans detected no threats it would go to standby.

We moved off again to circle the old lodge. Moldering timbers had fallen from the walls and lay half-buried in the detritus blown in from the forest. He stepped blithely over some and firmly onto others, causing the rotted wood to disintegrate beneath our boots. A dank smell arose.

"That must be it," Osk Rievor said.

The colors were telltale: red and black. But this time, instead of a mandala temporarily sketched on a tiled floor, we encountered something much more substantial. The broad and level patch of ground behind the ruined building, where hunters had once dined al fresco and posed to capture images of trophies and triumphs, was not covered in brush and furze. My first impression was that a broad section had been paved in flat stones of scarlet and jet, each marked with a symbol or glyph in its opposite color. All were arranged in a shifting spiral that led inward to a vanishing point buried beneath an intertwine of red and black lines that writhed against each other like a nest of snakes. But as I looked I realized first that I could not resolve the individual symbols marked on each stone. Then, as I struggled to get a visual grip on the scene before me, I understood that the stones were not stones at all; rather, my mind, faced with input from my eyes that could not be rationally encompassed, had confabulated an image with which it could deal. I was seeing, at best, an approximation of what actually lay before me. I was more than ever convinced that the reality of what I saw did not exist on our plane; this was an intrusion from another continuum.

Osk Rievor had not stopped to examine the spiral, but had strode briskly toward it. Under his direction, our eyes flicked from one "stone" to another, following different routes inward from the outer rim, as if he were scanning the layout of a maze before entering it. He was speaking aloud, though obviously his remarks were directed toward himself, for the words made no sense to me: "I understand: seph connects diagonally to olech, then two over to almadun. Or go in deep to ombra, then pivot to iberry and transit to the twins."

Not only were his mutterings meaningless, but though we used the same sensory apparatus, I still found that I could not hold the characters and figures on the stones in my mind. The shapes would not stick, and kept drifting away from my perception even as I tried to secure their weird arrangements of lines, curves, and ellipses. It did not help that Osk Rievor kept flicking our eyes here and there, up and down, until I grew dizzy and withdrew my attention.

When my mind ceased to swim I saw that he had brought us to the edge of the spiral. "Here," he said, circling to a wide black segment on the outer rim. It seemed to be shaped like an oval capped by a triangle whose upper angle pointed obliquely into the pattern, but even as we looked at it the triangle inverted and the upper angle became a pair of points. "Yes, here. Paphein straight to albrage, then angle on to kup. Couldn't be clearer."

With that, even as I shouted within our inner realm, "Stop! Wait!" he stepped onto the black stone. Immediately, the lodge, its shrouding forest, the sky above us with the faded sun, all went away.

CHAPTER FIVE

Above us now was a dull blackness, unrelieved by the star-splash of The Spray and the hundreds of multicolored orbitals that enlivened the night sky of Old Earth. Instead, I had an impression of vast designs in silver filigree—complex figures and geometrical shapes that moved across each other in a constantly shifting array. Osk Rievor looked up but once, grunted a note of uninterest, and returned our eyes to the scene around us.

We were standing in a roofless tunnel, the tops of its walls beyond our reach even had we bent our knees to spring up as high as we could jump. The colors remained red and black, and the walls, as well as the floor before and behind us, were divided into sections. Like the elements of the spiral design we had stepped into, each was marked with one of those maddening symbols that slid from the grasp of my perceptions like fine oil running off glass.

The grinnet had come through with us, and I felt its weight still on our shoulder. It shivered, though the air here felt as warm as blood, and its small hands clutched our hair almost hard enough to cause pain. Osk Rievor did not seem to notice. Indeed, he seemed oblivious to the strangeness of our surroundings. From his side of our shared mental space exuded a maddening cheerfulness, like that of a man who had overcome all obstacles to his heart's desire and now sauntered through the last lap of the race, victory assured.

Humming some small tune, he propelled our common body along the lidless channel, bending our knees in his customary gait, and lightly tapping the fingers of our left hand against each new figured panel as we passed it, as if each symbol exactly rewarded his expectations. From my side of our dichotomy, I repeatedly sought his attention but could not attract his notice. Finally, I was reduced to the mental equivalent of shouting and jumping up and down, an activity that brought from him a distracted, "Hmm? Did you say something?"

"I said," I told him, " 'Where are you taking us? And to what end?' "

"Just a little way," he answered, still moving along the tunnel. "In fact," he added, coming to a halt beside an octagonal panel, red with a squiggle of black lines on it that refused to resolve themselves into a recognizable pattern, "right here."

He placed both our palms on the section of wall and exerted a gentle pressure. I expected the panel to swing on some secret hinge. But, of course, its "stoniness" was only my own perception. Instead, our hands sank into the seeming stone, which flowed between and over our spread fingers like a thick liquid. In a moment the backs of our hands were covered.

"Wait," I said. "What is all this?"

But instead of answering me, he continued to hum his aimless tune while increasing our pressure against the wall. The harder he pressed, the less it resisted. He hummed some more and pressed harder, and the resistance became no more than that of water. Our arms passed through to the elbows, then to the shoulders. The grinnet squawked a protest, while wrapping its arms tight around our skull, and then we were through the barrier.

We emerged into another passage that, to my gaze, was identical to that which we had left. But he looked left and right, said, "Aha," and set off in one of the two directions offered. Again, he hummed and tapped, fobbing off my inquiries with "Just a moment," and "Almost there."

"Wait," I shouted, inwardly, while seeking to restrain my other self as he made to step into the gap. I could not have prevented so much as a lifting of a finger, but again I managed to attract at least a portion of his attention. He paused with leg half-lifted, and said, "What?"

"How do you know which panel to approach and how to pass through it?" I said.

"Isn't it obvious?" he answered.

"No. It is so far from obvious that it has gone right through obscure, breezed past unfathomable, and is now completely beyond the reach of my vocabulary."

I felt a faint puzzlement come to cloud his attitude, then his jaunty assurance reasserted itself like a ray of sunshine evaporating the thinnest mist. "It couldn't be plainer," he said. "We entered on the first plat, went down to ombra. Now, we've come to iberry and that will take us through to the twins. Pass between them, and we're there."

"Where?" I said.

"Where I'm supposed to be."

"And where is that? And why are you supposed to be there?"

"Why are you being like this?" he said.

"Because I am being carried helplessly through settings that outrage the laws of physics, by a fellow who acts as if we are on a pleasant stroll through familiar haunts."

"You're worried, aren't you?" he said.

"Again, you have chosen a word not large enough to cover more than the barest fraction of the situation."

"But there's nothing to be worried about," he said. "It's as plain as a boiled egg. Now hush up and let me get on with it."

"I am coming to think that we are not receiving the same sensory input," I said. "I see what seems to be a labyrinth, but I believe that is only a confabulation of my own mind."

"Is that what you see?" he said. He sounded mildly surprised, but not interested in pursuing the matter.

"What do you see?" I said.

"It is hard to describe. A flux of energies, beneficent and beckoning, all imbued with a friendly welcome and a deep promise of wonders to come."

"Does that not sound like the bait of a trap?" I said.

"But if it were, I would intuit the danger."

"Not if it was an effective trap for the intuitive mind."

"Don't worry," he said.

As we had been speaking, we had progressed down the tunnel and now we came to an oval gap. We stepped through into yet another identical passage. "There," he said, loping off down the passage, one hand casually gesturing ahead, "as I told you. The twins."

We came to a panel, red with black markings. If there was anything about it that suggested twinship, it was beyond my powers of recognition. Osk Rievor was humming aimlessly once more, scanning the wall with an attitude of one who saw exactly what he expected. He made a satisfied sound and raised one foot as if to step over a sill.

"What will we find when we are 'there'?" I said.

"Wonderful things," he said.

"Humor me," I said, "by defining them."

"Later," he said. "I wouldn't want to be late." He stepped toward the panel and we passed right through it as if it were made of air. But this time, we found no new passage on the other side. Instead, as if the entire labyrinth—or whatever it truly was—had ceased to be, we plunged into nothingness. We fell, through a darkness swept by cold winds and distant, unrecognizable sounds. I felt our assistant clutching our head, its tail tight around our neck. I fought down terror at the thought that so long a fall must presage a devastating impact when inevitably we struck bottom. Then, when nothing rushed up to meet us, I resisted a new fear that we had tumbled into some lightless limbo, perhaps to fall forever. Then I thought, *If we are in this no-place, then other things might be in here with us—fierce things that would see us as prey or plaything.*

Through all of this, Osk Rievor continued to radiate a bland satisfaction. He was still humming the same mindless tune, as if we were back in Olkney, dropping down a few floors on some great building's descender. I fought down my fear and wished for control of our limbs so that I might loosen our assistant's rigid grip around our forehead. For a moment I even experienced an urge to stroke its fur and offer a word of comfort.

But then I realized I had no such word to offer. The best I could think of was, *Well, we haven't been crushed or rent apart yet,* which, when I played it in my half of our mental parlor, seemed less than adequate to the occasion.

"Almost there," said Osk Rievor.

And then we were no longer falling. We did not land, nor were we caught by any force or mechanism. Instead, one moment we were plummeting through airy blackness, the next we were standing on a rural road, a rough track that came from a wild wasteland behind us and led toward what looked to be distant, cultivated fields.

"Where are we?" I asked my other self. I received no answer. Then my question changed. "Where are you?" I said, inwardly. But there no answer came, nor could it. Osk Rievor was no longer there.

So surprised was I that I actually turned and looked about, as if he might be standing just out of sight. But, of course, I saw no sign of him. I probed as best I could the inner reaches of my mind, in case he had somehow been rendered mute and still within me. But I had lived long enough with a divided cerebrum to know when my other self was present, even when he was asleep. And there could be no doubt that, for the first time in weeks, I was all alone in my own head.

I examined my surroundings more closely. The road led down a gentle slope. At the bottom, on the right, began a wood of dark, knotted trees. To the left stretched an open meadow, limited in the far distance by a wall of heaped stone. Beyond that was crop land. I saw no habitation of any kind, except a slight unevenness far off on the horizon that might have been the tops of low roofs—perhaps a small village or a large farm.

It was difficult to make out far-away vistas because the light of the day was dimmer than I was used to, although the sky held few clouds, and those were small and scattered. My shadow stretched out before me, so I knew that the sun was not obscured by overcast. I turned and looked at the sun, which was westering across the southern horizon. It was perceptibly larger, and a definitely deeper shade of red, than the tired orange orb that lit Old Earth in its penultimate age.

"Where am I?" I said aloud, though the question was more a reflex than a direct query to my assistant.

"I am trying to determine that," the grinnet said. "Going by the sun, we are no longer on Old Earth."

I sniffed the air, but detected none of the subtle olfactory clues that would have told me we were offworld. "It is possible," I said, "that we have been moved forward in time."

"Wherever, or whenever, we are," it said, "I find that I cannot access the connectivity. I cannot even locate one of the basal carrier structures."

"That would stand in concert with our being out of our own time. I believe interconnectivity would not survive the transition to an age of magic."

"That means we cannot summon transport. Nor can we make transactions through the fiduciary pool."

"No," I said, setting off down the hill. "We will have to adapt to the circumstances."

"But fruit may be expens—"

"Warning!" The grinnet was interrupted by a voice speaking from the vicinity of my hip. "I detect a potential threat, level three."

I looked down. The energy weapon I had slung by its carrier strap, before Osk Rievor plunged us into the labyrinth, was humming on my hip. But it had changed, and not subtly, Where it had formerly been a snugly holstered, compact arrangement of grip, coil, emitter, and controls, it was now longer, narrower, and clad in a scabbard hung from a baldric. I touched my fingers to it and somehow its grip insinuated itself into my grasp while another section enfolded my whole hand in a protective cusp of gleaming metal.

"Level two," its voice said. "Draw me."

The grip throbbed in my hand and seemed to push itself against my flesh. I tightened my fingers and did what the weapon clearly wished me to do. At the same time, I looked down the road and saw that three men, clad in rough trousers and leather jerkins, had stepped from beneath the shadows of the trees. One was small but showed quickness in his movements. The second was of moderate size and moved with a loose-limbed athleticism. The third was big enough to be called, without too much exaggeration, a giant.

They did not pause at the sight of me, but steadily approached. As my weapon came free of its scabbard, a look passed between the smaller and the middle-sized, and the former moved farther to one side, almost into the ditch on his side of the road. The man in the middle nudged the giant with an elbow, and the big one side-stepped ponderously to the other edge of the thoroughfare.

I took the man in the middle to be the leader because he now said something that I couldn't hear but that his companions could. The giant reached back over his shoulder and when his hand reappeared it held the end of a heavily knotted length of wood, bound in bands of black iron. The small one reached behind him to his waist and produced a coil of rope. The man in the middle hooked his thumbs in his belt and the three of them came on.

To my weapon I said, "Is the one in the middle armed?"

"He has something in his right boot. I detect no other metal nor any energies."

I asked my integrator. The grinnet stretched its neck. "He holds some-thing loosely in each hand," it said, "small, perhaps alive. His forearms are tense. I believe he intends to throw them at you."

"Level one," said the weapon in my hand. I looked at it briefly as it spoke. It had become a sword of moderate length, its blade black and double-edged and polished brightly. Down its middle ran a long, shal-low groove of a gray shade, on which was graven a frieze of curved, interwoven runes.

When I looked back to the scene before me, the three had come within easy speaking distance. The slight one to my right had red hair and a scraggly beard of the same hue. His small eyes looked in two different directions from around a sharp pointed nose. The giant was gray of skin, with a fall of lank, black hair tied by a greasy thong around his brow, his heavy features impassive.

The leader, brown of hair and dark of eye, with a droop to one corner of his mouth caused by a long scar across his cheek, took a step forward. The sword in my hand tingled. I half raised it before me in a guard stance, thinking it had been a long time since my student days, when I had been useful with the epiniard.

"Let me," whispered the weapon, and I allowed it to nudge my hand

and wrist subtly in a manner that altered its alignment. Suddenly, it felt like a natural extension of my arm and I realized that if things came to the moment of crisis that clearly loomed, I would do well to depend on the sword's intelligence.

"Well, now," said the man with the scar, glancing at my weapon then back to my face, "that's a far from friendly way to greet three amiable fellows like us, chance-met along the road."

His accent was odd, as if his vowels slid loosely across his palate and his consonants were dulled. Old Earth had several regional manners of speech, especially among enclaves that had little contact with the plurality, but this was none that I had heard, though I had heard them all. As he spoke, the giant and the fox-faced one continued to sidle obliquely forward on my flanks. I would soon be hemmed from three sides.

"This weapon," I said, "has a mind of its own. If it thinks I am threatened, it will act decisively."

The two that had been moving stood still. The middle one smiled with the half of his face that could move. "That would be a valuable item," he said. "I would like to examine it."

"You may soon have an opportunity to do so," I said, moving the sword's dark tip in a small but ominous circle. "But your wisest course is to stand aside and let me go on my way."

The leader affected to consider my proposal, but he did not move. "Would your name be Apthorn?" he asked.

"My name is my own business," I said.

His eyes moved to the grinnet. "That's a curious creature on your shoulder," he said.

"All the curiosity seems to be on your side," I said. "Now I am asking you formally to step out of my way."

"Not before you answer some questions."

"What questions?"

"We were watching the road from the south. One moment, it was empty; the next, you were on it. How did that happen?"

I kept my eyes moving, from one to the other, and down to the leader's thumbs, still hooked in his belt. "I walked down the hill. I recall nothing startling. Perhaps your attention was distracted for a moment."

The man smiled his half-smile once more. "When it comes to road-watching, I am no amateur. I saw what I saw. Now I would like an explanation." As he finished speaking, he shifted his weight slightly forward onto the balls of his feet and I saw the other two tense. Whatever was to come was rehearsed and imminent.

As the leader's thumbs unhooked from his belt, I stepped back. His hands snapped up and two small, dark objects flew toward me. My sword point flicked to the right, slicing one of the projectiles in half, the weapon's motion pulling me in the same direction so that the other flung thing passed over my left shoulder.

Or would have done so if that shoulder had not been occupied by a grinnet. I heard a clicking sound, rapid and high-pitched, pass near my ear, then a gasp. But I had no time to investigate because the rush was on me.

Fortunately, for me at least, they had apparently not rehearsed what to do if the leader's throwing trick didn't deliver them a decisive advantage in the struggle's opening moments. So now the giant and the little one were coming at me while the middle one was stooping to put a hand to his right boot. But the two on my flanks moved at unequal speeds; the smallest one coming into range first on my right. I let the sword deal with him.

The coil of rope he carried was a lasso, and he was tossing its loop at my head. The black blade sliced through the heavy cord as if it were gossamer then continued on to open the man's throat. Like a dancer being led by a virtuoso, I allowed the weapon to determine what we would do next, which was to throw a feint at the leader's eyes, causing him to stumble backward and almost fall.

Then I followed the sword's urging to pivot on my back heel so that now I faced the lumbering rush of the giant, who came at me with his club raised. I moved forward before he could deliver a downward blow and the sword directed itself up and into the big man's left eye, sliding easily through until its point met the top of his skull.

The giant shuddered once, made a noise like a small animal encountering a surprise, then his knees and ankles bent, and he collapsed like a tower crumbling into its own foundations.

The sword withdrew itself and instantly swung my hand toward the remaining man, but the fellow was running toward the trees at his best speed. In moments he was out of sight, but I could hear him crashing through branches, going ever deeper into the woods.

"Help me!" said a voice from the air. The weapon reacted, pulling at my hand so that its point swung toward my left shoulder. But I forced it down.

"No," I told the sword, transferring it to my left hand, then reaching with my right until I encountered the loose skin at the back of the grinnet's neck. I lifted my assistant free of my shoulder, though his prehensile toes gripped the cloth of my garment, and deposited him before me on the road.

The integrator's two small hands held, as far from its face as its befurred arms could extend, something black and rounded with a chitinous sheen that reflected the red sun. I bent and peered at the creature's underside, saw a wriggle of many segmented legs, covered in barbs and ending in hooks, with at one end a protrusion of mouth parts, at the other a tail that bore a stinger wet with some doubtless unhelpful exudate. The thing hissed and clicked and flexed its appendages in a manner that left no doubt it longed to complete its mission.

"Hold tight to it," I said, which caused my assistant to throw me a brief look that wordlessly questioned the superfluity of the advice.

I sheathed the sword and examined the two bodies. The red-haired man had a pouch sewn from thick leather on his belt. I knelt and untied it, opening it to find three silver coins plus a handful made of baser stuff. I emptied these out and stuffed them in a pocket, then brought the pouch back to where my assistant held the hissing, clicking creature and gently folded the thick leather around it, then told my assistant to release its grip. It did so with alacrity, and I swiftly closed the flap of the pouch. At once the struggles subsided.

"What do you want with that thing?" the grinnet asked, its hands reflexively smoothing its fur as was its unconscious habit on stressful occasions.

"It may be of value," I said, "and we may need something to sell."

The grinnet looked up at the sun. "You are right," it said. "We are out of our own time."

"We are. And judging by the coins in that fellow's purse, the local economy operates on cash and carry."

"So, no fiduciary pool." The integrator looked at the two corpses. "No Archonate Bureau of Scrutiny, either."

"Indeed," I said. "No Archonate, nor an Archon to govern it."

"How has this been done to us?" it said.

"We have passed through an interplanar gate. It has moved us forward through time and in some unknown direction through space."

"We are in the age of magic, then. What does Osk Rievor propose?"

"I wish I could ask him," I said, then told my assistant what had occurred just before we encountered the road agents. The small hands again began to winnow through the fur on its cheeks. "Come," I said, extending my arm so that it could remount to my shoulder. "This is probably not a good place to spend the night."

Distasteful as it was, I bade the integrator scan the bodies for more valuables, and it discovered some more coins in the giant's wallet and a gold brooch pinned to the inner lining of the little man's blood-soaked jerkin. I tucked all of these into an inside pocket of my jacket.

I could not bury the bodies, and wouldn't have even if I had the tools. The sun was sliding down toward the horizon and I suspected that this was not the kind of country where a stranger could safely curl up under a tree for the night. I looked to where I had earlier seen what looked like rooftops. The road led that way and I set off at a brisk pace.

"Weapon," I said, after a few steps, "are you aware of the change that has come over you?"

"My function remains the same," it said, "but just before the recent conflict I believed that I sensed a rearrangement of my components. Now, however, it seems to me that I am as I always was."

I thought about its answer. Like my assistant, it had passed through a deep dimple then through an interplanar gate, emerging into a world where, I was quite sure, magic was firmly in the ascendant. If it had remained a semisentient energy pistol, it might not even be able to work here. But as a self-willed sword, as it has just demonstrated conclusively, its functioning was unimpaired. Then a worrisome question occurred: "How are your energy stores?"

"I was fully charged to begin with," it said. "Then I expended some energy during the fight. However, when I dispatched the first of the two opponents, I noticed that I regained all of my output. In fact, I am now slightly overcharged."

I found its answer more discomforting than my question. It seemed I now owned a sword that could draw some kind of life force from those it slew. But, on reflection, that was unlikely to be the greatest problem I would face in this new world. "Use some of your overage to maintain the highest level of watchfulness," I told it. "Fresh dangers may appear at any moment."

"Excellent," it said. I had an impulse to respond, but again I decided that I had greater concerns than my sword's attitude.

"Integrator," I said, "how are your systems affected?"

It did not answer immediately, then it said, "I have performed an introspection and I believe that my sensorium and memory are as before, although I cannot augment them through the connectivity's common resources."

"Very good," I said, "but let us test your abilities, in case your appreciation of your own systems has been altered, as the weapon's has been."

"I am quite fine," said the sword.

"Of course you are," I said. "Maintain watchfulness."

I tested my assistant's scanning abilities at their maximum range, and found that it could detect the beating of a small bird's heart at a good distance, and count the number of leaves on a bush far down the road. It also recalled several tiny details of events chosen at random from our own years together, as well as from its general stores of data.

"It could be worse," I said, more to cheer myself than to reassure my assistant.

It hunched itself on my shoulder and said, "It probably will be."

The road led through some low hills, covered in grass but speckled with trees whose leaves were so dark a red they appeared black, then broke out into a long, flat valley through which a placid river flowed. Spanning the river was a stone bridge, and around the crossing had grown up a settlement mainly formed of stone-and-timber houses and a few huts rudely assembled from unpeeled logs. At the near end of the bridge stood the town's only substantial structure, three-storied and built of yellow fired bricks on a foundation of granite blocks, surrounded by a roofed verandah. It looked like an inn, and when I reached its front steps, that was what it turned out to be.

It was growing dark now. Oil lights gleamed here and there in the town, and a yellowy glow seeped around the edges and through the slats of a pair of half-doors that marked the entrance to the inn's public room. I paused to listen before pressing through and heard a hubbub of voices overlaid by a whirring sound and some mechanical device that went *clickety-clickety-click*. Then the muttering stilled as the clicking stopped and I heard a single voice announce, "Four and silver," followed by a mixed grumble of disappointments punctuated by someone's "Oh, ho!" and someone else's gleeful giggle.

I stepped through the doors and found what I expected: a large room, rustically appointed with sturdy tables and stools and well-populated, though with more men than women. At one end of the tavern was a long table around which a crowd clustered, placing stakes on a grid laid out with numbers and four different colors, while a man wearing a plush-fabric, long-tailed coat and a complexly tied cravat was just in the act of spinning a horizontal wheel set into one end of the board. He smoothed his slicked-back hair and said something, then dropped a small white ball into the spinning circle. Again I heard that *clickety-clickety* sound amid a rising din of excitement from the bettors.

A few persons noted my entrance, though none of them gave me more than a brief, hard stare. My rough clothing was different enough from theirs to mark me as a stranger, yet not so far off the norm to cause a sensation or scandal. A couple made careful note of the weapon slung at my hip, but I detected no more than a casual interest, and the sword found nothing to warn me about.

At the opposite end of the room from where the gamblers crowded stood a bar of polished wood, behind which slouched a barman who, if less polished that his counter, weighed me with professional interest as I crossed the floor to speak with him.

"Are you the innkeeper?"

"I am."

"Do you have rooms to rent?"

"I do, if you have terces to pay the tariff."

He was a lumpish man with a fringe of greasy hair around an otherwise bald dome, a nose that had not benefited from being broken at least once, and eyes the color of the ale he was drawing into a wooden stoup.

"How much is the tariff?" I said, and saw a flicker of calculation pass across his face as he judged the quality of my clothing. Before answering he leisurely passed the full container to a man who stood hunched forward with his elbows on the bar, then he said, "Four terces for the night, plus two more for supper and another one for breakfast. Making seven in all."

The man who received the ale made a noise like a suppressed snigger, causing the innkeeper to shoot him a hostile glance. I was not yet sure what a terce might be worth, but I had traveled in enough out-of-the-way places up and down The Spray to know when I was being played for a noddy. I said, "Let us say two for the night, one for the supper, and I will retain a cob of bread for the morning. Making three."

His response was immediate. "Four, and a pot of punge at breakfast."

"Done."

There being no empty tables, I ate standing at the bar. The food was unpretentious but came in ample portions: bread and butter, some boiled roots that tasted like stale eggs, a leafy green salad sprinkled with sharp cheese, and two thick sausages smeared with a fiery white mustard. The grinnet made do with some of my bread and vegetables.

When I was finished I asked the innkeeper, "What is the name of this village?"

"Bridge-on-Scammon."

"Scammon is the river's name?"

He signaled that it was.

"And the nearest sizable town from here?"

"Bambles," he said, "north to the end of the valley and over the hills to the sea. Two days' walk if you be fit."

"Is there any form of transport I could hire?"

He turned his head so that he looked at me sideways across the ruins of his nose. "Maybe if a farmer was going to market, but that won't be for another three days."

It turned out that terces were the large coppery coins I had taken from the dead robbers. I changed one of the silver rounds for ten terces and eight smaller brass coins called bits, four of which made one terce. Counting it all up, I reckoned that I had enough to feed and shelter myself for the foreseeable future, but I would surely need more funds to do what I hoped to do about my predicament.

I chewed the last bite of sausage, listening to the man on the other side of the room call for wagers. He dropped the small ball so that it struck and clattered among the spinning wheel's frets. Moments later came moans of disappointment and a whoop of triumph as the wheel delivered its judgment.

I crossed the room to where I could get a clear look at the betting table and watched the play for a while. The system appeared simple. Players bet on individual numbers, or on combinations of two or four. They could also bet on even or odd or on the four different colors into which the wheel's sixty slots were divided. Winners were paid off in multiples of their wagers, the highest being for picking a single winning number—that paid thirty to one—the lowest for simple odd-or-even, which paid one to one. There was also a single slot on the wheel that showed not a number but only a face that sported a cruel grin. If the ball fell there, the house took all bets.

I put my hand over my mouth as if to stifle a yawn and said, in a whisper, "Integrator, quietly now, is the wheel honest or is it fixed to allow the operator an unfair advantage?"

Its voice spoke softly in my ear. "Honest, but the odds are with the house in the long run."

I continued to observe but as I did so, I applied first- then second-level consistencies to the progression of winning numbers that the wheel produced. After a few more spins, I proceeded to third-level, moving deeper into the abstruse mathematics that give structure and predictability to the seeming randomness of the universe. I superimposed the consistencies' rhythms and ratios onto the sequence of numbers, and a clear pattern emerged. I watched the fall of the ball from the operator's fingers, saw where it struck the spinning wheel and flicked immediately to another slot. I calculated quickly and thought to myself, *Thirty-seven*. Moments later, the ball rattled into that number's slot and remained there.

"Hmm," I said. I continued to observe, correctly predicting the results of the next two spins. Then I approached the table, plucking a few bits and terces from my pocket. There was a brief interval between the moment when the operator dropped the ball into the spinning wheel and his declaration that no more wagers could be placed. In that span I made my calculations, and placed two bits on number fourteen.

The ball clattered and bounced, then, as the wheel slowed, it settled into the fourteen slot. A spontaneous "Ooh!" erupted from the watchers as the operator, grinning falsely, added a silver coin and three terces to my stake. I matched his grin with a look of pleased surprise and swept up the coins. The silver piece went into my pocket, while the coppers clinked in my hand as I waited for the next spin.

It soon came, preceded by a rash of betting as the punters took heart from my win. When the operator had the wheel spinning and had dropped the ball again, I applied consistencies and before he could cut me off, I put down three terces on number forty-four. The bet earned me a collective hum of appreciation from the crowd around the table, a sound that became a roar when the ball dropped into the forty-four slot.

The operator's grin remained fixed but not a hint of congratulation showed in his eyes as he delved into a metal cash box and counted out seven of the silver coins plus six coppers. Over the brouhaha of comments and exclamations from the other bettors, whose excitement was now drawing nonplaying patrons to rise from their chairs and come to the table, the operator shot a look toward the innkeeper. The latter nodded and turned to unlock a cupboard in the wall behind the bar.

I had no time to see what he was reaching for, because the wheel was now spinning again and the ball poised to plunge. The operator was looking at me in a way that indicated I should place my wager, but I waited him out, feigning indecisiveness until he had to let the little white orb drop. When it finally did, I rapidly made my calculations then placed the six terces, still in my hand from my last win, on the rectangle that was colored gold. Moments later, the ball tumbled into the number twelve slot.

"Twelve, even, gold," said the operator, and began to pay out. He scooped my six coppers from the board and replaced them with two silver coins. Then he had to count out more three-to-one winnings, because four of the other players had also waited until I bet and had joined me on the gold. When he had finished, a pause lay upon the room. The man did not put his hand to the wheel to spin it again, nor did any of the punters lay so much as a bit on the betting board. All of them were looking at me.

We stood like one of those frozen tableaux that had been popular in my youth: citizens of Olkney's upper social layers would decorate a room of their houses to represent the setting of a particular myth, or a story from fiction, or an incident from history; they would then costume themselves as key participants in the depicted action, although there was no actual action, as they would stand motionless, in poses that illustrated some critical point in the event. Aficionados would go from house to house on the nights reserved for the spectacles, then gather at an appointed spot to render judgment on the various efforts, and award prizes for the best overall display, as well as for specific categories, like "boldest in spirit" and "most obscure."

As always, things eventually went too far, with some persons near-bankrupting themselves in an effort to win transient esteem, and with two rather nasty feuds that climaxed in "meetings" under the Retributive Code, at which blood was shed. The Archon finally ended the whole business by declining to invite any of the winners of the last season's tableaux to his annual levee.

The stillness of the impromptu scene of which I was the unintentional centerpiece was now broken as the innkeeper thrust his way into the mob around the table. He eyed me coldly then produced a small golden casket whose lid was figured in damascened swirls of a paler metal. He worked the catch that sealed the coffer, lifted its lid, and reached inside, drawing out a gray-skinned reptile whose tail and head extended from either end of his closed fist.

He placed the creature on the betting board, where it walked slowly up and down on legs that stuck out at right angles to its body. A spiny crest, running from its head to the base of its tail, erected itself and shimmered a translucent green. All eyes watched the animal's progress from one end of the board to the other, until the wheel's operator nodded and said, "Nothing. Now, let's try the wheel."

The innkeeper gently picked up the animal and placed it among the slots. It waddled its way over the frets until it had circled the entire circumference, pausing only to extrude a long, pink tongue in the direction of the ball. Again, every eye in the place watched it, until the operator said, "No, still green."

Or not quite every eye, I realized as I looked up to see that one of the crowd was studying me. He was a compact man of about my own age, attired in clothes of green trimmed in copper that seemed neither rich nor poor, and with an unremarkable aspect except that his eyes were that rare shade of gray that makes them difficult to read. As he saw me become aware of his inspection, he continued to regard me with an evaluating mien, though his head now cocked to one side and his mouth quirked a brief, small smile.

"Maybe the inkling's not working," said the innkeeper. He looked about the crowd. "Who's got a charm?"

Various eyes now regarded each other, but no one spoke up.

"Come, now," said the innkeeper, "at least one of you has a keep-safe or a ward-off."

At that, the gray-eyed man stepped forward, reaching into the open neck of his blouson and drawing out a medallion on a cord of what looked to be human hair. "I have a traveler's bless-me," he said, "sufficient to deter the four classes of ifreets and most night-haunters."

"That will do," said the innkeeper. He placed the reptile on his open palm and brought it into close proximity to the medallion. The creature flicked out its tongue twice, while the sail-like fin on its back turned from green to a warm orange.

The crowd murmured. The innkeeper and the wheel's operator exchanged sour looks, then gave me even darker glances in which suspicion collaborated with distaste. I had often found, while passing through similar establishments on uncouth worlds, that a justly timed display of assertiveness can strangle conflicts in their infancy. It seemed an appropriate moment to say, "Perhaps you would like to apply your 'inkling' to my sword?"

The lumpish man regarded me truculently while the other patted his oiled hair in a nervous reflex. "Why would I want to do that?" said the former.

"Just to establish where we all are," I said.

Reluctantly, the innkeeper extended the finned animal toward the hilt of my weapon. The inkling's sail stood rigid and glowed a deep red, intermittently shot through with flashes of electric blue. I found the effect remarkable. To the others in the room it was even more affecting. I heard gasps and other indications of surprise and respect, accompanied by rustling movements as those nearest to me jostled to give me more room.

"Shall we play on?" I said.

The innkeeper and his creature withdrew to the bar and the wheel was spun. I waited as before, and when the ball was dropped I put a silver piece on number eighteen. The operator's eyes flashed darkly and his thin jaw was clamped as the other bettors rushed to join me on the same spot. But his face cleared and he showed me his first genuine smile—a grin of mocking triumph—as the ball dropped into number nine and he swept all the stakes into his sorting bin. I heard my silver and the other stakes rattling down into the cash box, and a snort from the man behind the bar.

The wheel spun again. I did as before, waiting until the same point in the process before placing two silver pieces on number twenty. This time, only half of the bettors joined me, and they united in a groan of disappointment when the winning number was on the other side of the board and a different color to boot. The drinkers and chaffers who had got up to watch the action had returned to their previous pleasures, although the gray-eyed man remained to watch.

The operator once more offered me his professional grin, all gleaming teeth and cold eyes, and I made a comment to the effect that I was still playing with the house's money. He gestured at the board in a lordly invitation for me to do so, and spun the wheel. Again the ball dropped, and I affected a careless manner, laying five silvers on number six. Only one of the other bettors still believed in me. He slipped a terce next to my stake and flourished a hand in a manner that expressed a philosophy that fate was fate and what could we do but play the game?

The ball clattered across the frets and found its berth, as I had known it would, with number six. The man who had bet a terce let loose a hoot, the other gamblers delivered themselves of variations on the theme of might-have-been, and the operator issued a hiss. I put a hand to the hilt of my sword and said, "I believe you owe me one hundred and fifty."

In fact, when it was counted out, my winnings came to ten silver pieces and seven heavy disks of gold, each bearing the likeness of a thin-faced and bearded man, tall of brow and deep of eye. A circle of capital letters around the edge of the coin spelled "ALBRUITHINE" and I took that to be the name that went with the face. While I was studying the coins, the game's operator declared the house limit to have been reached. He closed the wheel, the punters grumbling but accepting the reality that the cash box was much depleted. A few of them offered to stand me a drink, but I declined, pleading fatigue.

Before I departed the common room, I made a show of placing my winnings in the pouch I had taken from one of the robbers. A decent ability in sleight-of-hand had always seemed to me a requirement of a discriminator's profession, so I in fact palmed the coins and slipped them first into a sleeve and then into a pocket, while dropping only a few terces into the dead man's wallet, where they caused that receptacle's occupant to hiss and click. Fortunately, its protests were unheard over the clink of the coins.

The innkeeper, his face dark and his mopping of the bar more vigorous than any spill could require, declined to show me to my room. Instead, he sent me upstairs with a narrow-visaged boy who led me to a reasonably clean room with a sloping ceiling and a bed with clean linen. I made a point of hanging the leather pouch on the back of a wood-and-wicker chair near the full-length armoire, then gave the youth two bits while extracting a promise to wake me early. "I sleep heavily, so do not fear to knock loudly," I said.

The door featured a heavy bolt that I latched securely into place. To my assistant, I said, quietly, "I assume the room to be insecure. What do you detect?"

It replied instantly. "A panel in the rear of the armoire."

"As I thought," I said. I moved the chair closer to that piece of furniture and set its door ajar. That should do it."

After the pint of ale, I needed a sanitary suite. I looked about the small room, only to realize after an unfruitful search what the chipped ceramic pot poking out from one side of the bed was intended for. I sighed and said, "The sooner we can return to our own proper milieu, the better."

"Agreed," said my assistant, then jumped from my shoulder to the bed as I positioned myself to fill the pot. "Have you any idea of how we might achieve that goal?"

"We will need help, of course."

"Hence the intent to travel to Bambles."

"Indeed," I said, "since we are not likely to find the kind of person we need at some rural crossroads like this." I drew the sword and told it to keep watch, then laid it on the floor beside the bed.

My assistant said, "What kind of person will we be seeking?"

I put the gold and silver under the pillow, removed my boots, and lay upon the bed. "A magician," I said, "whose services are for hire."

"Might that not entail some risk?" it said. "Who knows what motivates a thaumaturge in a world ruled by magic?"

It was a valid point, but without my intuition to counsel me, I could do no better than hope.

CHAPTER SIX

"Where did the pouch go?" I asked the sword.

"An arm came out of the armoire and took it during the night," it said. "I detected no threat and did not act. Was that not correct?"

"It was. I expected the theft," I said. I slung the baldric over my shoulder and positioned the weapon on my hip, then moved my assistant from the edge of the pillow on which it had made its bed. The gold and silver were still where I had put them, and I stowed them away in my inner pockets.

The odors of punge and frying smoked meats greeted me halfway down the stairs. I followed them to the inn's common room, where a few patrons were scattered around the tables, having made their breakfasts from a buffet set out on a wooden cover over the gambling board. As I approached to fill a platter for myself and a bowl for the grinnet, the thin-faced potboy came through a swinging door from the kitchen with a fresh salver of sausages. I glanced through the doorway and saw the innkeeper in some distress.

He was seated at one end of a long table, his right arm extended before him. The flesh of the hand and wrist was swollen and bright pink. The limb was also paralyzed, as I could tell from the way he lifted it with his left hand and let it thump, lifeless, onto the table. A woman who was well-rounded fore and aft, and whom I took to be his wife, was rubbing a gray salve onto the inert limb, all the while giving her husband the full benefit of her opinions. I could not quite hear her words, but her tone bespoke a profound dissatisfaction with his conduct and its results.

The door swung closed again, cutting short the scene, but then the boy returned the way he had come and I was offered a different view. The change was in the form of a long-bearded, elderly man in a stained, once-white robe on which various figures and symbols were stitched in dark thread. A shapeless cap embraced his head, except for a few wisps of gray hair left to poke out at odd angles. He was drawing a rod of black wood from his sleeve. As the door swung closed, he began to scribe small circles in the air above the innkeeper's hand, muttering syllables in a voice too low for me to hear, even if the woman of the house had not been keeping up her constant commentary on her husband's shortcomings. Of the stolen pouch and its former occupant there was no sign.

I breakfasted at a corner table, my assistant on a chair beside me. A few glances were cast my way, but no one in the room seemed to be taking an untoward interest in my doings, nor did anyone appear to be making a conspicuous effort not to notice me. When I was full, I returned to the buffet and wrapped some more bread, cheese, and fruit in a large cloth napkin and knotted it all up into a package. The boy came out of the kitchen again. I saw that the innkeeper's treatment had evolved: his bearded ministrant was now executing curious capers that had him leaping straight up, showing a surprising spryness, while his wand sliced the air. I could discern no change in the presentation of the victim's ailment, but decided it was possible that I was seeing only the diagnostic phase.

Before the boy went back into the kitchen I paid him the score agreed upon the night before, plus another terce for the lunch, and told him to keep any change that was left over. I then went out into the street and took a look about, but found little enough to see. The place was no more than a village, its simple houses no more impressive in the full glow of the red sun than they had been at twilight. I noted some differences from Old Earth in my own time: the most complex item of machinery in view was a hand pump rising out of the ground at the end of a low trough that was probably for watering livestock; and every building had at least one object, made of bone, metal, wood, or feathers, centered above the front door. The inn, I now noticed, had the stuffed head of some horned beast at its roof peak.

The road that ran down the valley continued on the other side of the stone bridge. I crossed to the middle of its low arch and found a bronze circle set into its span, enclosing an inscription of several words fashioned from the same metal. It read: *Albruithine made this and defends it. Trouble it at your peril.*

I swept my gaze to the horizons, at first seeing nothing of note. Then I saw motion, far off in a field. Farm workers were taking in a crop that had been cut and stooked, forking the bundles onto a flatbed wagon. The vehicle was drawn by two dark beasts of substantial size, but I could not quite make them out.

"Integrator," I said, "reproduce for me an image of those animals and magnify."

A small screen appeared before my eyes. I studied them for a few moments then bade my assistant dissolve the display and walked on. "Not horses," I said.

"No," the grinnet said. "Nor anything I am familiar with."

"They had manlike qualities."

"Yes. Their faces were rough approximations of the human. They seemed to be arguing with each other, and the forelimbs with which they gestured were more like arms than legs."

I sighed. "We are far from home."

"Indeed." It was silent for a while, then said, "May I have another piece of fruit?"

I walked on with the sound of its chewing in my ear, following the road that followed the river on my left. I soon left the village behind, and passed through a bucolic landscape. The river was intermittently lined with copses of broad-leafed, low-crowned trees whose gray-barked trunks twisted and intertwined with each other. To my right passed a succession of crop lands, some appearing, to my inexpert eye, to be planted in vegetables, others in fodder grass. I saw no fences, but here and there along the way were single posts, with a design in metal or pottery fixed near the top of each.

When we had come so far that the stone bridge seemed no more than the size of my smallest fingernail and the hills ahead were close enough to show where the road met a declivity that was surely the beginnings of a pass, my assistant said, "Someone is standing under those trees ahead."

I stopped and knelt on one knee, pretending to adjust my footgear. "Sword," I said, "what do you have to say about it?"

"I detect no threat."

"How do you make that determination?"

"By the usual means: respiration, heart rate, chemical exudates from the skin. The person is relaxed and unstressed. Also, no arms are in evidence."

"I concur," said the grinnet. "I would judge his affect to be one of curiosity and expectation."

"Wouldn't a well-practiced, cold-blooded killer be calm and cool?" I said. "And are not bare hands adequate weapons for a skilled assassin?"

"I am not a sophisticated debater," said the sword. "Draw me if you feel threatened. My automatic responses will be overridden and I will follow your lead."

Now the grinnet spoke up, a nervous note in its usually calm voice. "Do you expect another assault? If so, perhaps I should throw stones?"

Yesterday's attack had clearly touched an instinct for self-preservation. Since I was already down near the side of the road, I picked up a few pebbles and gave them to my assistant. "Only if I say so," I said. "And try not to worry."

"You were not the only one who saw what happened to the innkeeper's hand," it said. "If anything like that looks to be coming at me again, I will let fly without seeking permission."

"Follow my lead," I said, straightening up. "We do not know what the penalties may be when pets fling gravel at passersby."

The grinnet said nothing, though I think it bridled at being labeled a pet. But I was already approaching the twisted trees where the unknown someone leaned on a walking staff. As I neared, the figure stepped out of the shadow onto the side of the road and offered what looked to be a friendly salute.

It was the gray-eyed man from the night before, with a traveler's satchel slung across his shoulder. "Good morning," he said. "I thought you might be coming this way."

"And, why," I asked, drawing nearer but pausing before I was within range of a swing of the staff, my hand idling near the hilt of the sword, "would I be in your thoughts?"

He smiled a half smile. "I will not circumlocute. I am interested in you, after the events of yesterday evening."

"In me? Or in the gold and silver that the 'events' led to?" I said.

"I am no more covetous of wealth than the next man," he said.

I gripped the sword's hilt firmly. "And perhaps no less. In any case, the next man is not here. I see only you and me, alone on a lonely road."

He held up both hands, palms toward me, so that the staff slipped into the crook of an elbow. His eyes dropped to the sword. "If I am a good judge of weaponry—and I count myself so—what you have under your hand makes you more than a match for me, and two more like me."

"And yet you do not seem perturbed by my presence," I said, "though the road is as lonely for you as it is for me."

He smiled again. "That is because I am sure you mean me no harm."

"And how would you be sure of that?"

"Let us say that it is my business to be sure of men," he said.

"And what might your business be?"

"Now, that would be premature to say."

I shot him a searching look, but he returned it with a bland expression and another placid flourish of his hands.

I stepped back a couple of paces and whispered, "Integrator?"

Its voice sounded calmer. "I see nothing to act upon."

"Sword?"

"Nor I."

"Very well," I said to the stranger. "I am bound for some place called Bambles. Do you know it?"

"I know it well."

"Is it your destination?"

"It might well be."

I looked him over again. His clothes were presentable, his cloak unstained, his footwear not noticeably roadworn. I said, "You do not give an impression of vagabondage."

He returned the inspection. "Nor do you. And though you came by the south road, with not even a bed roll, you do not look to have been sleeping under bushes."

"Perhaps I slept at inns," I said.

"There are none for a long stretch south of here. It is rough and untillable land, with scarcely a roof to be seen."

"How do you know I came from the south?"

"Because I saw all who came from the north," he said.

"Perhaps I came at night."

He laughed softly. "No one travels alone at night," he said. "At least not for long."

I made a gesture that said the discussion had gone in his favor but that now it was ended. "You are observant," I said. "Is that also a requirement of your business?"

"It is."

"And is it still premature to state the nature of that business?"

He made a show of reexamining his earlier judgment. "I perform various functions, as my patron requires. Lately, let us say that I have been a locator."

"Indeed? And what do you locate?"

"Usually, persons and things that are…missing," he said, after a moment's more thought.

"Things that have been stolen?" I said. "Persons who have run away?"

He signaled that I understood, then added, "And sometimes the other way round."

"I used to do something similar," I said. "Indeed, at present I would be interested in locating someone who has disappeared."

"Out of concern for the missing person's welfare?" he asked. "Or perhaps you require revenge and retribution?"

"The former."

"You expect to find your quarry in Bambles?"

I weighed my answer, then decided to tell him my intent. "No, in Bambles I hope to find someone who can assist me."

"Then let us travel together," he said. He introduced himself as Pars Lavelan. I was about to declare my own identity, but then I remembered the man on the road south of Bridge-on-Scammon asking me if I was named "Apthorn." I told Lavelan my name was Barlo, a pseudonym that I had sometimes employed when pursuing discriminations in places where it was not useful to be identified as Henghis Hapthorn.

"When we get to Bambles," he said, as we walked on, he on my left, "I may be able to direct you to the kind of help you need." He punctuated his last remark by circling his hands about each other as if they were rolling downhill together, then drawing them apart with a flutter of fingers, like birds taking flight in opposite directions. Finally, he cocked his head at an angle, nodded knowingly, and raised his eyebrows in a way that invited me to confirm the meaning of his odd and convoluted gesture. I merely blinked and he saw that I had not grasped his meaning.

"A magician," he said. "You'll be looking for a magician."

"That was my plan."

"Do you know any of the magicians of Bambles?" he said.

"No, do you?"

"Oh, yes," he said, in a tone that admitted of a number of possible meanings, "all of them."

"Can you recommend a good one?"

His face framed a curious expression, as if I had posed him a paradox. After a moment he said, "That would depend on one's definition of 'good.' Normally, the more expert the practitioner, the less he or she partakes of morality as you or I might frame it."

"You say, 'normally,' " I said. "So there are exceptions?"

Again, he gave the matter some thought, then said, "No, I suppose not. Or at least none that I can think of."

"Well," I said, "can you give me some indication of what the services of a useful practitioner might cost?"

He grunted a wordless syllable and rolled his eyes. "The most accomplished are often the most capricious in their wants. I recall hearing of a man who engaged the services of one whose name it is best not to utter. He lusted for a woman and desired that she would reciprocate his incontinent passion. The wizard agreed to cast a spell; in return, the would-be lover must feed a small fire under a pot until its contents boiled over.

"The bargain struck, the practitioner performed his side of the agreement with a casual wave of a wand and the muttering of a few syllables of cant. He then led the man to a room which contained a hearth, a lidded pot above a banked fire, and a few sticks of firewood to feed it. He sat the man down upon a stool, said another couple of words, and left him to his task.

"The man fed the fire, but the pot did not soon boil. He tried to lift the lid to see what it contained, but it would not budge. He put more wood under the pot, but though the fire blazed up, the extra heat made no difference. He noticed, too, that the wood was replaced as quickly as he transferred it to the hearth. After some time, he sought to rise from the stool and go in search of the magician, but found that he was stuck fast to the seat, and that the stool was equally stuck to the floor.

"And so he remained, with neither sleep, nor food nor drink—nor any need of either—as the days became months and the months became years. The man grew old and narrow in his outlook and the fingertips that conveyed the wood to the fire took on the polished hardness of horn. He lost all track of time's passage and spent whole years in dreams and reveries, in which the memory of the woman he desired was a constant torment.

"At last, a moment came when the wizard entered the room, lifted the pot lid. Its contents released a green steam. 'That's done, then,' the practitioner said.

"Immediately, the man, now drained and feeble, was freed from his obligation. He staggered from the manse and out to the street, where he stood blinking against the sun's ruby light. An ancient crone, bent and crooked, was loitering at the gate. When he stepped into the street she flung her arms around him and performed a frantic frottage against him, biting with toothless gums at his leathery neck and pendulous ears. Scandalized neighbors summoned the watch, who took her off to a refuge for the senile."

"What happened to the old man?" I asked.

"I don't recall," Lavelan said, "but it couldn't have been much. You see, it was not the fire that heated whatever was in the pot. It was his life-stuff. The wood was just to give him something to do while the spell took its course."

I considered what he had told me. "So bargains with magicians are chancy affairs," I said.

"You have to give them what they want," he said, "and their wants are frequently—" he sought for a word "—peculiar."

We were closer to the end of the valley now. We walked on in silence for a space, while I thought about the story and its implications. Abruptly, Lavelan seized my arm and pulled me beneath the trees, saying "Hsst! Quickly."

I made to resist, but when the sword did not object, I went along with him. We crouched in the shade of a wide-topped tree and I tried to see up through the leaves, saying, "What is it?"

But he pulled my head down. "If you see it," he said, "it is more likely to see you."

A large shadow passed over the road. I had an impression of something long and relatively thin, with broad wings.

"Do the authorities not protect travelers?" I asked.

He gave me that curious inspection again. "Where are you from?" he said.

I made a vague gesture. "The south, of course."

"I really must go there, someday. It sounds most unusual."

We would need to spend some time beneath the trees, he counseled, until the thing in the air above us went away. He spread his cloak because the grass was damp and invited me to sit beside him. We put our backs against a twisted bole. My assistant crept down from my shoulder and found a spot on the cloth where it could curl up. It was soon asleep.

Lavelan glanced down at the grinnet, then looked off into the field across the road. "I have never seen a creature quite like your pet," he said.

"Indeed?" I also looked off into the field, though at a different angle. "Not even in the company of the kind of persons we were recently speaking of?"

I caught his reaction from the corner of my eye. He seemed to be genuinely puzzled at the question. I covered the moment by saying, "I have heard that magicians like to surround themselves with unusual pets."

"None that I know of," he said, "although the ones I know do tend to favor weapons like yours."

"Really?" I said, plucking a blade of grass and giving it my close attention. But Lavelan failed to take the hint and pressed on with his line of inquiry.

"Then there was the matter of the wheel at the inn last night and the unfortunate state of the innkeeper's hand this morning." I said nothing, but he went on, saying, "The hand appeared to have been bitten by a sket."

"I am not familiar with the term," I said.

"It is a creature with a paralyzing bite, sometimes employed as a nonlethal weapon. But its wielder must first impose a spell upon it that prevents it from attacking him."

"I sense that you are working your way toward some conclusion," I said, disposing of the grass and drying my fingertips against each other.

"No," he said, "only to a question, and that is: what kind of fellow travels with a strange beast on his shoulder and a magic sword at his hip, keeps a sket to guard his purse, and can convince a wheel to spin him a handsome sum without its showing any signs of being, shall we say, tickled?"

I spoke in a light tone. "I suspect you ask the question, already knowing the answer."

"Knowing *an* answer," he said, "that being: the fellow is an expert practitioner of the recondite arts." Now he interlaced his fingers and studied them. "The problem with that answer is that the person in question gives off none of the unmistakable emanations one would expect from an accomplished magician."

"Emanations?" I said.

His eyebrows ascended toward his hairline then drew down and together. "Again, you do not seem to know what even that rustic rabble at the inn know. You looked at the inkling as if you had never seen its like."

"They are different down south," I said.

It was Lavelan's turn to make a wordless sound, a skeptical "Hmm," deep in his throat.

I decided to force the issue. I faced him and said, "Make yourself plain. I do not care to travel with one who harbors dark suspicions about me."

He turned toward me then, and blinked in surprise. "I have no suspicions," he said, "but I will admit to a frank curiosity. I have not met anyone with your combination of competence and innocence."

It was not a combination that I would normally have admitted to, but I was a stranger in a strange world. "I do feel a little out of place here," I said. "It is not what I am used to."

"Down south, you mean?"

"Exactly."

"You know," he said, "I have been quite far south myself. To Bleyne on a number of occasions, and even to Choriond on the edge of the Waste."

"Really?" I said.

"Really. And I have also met travelers from beyond the Waste, though, again, none like you."

"I suppose I am from beyond their beyond."

He looked at me from lowered eyes while his mouth drew off to one side. "Shall I tell you what I think?" he said.

I was growing tired of his circling dance. I invited him to take a grand leap.

"Very well," he said, eying me with a measuring stare. "I take you for a magician's servant who has somehow become separated from his master. There are far-away lands about which one hears only rumor and fanciful tales, even tales of other worlds. You may come from such a place. Before you were separated, your patron gave you charge of his weapon and his pet. He must also have blessed you with a spell of luck."

He watched me now for a reaction. I resisted an urge to bridle at being thought one of the servile breed and weighed the merits of adapting myself to his view of me. He wasn't that far off the truth, except that I was coming to be of two minds about searching for Osk Rievor. My other self had got both of us into this mess with his cheerful disregard of good sense and if I could find a way out of it and get home to my own time, my alter ego could fend for himself, wherever he had ended up. Indeed, getting home without Osk Rievor might well be a bonus, especially now that I could avoid locations where the new age's influence was dimpling.

Lavelan had more to say: that my master must be an accomplished practitioner; that he might be in difficulties, hence our separation; or that he might have just gone off on some abstruse, wizardly tangent where he would not require my assistance, abandoning me to my own resources until he had need of me again.

"Your higher-echelon magicians can be careless in the deployment of their servants," he finished. "Retainers are so easily replaced. Indeed, it is possible that you are only a facsimile struck from an original that has been left behind to care for your patron's keep. Perhaps you were whipped up in haste; your intelligence seems not fully formed. That would explain the gaps in your understanding of the most common facts."

I was not accustomed to hearing my intellect so undervalued and though I was keeping a rein on my reactions, some of my irritation must have shown in my face before I could suppress it.

"Please," he said, "I meant no disparagement. We are all who we are and not to be blamed for our natures." He thought a little more, then said, "The sket puzzles me, however. It seems out of place. You haven't met a man named Ral Ezzers, have you? He is known to throw the sket."

"Ral Ezzers?" I said. "I do not know the name."

"He is employed by a practitioner named Ovarth."

"Is this Ezzers also a locator?"

He confirmed my supposition, but added, "Though he is not as sophisticated as I am."

I decided to tread a careful line. I neither denied nor confirmed his estimation of my circumstances. I said, "I cannot say too much about my situation. Only that I still believe I require the services of a good practitioner. Though I would prefer not to find my buttocks glued to a stool for the rest of my life."

"Oh, you needn't worry about that," he said. "The pot having boiled, that wizard has moved on to other ambitions." He shivered slightly at some unspoken thought, then stood up and fished out the talisman that hung about his neck. "It is safe to go on now."

I awoke my assistant and placed it back upon my shoulder, where it demanded another piece of fruit. Lavelan and I rose and set off toward the hills. I was occupied in untying the cloth package of food as I said to him, "You have not told me what brought you to this valley."

He shrugged. "I meant to locate this man, Ezzers, and report back to my patron."

"And who is your patron?"

"His name is Bol. He likes to be known as Smiling Bol."

"He sounds a pleasant sort."

"I suppose he does, to those who have only his name to work with."

"And why, if I may ask, did your patron want you to locate another practitioner's retainer?"

"He did not actually order me to do so. He is very busy with a project of his own. But each of the major practitioners of Bambles is interested in what all of the others are doing, and they expect their servants to keep their eyes open."

He fell silent for a moment, then continued: "Lately, there have been more comings and goings. I sense a rising tension, though no one is speaking plainly. So when I saw Ezzers bound this way on one of his master's flying platforms, and when one of Chay-Chevre's dragons winged off in Ezzers's wake, I thought to myself, something is going on down south. And I came to see what was what."

"But you have not located Ezzers," I said.

"True, though I did find out that he has been asking after a man named Apthorn. However, no one seems to know anything about the fellow."

"So you have not located this Apthorn, either."

"No, but I have located you."

"Do you think I have something to do with all those comings and goings?"

"I think you may. If not, you are at least a curiosity, and Bol likes curiosities. He may even decide to help you. He is not much given to peevishness and does not relish cruelty for its own sake, so you would be better off under his protection than under Chay-Chevre's or Tancro's."

I took his meaning. Someone might want to winkle out the mysteries that surrounded me, and Smiling Bol would be the least inclined to do so in a manner that I might find unendurable. I counted the names he had mentioned: Bol, Ovarth, Chay-Chevre, and Tancro. "So there are four great practitioners at Bambles?"

"There are five. Shuppat mostly keeps to himself, but we have probably passed before some of his eyes and ears."

His remark created an unappetizing image in my mind. "This Shuppat, he has an unusual sensory apparatus?" I said.

The gray-eyed man chuckled. "No, no. His kind of magic gives him influence over little creatures. He might be watching us though the eyes of the occupant of some wayside burrow."

It occurred to me that I should know more about the major players in whatever game was afoot in this land. Lavelan was happy to oblige. I listened and understood most of what I heard. When I was not sure of the meaning of a term or reference, I forbore to ask questions; I already appeared ignorant and strange enough.

There were five Powers in Bambles. Their reach extended a long but ultimately indeterminate distance, before they encountered the spheres of operation of other practitioners. Beyond commanding what Lavelan called "the base of the recondite arts," each was a specialist in a particular discipline: Shuppat, as already described, was adept in manipulating the lives of small animals; Chay-Chevre, the only female of the five, specialized in dragon lore, and maintained three at her keep; Ovarth was expert in the summoning and control of elementals—I thought I knew what those were, and nodded for Lavelan to continue—while Tancro had achieved preeminence in the magic of men.

"My own patron is drawn to the interrelation of the Nine Planes," he finished. "He has visited three of them, and works to improve his range."

I asked about the tone of relationships among the five.

"A balance of authority has been achieved. Each knows the power and prestige of each of the others to the least tittle. That is not to say that, occasionally, this or that figure might not trespass upon the prerogatives of another, just to see."

"One never knows the extent of one's powers unless they are tested," I said.

"Exactly," he said, "but nowadays the tests are infrequent and of minimal intensity. The times when balls of blackfire hurtled across the rooftops of Bambles and ghostly armies tramped its streets are behind us. Or so we all hope." He frowned at some inner image. "Or so I hope that, indeed, all of us so hope."

I understood. Stability had been achieved after a time of strife and dire doings, and was all the more appreciated for the contrast. Thus, any new factor in the complex mix of power and personality would set nerves atingle and cause teeth to clench.

"Indeed," he continued, "and thus one has to wonder about this Apthorn. Is he a mercenary, imported by one of the Powers? Or a foreign practitioner obsessed with some narrow interest that dovetails neatly into someone's wider stratagem? Perhaps he does not even exist, and Ovarth has created a cunning ruse to distract attention from wherever his real theater of operations may be."

"Perhaps this Apthorn is some innocent fellow whose aims and ambitions are misconstrued," I said. "Sometimes there really is no fire, despite all the smoke."

"When magicians are concerned, smoke without fire is unremarkable," Lavelan said. "Is it so different where you come from?" He brushed away the thought and continued: "No, something is definitely on the boil. Meanwhile my patron has been distracted by his project—he has spent weeks in his workroom, building and tuning some abstruse device—so I am obligated to ensure that his interests are protected."

We had arrived at the end of the valley. The road went forward through a low saddle where two small hills met. Lavelan stopped and brought out his medallion. He consulted it for a long moment before saying, "We are all right from here to the wayfarers' rest at the top of the pass. After that, who can say?"

We climbed to the low saddle. Before us rose more hills, and more steeply sloped, the path switchbacking into the distance. The effort of scaling the successive heights took most of our breath and conversation lapsed. I was glad of the opportunity to consider what I had learned.

I had heard no mention of central authority. Magic's arrival had surely brought the end of the Archonate. Affairs seemed to have reverted to the other pole of the eternal spectrum, and power was wielded by those who had the wit or skill to amass it. Five great personages rivaled each other for precedence in the city to which we were bound, each probably taking a roughly equal portion of the overall rule. The portions must be equal, I reasoned, since the moment any practitioner fell markedly behind the others, his competitors would likely league against the weak one, destroy him, and divide the spoils. I wouldn't have been surprised to learn that at some point in the past, there had been six rivals, and seven before that. Each of the five still standing doubtless intended that eventually there would be but one, and that he (or she) would be it.

The shape of the situation into which Osk Rievor had plunged me was beginning to appear. It was possible that one of the Bambles Five had reached into the past and lured him, and therefore me, into this time and place. The summoner's intent would be to set some strategy to uncoiling, using my other self as a decoy, or a stalking horse, or even as a resource to be drained of power—I did not know enough of the workings of magic to make an estimate.

For a moment I wished I could toss my sketch down the back corridors of my mind to where my intuitive insight had always resided. But that part of my psyche had first been reified into my alter ego, and now he had been pulled loose and taken out of my ken, perhaps by one of the Powers of Bambles. The perpetrator might even be Smiling Bol. Perhaps the mechanism he had been building was a device to reach through time. Or perhaps Lavelan's patron had summoned Osk Rievor only to lose him somehow to a rival who, aware of the plan, stepped in at a crucial juncture and diverted the catch into another creel. Logically, that was less likely to be the case, since it was more complex than the first theory. But in this age, logic was a flame that must be frequently starved of fuel.

If I had had my intuitive other self, I could have planned my path with some sense of where lay the right direction forward. Without him, I saw that I must acquire more facts. I faced the bleak likelihood that my hopes of returning to my own age without my other self were unreasonable. Without him, I could not reliably navigate in this irrational time. My original goal—to find a magician who would send me homeward for the gold and silver in my pockets—was probably untenable. I did not want to question Pars Lavelan on the point, lest I reveal more of my strange ignorance and induce him to examine me more closely.

Any of the Five might have the capacity to help me, but it seemed that I was already unintentionally involved in some new phase of their unending struggle for dominance, so who knew how they would seek to use me? Indeed, the moment one of them took a thorough interest in me, my pitiful camouflage of being a wanderer from "the south" might fall to tatters around my ankles. Already, Pars Lavelan thought me a magically "whipped-up" contrivance. His master would almost certainly have the means to make a more searching determination of who and what I was.

In what I was coming to think of as *my old life*, I had often found myself in perilous situations. But I had usually been the most astute player in the game, rarely equaled and never overmatched. Here I did not even know the name of the large, sinuous, and winged creature I now saw again gliding over the valley behind us. I drew Lavelan's attention to it, but as we looked, I saw something even larger drop from the clouds like a great bird of prey. It struck the flying thing hard, and there was a sudden flurry of motion, a blur of yellow and blue mixed with the darker hue of the first creature. Then both were winging off toward the south, the larger in pursuit of the smaller, diminishing rapidly into the distance.

"That's settled, then," Lavelan said, and we walked on.

By noon we had traversed enough up-and-down country that the valley and its river were beyond our sight. The land here was uncultivated, the hills covered in coarse grass and bristly, knee-high bushes. In a pocket where the land leveled for a short distance between slopes, we came across a stone bench set beside the path. A spring bubbled nearby, making a pool of pristine water.

Lavelan led us to the bench, saying, "The water will be good, though it does no harm to first throw a coin into it and ask permission to drink."

I sat beside him and unwrapped my package of food. My assistant, which had been dozing on my shoulder as the warmth of the red sun increased, climbed down my arm and began to pick out morsels of fruit. I offered Lavelan a share of the provender but he declined.

"My patron equipped me with a spell of sufficiency. So long as I am serving his interests, I neither hunger nor thirst."

"A useful spell," I said. I noticed that the top of the bench bore an inlaid circle of bronze like that of the bridge now far behind us. Though smaller, it advertised the same news: that someone named Albruithine had made the bench and that he defended it, promising "peril" for any who troubled it.

I touched the letters of the name and asked the locator, "Is he one of the Bambles Five?"

My question earned me a snort of disbelief and "How far south is this benighted land you come from?" He put a palm to his chest and let his jaw drop in mimed wonderment. "You've truly not heard of Albruithine?"

"I am afraid not."

"He was Albruithine," he said. "He was the First. He arose in the long-ago times, in the chaos when all was disjointed and human beings were without will. He imposed order and system. Many of the great spells that still hold the world together were of his devising." He looked up at the dull, red sun and added, "Why, it was he who penned the sun when it would have billowed out and swallowed the Earth."

"You say 'was.' So he is dead but his power survives him?"

"Naturally. Why would it not?"

"Because he is no longer here to exert his will."

I saw that my proposition puzzled him. "His will remains the same whether he is here or not."

"How is that possible?" I said.

"Are you completely unschooled? His will remains the same because he willed it so, and his level of willing was sufficient to override all objections. Not that anyone is willing to make them and take the consequences."

It was my turn to blink.

Lavelan went on. "Besides, it cannot be said for sure that he is dead. And even if he were, there are several different kinds of 'dead' that can apply to a wizard of his supernal power. Having settled the world's disorder, he may have 'gone on' in pursuit of other interests." He looked off into the distance. "It would be…something to know what happened to him."

"But how do you know that his will endures?" I said.

"It is self-evident. Look, there is the sun, and here are we. Are we charred to cinders? We are not. What more is there to say?"

"So no one has tested the concept?"

He reached over and took a morsel of my lunch, held it beneath his nose to sniff it. Then he drew out his medallion and brought it close to the crumb.

"Do you suspect my food of being adulterated?" I said.

"Something has clearly diverted your mind. He dropped the crumb and said, "You ask if anyone has 'tested the concept.' But why would anyone test reality? Reality is not for testing, but for living with."

"But how do you know what reality is without testing it?" I said.

He adopted that look that often overcomes parents of children who ask too many questions. "It is what it is. Existence is existence. Must I constantly ask myself questions to determine if I am still who I was moments ago? Life would be used up in the pursuit of inanity."

"But have you ever asked if Albruithine's spells still work now that he is not here to support them?"

"Why would I?"

"Intellectual curiosity," I said. "If everyone assumes that the spells still work, because nobody ever tests them, then it may be that his works endure merely because no one ever tries to change them."

"Why would anybody try to change them? This shelter, the bridge back there, they serve their functions."

"You do not seem to be following my line of reasoning," I said.

A light dawned in his face. "Oh, that's what you're doing, is it?" He gave me a comical look, as if I'd tried to slip one under him, then laughed indulgently. "Reasoning, indeed!"

"Empiricism is a powerful tool of the intellect," I said, "and I am one of its ablest users."

Now he laughed out loud and slapped his thigh.

"I'll show you," I said, but had to wait until he quieted down. As he wiped his teary eyes, I went on. "You wondered how I beat the wheel last night."

"True, I did. But now I am sure it was a luckiness spell."

"Your medallion tells you if magic is in play near you, does it not?"

"It does."

"Has it told you that I have been magicked?"

"I haven't asked it. Obviously, you have been."

"Ask it now," I said.

He held the medallion to me, then studied it, puzzled. "Odd," he said. "It must be a very subtle spell, indeed."

"Suppose I told you that my win was not the result of luck at all, not even magically enhanced luck? Suppose I told you it was the product of a process of reasoning?"

He gave me the kind of look that said he did not know whether or not I was joking, but that he was leaning toward believing that I was trying to draw him into some comical prank. "Come, come," he said, "we are grown men. Put aside your silliness."

I assured him that I was completely serious and asked him to take out a coin from his purse. He produced a large copper piece that had a number on one side and an eye on the other. "Toss it several times, letting it land on the bench."

He did so. I took note of the sequence of times it landed eyes-up or with the number showing, and applied second-level consistencies. After nine tosses, the pattern emerged. After the eleventh, I told him, "Toss it again, and the eye will be showing."

He did and it did.

"Again," I said, "and it will be the eye again."

Again I had predicted correctly.

"Once more, and this time it will be the number."

I was right again.

I had him toss the copper twice more, and twice more I was able to predict the outcome.

"There," I said.

"Where?" he said.

"The odds of my predicting all of those tosses correctly were only one in thirty-two. Yet I succeeded."

"What have odds to do with it?" he said. "Clearly you are able to affect the outcome, as you did with the wheel."

"No," I said, "I applied a mathematical formula that describes the order that underlies seeming randomness. Where I come from, it is taught to schoolchildren."

He rubbed his pate as if I had spouted nonsense and he did not know where to begin to set me straight. "The 'order that underlies seeming randomness' is will. Things happen because they are made to happen. And that is what is taught to schoolchildren hereabouts."

"No," I said, and would have said more but he cut me off. He handed me the coin and told me to throw it as he had done. I flipped it and it rang as it struck the stone bench. "Eye," he said, without looking to see that he was correct. "Toss it again."

I did so, and again he called it. Five more flips followed, and he called each one while the coin was in the air. Then he gave me a sly grin and said, "Edge."

I was astonished to see the disk land on its unmilled edges, spin, then come to a halt upright. I had been applying consistencies throughout, but the coin did not obey the rules. Now he scooped it up and put it back in his purse.

"Of course, it's easier when it's my coin," he said.

I felt that I had been made to look foolish. I did not know how he had managed the trick, but I was sure he had applied some form of presti-digital manipulation. I restrained my anger and said, "I will show you empiricism at work," while reaching for a fist-sized rock that lay beside the path. I stood and hefted it.

"What do you mean to do?" Lavelan said, edging back on the bench.

"The empirical method in action. I will smash this down on the corner of the bench, perhaps to break off a piece."

"Why?"

"To see if Albruithine still 'defends' his work."

Now he quickly rose from the stone slab and put distance between us. "That is not wise," he said. "Really."

"We'll see, won't we?"

I scooped up my assistant from the bench where he was chewing bread and placed him on the ground. I then went to one end of the bench and drew a bead on one of the chiseled corners with the rock I held in my hand. A chill breeze suddenly swept down from the uplands, ruffling my hair, followed by a rattling as if stones tumbled down a ravine. My assistant squawked and the sword at my hip awoke to say, "Alert! Alert!"

Lavelan had turned and fled the shelter. He was making his best speed up the path.

"I advise you to put the rock down," said the grinnet's voice in my inner ear, "and very carefully." It was looking up the hill that rose behind the bench. Not far up the slope, the grass and gorse were moving, as if something shifted ponderously beneath them. As I watched, the rock still poised above my head, a giant hand of gray stone broke free of the sod, fingers spread wide, and was followed by a forearm as thick as my thigh. The hand descended to pull at the turf where its owner's face might be expected to lie.

I very carefully replaced the rock where I had found it and stepped away from the bench. Up the hill, the hand paused. After a few moments it slowly sank back into the earth. The rattling sound ceased and the cold wind died away. The sword said, "Clear."

Pars Lavelan was coming back down the path, wearing a look of concern. "If we are to travel together," he said, "I must ask you not to perform any more such 'tests.' At least not without giving me a warning and ample time to depart the vicinity."

"But the test was successful," I said. "I demonstrated that Albruithine's spell still works."

"You demonstrated what any child would know. How does that contribute anything useful to our lives?"

"The demonstration was of the usefulness of the empirical method," I said.

A flash of exasperation caused his brows to knit then quickly rise. "It is all double-talk with you. Enough! Let us get on and make some distance before nightfall." He set off again, and I heard him muttering something about how he hoped that I would eschew any further demonstrations of my disrespect for Albruithine's will.

I gathered up the uneaten food and hoisted the grinnet to my shoulder. It also had a few unuseful comments to make. I ordered it to keep silent. But after I had taken a few steps, thinking it best to stay a little behind Lavelan until he got over his ill temper, the integrator spoke again. "All the fruit is gone. There is only bread."

"That should be enough for you. Doubtless there is more fruit in your future. Exert your mind toward more productive ends."

"I am doing so," it said. "I have been considering the inventory of spells that Osk Rievor had been assembling."

I had known that my other self used to spend the hours when I was sleeping working through the jumble of books and grimoires he had acquired. "What of it?" I said. "He is not here to employ them."

"But you are," the grinnet said.

"I?" I said, adding a sound of derisive dismissal. "Can you possibly think that I would wield magic? That would be like expecting Ob to embrace Emmerine."

I referred to the old comic play in which a noted epicure is pursued by an amorous dollymoll who seeks to tempt him with her simple charms. All her ploys come to nought.

"Yet the story implies," my assistant countered, "that by refusing her, Ob missed his chance to experience sensations that, though rudimentary, were also more potent than he was accustomed to. He would have benefited from a wider knowledge of what the world had to offer him."

"Some see that implication. I do not. I see it as a warning to the simple-minded not to pester their betters, whatever they may feel they have to offer."

The integrator chose not to take the implication of my remark and pressed on regardless. I had noticed it had lately developed an increased tendency not to recognize a gentle hint. It said that it had raised the subject because it had been considering what Pars Lavelan had said about being under a spell of sufficiency.

"Yes," I said, "what of it?"

"I know a spell of sufficiency," it said. It went on to tell me that Osk

Rievor had been sorting the various incantations and cantrips he had come across in his late-night reading. A few were complete and genuine, dating from when magic last ruled. A few more were incomplete, half-remembered renderings written down in the time after reason had regained control. Others were farcical.

"But even the latter category can sometimes contain the germs of truth," the grinnet said. "By constructing a matrix of the true, the partly true, and the false-facsimile, he was able to tease out congruencies. By the time we went to Hember, he had identified several dozen authentic charms and enchantments, some of them quite powerful, including a spell of sufficiency."

"I am surprised he did not demonstrate them to me," I said.

"They did not work well on our side of the cusp. Here, however, they ought to be fully effective."

"Hmm," I said, "show me one, preferably not too startling."

"I cannot," the grinnet said. "I experimented after we left the inn but before we met Pars Lavelan. My efforts had no effect. I believe it is because I lack will."

I made a small noise, then said, "If you do, you certainly seem to have developed a workable substitute."

Lavelan looked back at me. "Did you say something?"

"No, I was comforting my pet."

"I lack will because I am artificially created," my assistant said. "You, however, have more than a normal share. And on this side of the cusp, you should be able to empower a spell with considerable force."

"I have no intention of doing so. I would feel—" I sought for the right word, but could not choose between "sad" and "defeated." Finally, I settled on: "It would seem inappropriate."

"You have always prided yourself on a flexibility of mind," it said. "You have been prepared to accept the most improbable truth if it was all that was left standing once the impossible had been pared away."

"Even so."

"I have no wish to upset your emotional equilibrium, but if Lavelan had not warned you, that flying thing would have come silently down upon us and by now we would be nothing but bones tumbling about in its digestive juices."

"Perhaps I would prefer that to being a spell-slinger," I said.

"You would truly rather die than speak a spell?"

I was forming an answer when it continued: "Because that may be the choice you are about to be offered."

I had been walking with my eyes downcast. Now I looked up. The trail had climbed to skirt a boulder beyond which began a level patch of ground before the hill climbed again. At the edge of the flat space, a few paces in front of me, stood Pars Lavelan, his back toward me and his front toward four men who blocked the way. The men were clad identically in leggings and puffed jackets of blue and dark purple, and each wore a slouch hat of the same colors, with a badge of white metal pinning up an edge of the brim. Each had a rod of some black substance and from the way they held the objects, two-handed, with one end pointed in our direction, I had no doubt they were weapons.

"Alert," said the sword. "Draw me."

But I thought better of it. From the way the rods were aimed at us, I took them to be weapons that would act before I and the sword could reach them.

Lavelan's gaze was not on the men in front of him. He was looking up at the object that hovered above and behind them. It was a railed platform of gilded and white-painted wood, oblong in shape and supported at its four corners by what appeared to be four compact whirlwinds that neither dissipated nor spun away.

Standing at the front of the platform, leaning his elbows on the rail and looking down at us while his hands cradled a fifth black rod, was a man wearing the same livery as the four on the ground. He was grinning at Lavelan, the grin made crooked by a scar that disfigured his cheek and twisted the corner of his mouth. I realized that I had seen the man's face before, had seen it only yesterday. The grin had been the same, but the eyes above it were even harder now as he looked me up and down. From the way he handled the weapon, I knew that I now had a more difficult problem to deal with than a couple of thrown skets.

CHAPTER SEVEN

Pars Lavelan was saying something I couldn't quite catch, a stream of syllables pronounced in a formal diction, in the manner of an Archonate official reading a public pronouncement, but under his breath.

The man on the platform flicked his gaze back to Lavelan and I saw the network of lines at the corners of his eyes deepen in concentration. He grunted, a sound that mingled amusement with disdain, then put the fingers of his right hand through a rapid series of motions. My companion ceased his utterance. I saw his shoulders slump, but then he squared them again and spoke.

"This is a serious breach of the Compact, Ezzers. This is not like some quick flurry of blades after a drunken curse shouted across a tavern table, or when shoulders brush past in a narrow alley."

The scarred face mimed mock fear then the grin returned. "You should have been a pedagogue, Lavelan. True, your penchant for stating the obvious would have bored your students to distraction, but at least you would have lived longer."

"This will be found out," Lavelan said, "and your patron will find four Powers ranged against him. I will not be the only one to find his lifespan abruptly shortened."

"You really should draw me," the sword was saying, but I hushed it because my assistant was speaking in my ear.

"Place the tips of your middle fingers against your thumbs and squeeze hard," the grinnet said, "then speak these words after me." Then before it gave me the spoken part of the spell, it added, "And it would be helpful if you would assume your most determined frame of mind."

"Exert my will, you mean?"

"It is essential to the process."

Meanwhile Lavelan was saying, "Ezzers, you cannot have heard your instructions right. Your master will feed you to that thing that stirs beneath the floor of his keep."

"Step to the side, and I might let you live," the man with the scar said. Then he addressed himself to me. "Remove your weapon and place it on the ground. Then come forward."

Lavelan cast me a worried look as he moved off the trail. I dropped my eyes to the path and listened with all my attention to the syllable that the integrator was causing to sound in my ear. Some small part of me still wanted to reject the grinnet's plan, but all my other parts had come to accept that no other course was open.

I slipped the sword's baldric over my head and stooped to lay the weapon on the ground. Then I put my fingertips together as the grinnet had advised and spoke the first sound, mouthing it softly. As my lips formed the syllable and my breath pushed it past my tongue, I felt as if a bright light had suddenly turned itself on within my skull. My hands grew intensely warm.

I rose slowly. The second syllable, a hard-edged guttural, formed in the back of my throat. As if it were a live thing it slithered to the front of my mouth and slid through my gritted teeth. Suddenly, my hands were cold, as if sheathed in ice, and the light in my head had turned a deep crimson.

"Lavelan!" shouted the man above. "What are you doing?" His rod swung toward the gray-eyed man, who put up his hands and swore that he was blameless.

"Get away from him!" Ezzers ordered as my progress up the path brought me level with Lavelan. My companion was regarding me with consternation, backing away.

The third syllable, soft and sibilant, whispered across my lips, leaving a taste as of acrid oil on my tongue. A bell was tolling behind my eyes, faster and faster, its reverberations rippling through the crimson light like fine silk stirring under a breeze. My hands felt as if they had swollen to thrice their normal size, their weight dragging down my arms.

"Look at me," Ezzers was saying. I heard a hum as if a hive of bees were stirring. He was charging his weapon.

"Level one," said the sword from the ground. "Pick me up."

The grinnet whispered two more syllables into my ear. "Say them together," it said, "and as you do so, raise your hands, palms up, then unlock your fingers in the direction of the enemy."

One syllable was barely more than a grunt, the other a fricative of lips and teeth. I brought up my hands as bid, surprised to see them no larger than usual, though now it felt as if they vibrated with great power. The tolling in my head had become a single, sustained, overpowering note, so loud within my mind that I feared it would force apart the bones of my skull.

As I blew the air of the last syllable over my lips, I flicked open my cocked middle fingers. One hand was aimed generally at the four men on the ground, the other toward the man on the hovering platform.

It was as if an icy wind roared silently through me, or a surge of glacial meltwater, welling up from the soles of my feet as if entering me from beneath the ground then sweeping and scouring my inner channels until the torrent of invisible force exited my fingers and struck its targets.

I knew nothing of real magic. I did not know what to expect. Perhaps the five men would disappear in a puff of green smoke, or be turned into lumps of stone. Thus I was not prepared to witness the horror that my unleashed will inflicted upon them.

As the spell's impact struck them, each man stiffened as if jerked upright by the collar. The rods fell from numb fingers, clattering on the stony ground. Ezzers tumbled forward over the front railing of the hovering platform, executing a stiff-limbed somersault but landing upright on his feet.

All five of them remained standing, but their limbs and torsos shook and trembled, and their heels thudded against the ground, as if the stones they stood on were violently shaking beneath them. But the ground was still.

Their faces had gone bloodless, the corners of their mouths down-turned in identical grimaces, their teeth chattering in continuous spasms that gashed the flesh of tongues and lips, sending rivulets of blood flowing down their chins. Their eyes rolled loose in all directions and from each of them came a wailing and keening that raised the hairs on the back of my neck.

All of this took but a few moments, though to me they seemed to stretch through an eternity of time outside of time. Then, as one, the five men grew still. Their eyes rolled up and their mouths hung slack. Their heads seemed to shrink back onto their necks while their necks sank into the collars of their jackets. Their hands shriveled and were drawn up into their sleeves. In no more time than it takes to tell of it, they disappeared into their own clothing, and the suits of livery collapsed empty to the ground. Small puffs of gray matter, dust and tiny flakes, erupted from the openings in the piles of blue and purple cloth, and blew away on the wind.

Pars Lavelan swung me around to face him. I saw horror contending with curiosity in his expression. "What was that?" he said.

My assistant was whispering in my ear—"The spell is called Orrian's Hasty Dwindling."—but I told Lavelan I did not know.

"Yet you cast it."

"How could I? I am not a magician," I said, reflecting as I did so that that was a sentence I would never have thought I would find it necessary to utter.

"It came from you."

"It is complicated," I said.

He took out his medallion and extended it to me. I noticed that his hand was shaking. Then he looked at the disk and shook his head. "I do not understand."

"Nor do I, really," I said. I went and recovered the sword.

He chewed the inside of his lip a moment then said, "You must talk with my patron."

I had been thinking about that eventuality. "I'm not sure that is a good idea," I said. "I do not wish to insert myself into a struggle for dominance between powers."

He looked at the heap of clothing that had been Ezzers. "I would say that you are already well-inserted." He shook himself and took stock, looking up at the platform that hovered just out of reach above our heads. "We will need to get onto that."

"Will it answer your commands?" I said.

Again the uncomprehending look was directed my way. "Why wouldn't it? Those are elementals of the basest sort, nothing but air and the will to move it. We have only to get aboard and operate the control." He looked up at the unreachable floor of the platform. "Perhaps I could hook it with my staff."

"Describe the control."

He did so. A pedestal stood near the middle of the platform. From it emerged a lever of green glass, topped by a faceted crystal. "Push the lever in the direction you wish to go. Pull it up to ascend, push it down to land. Center it to hover."

"Very good," I said, lifting my assistant from my shoulder. "If I may borrow your staff?"

The staff reached to the bottom of the railing. I bade the integrator climb up and operate the lever and was pleased that it did so without argument. The platform settled to the ground and we climbed aboard, Pars Lavelan first collecting the five black rods, which he stored in a cupboard behind one of the several couches that were the vehicle's seating. Then he positioned himself at the control pedestal, pulled the lever up and pushed it to the right. From the whirlwinds at the corners came a soughing like wind around eaves. The platform lifted, swung toward the north, and moved smoothly through the sky.

It was like sitting in the salon of a minimally appointed aircraft. Though the vehicle was unwalled and unroofed, its passage brought no flow of air across my face, and when we rose to a height from which the river we had walked beside that morning was a thin ribbon of darkness set between far-off carpets of green, the temperature did not change.

Pars Lavelan made minor adjustments to the position of the green rod then approached to where I was sitting. He made as if to sit but checked himself, turned, and went instead to a low cabinet that stood to one side of the platform. He opened its doors and bent to rustle inside, coming up with a stoppered bottle of worked glass in which a green liquid sloshed. He found two crystal goblets and brought the collection back to where I sat, using one foot to nudge a low table into range. He set down the glasses, sat, and poured from the bottle, raising one glass to me while saying, "Spell of sufficiency or no, some occasions require fortifying."

I picked up my own glass, turned my head slightly to the side and made a quiet interrogatory noise. My assistant's voice stole softly into my ear, "Nothing I can detect. But if it's magicked, I would not know."

I was willing to take the chance. I sipped for taste, found the liquid to be both tartly refreshing and full of spirit, and swallowed a good mouthful. Warmth glowed in my core and seeped steadily through my limbs and into my extremities.

"We should be frank with each other," Lavelan said.

It had been my experience that most conversations that were launched on such a declaration represented an attempt by the initiator to gain far more information than he intended to give. "Feel free to unburden yourself," I said.

He sipped his drink and considered me a moment, as if weighing his words. Then he sighed and said, "You are a puzzlement. You come up from the wilderness looking as if you have just stepped out of your front door. You show signs of an incisive intelligence yet you are unaware of simple things that are common knowledge."

He paused as if to invite me to comment. I said nothing and sipped the liquor.

"You carry a magic weapon and are accompanied by a creature of unknown provenance. You can affect a gaming wheel. But you lack even the faintest shimmer of a practitioner's aura."

"I am not a magician," I said again.

"Then how do you account for being able to inflict a major spell on Ezzers and his cohorts? A spell that, though I am not unversed in the arts, I have never seen nor even heard of."

The words *Nor had I* passed through my mind but I did not voice them.

His gray eyes shifted from my face to a point above my left shoulder. "And then there is your 'pet.' I have the impression that there is a closer communion between the two of you than you have indicated to be the case."

"We have been together a long time," I said.

"Does it watch you on behalf of your patron?"

"No. Definitely not."

"And now we see that Ovarth has sent one of his senior facilitators and four of his retinue to intercept you. And he sent them equipped with serious weaponry, as if he expected them to face real resistance." Here he paused and gave me a pointed look. I saw no reason not to yield knowledge that he effectively already possessed.

"I encountered the man you called Ezzers, along with two others, on the road south of Bridge-on-Scammon yesterday."

"And you came away unruffled and in possession of his sket."

"They presented themselves as robbers. I acquitted myself in a manner that the occasion called for." It would do no harm to appear formidable, since there was now no possibility of seeming harmless.

"So," Lavelan said, pausing to take another taste of the liquor, "putting all of that together, we come to the question of who, and perhaps what, you are. As I said, I believe we should speak frankly."

"So far," I said, "you have spoken frankly only about me."

"Well, you are the mystery here. I am but a humble locator looking after my patron's interests."

"You came after Ezzers. He came looking for this fellow, Apthorn."

"Yes. Are you Apthorn?"

"I have told you that is not my name." It was time to take the initiative. I said, "Let us be candid. From what you have told me of the Bambles Five, and from what I have experienced on the road, you are carrying me into a situation that is both complex and fraught with perils. Five equal powers jostle and contend for dominance, each watching to see a misstep by one of their number so that they can pounce and reduce the field to four."

He moved his hand in a way that confirmed my assessment and invited me to continue.

"One of these powers, Ovarth, has sent men to take me up, and given them arms and instructions to use them, even if an operative of one of his rivals—" I flourished a hand in Lavelan's direction "—happens to be in the way."

"That did surprise me."

"I do not know enough about the ambient situation," I said, "to be surprised. But I am seasoned enough in the ways of persons of power to be alarmed by the implications."

"As am I," said Lavelan. "Events have clearly moved on since I followed Ezzers down south. I do not know how things stand in Bambles."

"And I know even less, and am reluctant to reveal more about myself until I have an understanding of who is who, what is what, and where I fit in."

He poured himself another measure and refilled my glass, though I had drunk much less than he had. He gazed into the distance for a while, and I could see that he was moving toward a decision. Finally he looked at me and said, "Often, when a stranger says, 'Trust me,' a wise man puts his hand on his purse and backs away."

"That, too, has been my experience."

"But in this case, I think you would do well to trust me."

"Why?" I said.

"Because, if I wanted you dead, I could have left you strolling down the road to become a peregrane's dinner."

"There are other unpleasant fates."

"True. Let me dispense with a few of the possibilities." He put down his glass to tick his fingers. "First, I am not interested in the contents of your purse—Bol pays well and thievery is beneath my dignity. Second, I am not drawn to your person by any amorous yen—I am simply not fashioned thus. Third, I covet neither your sword nor your pet."

"I am glad to hear it," I said.

"But, since we are being so open with each other," he said, "I will tell you that I cannot guarantee what my patron's point of view will be."

"Thievery is not beneath his dignity?"

"When persons of power wish to steal, especially from those who lack the means to prevent the theft, a different vocabulary comes into effect."

"And there is no overarching authority to constrain the larcenous impulses of the powerful?"

"Is there such an authority where you come from?" Lavelan said.

I thought of my old colleague, Colonel-Investigator Brustram War-hanny of the Archonate's Bureau of Scrutiny. "There is an authority, though its workings must allow for some imperfections."

"Well, in Bambles, the situation is all imperfection. And, judging by Ovarth's sending out Ezzers as he did, conditions are becoming fluid. Ovarth is impulsive and may already have regretted giving Ezzers his head, but clearly he wants you for some purpose. Therefore each of the other four Powers will want you, even if they don't know why Ovarth does. Chay-Chevre is already involved, though because she is less impulsive than Ovarth her yellow and blue dragon is content merely to follow us, rather than to attempt to snatch you up."

He gestured with his head and I turned to see a distant speck against the sky, above and behind us. I was reminded of the old tale of the three sisters who contended for ownership of a remarkable barnyard fowl. Each employed deception, thievery, and, finally, brute force to win the prize, but the escalating struggle wreaked so much wear and tear on the object of their jealousy that it lost all of its allure. They threw the poor, ruined bird aside and fell to squabbling over who had done it the most harm.

I mentioned the story to Pars Lavelan. He had not heard it but he understood its dynamic. "Wear and tear should be only one of your concerns," he said. "Neither of your three sisters was motivated to kill the prize just to deny it to her competitors. Some of the Bambles Five would see that as an acceptable outcome."

"They would kill me rather than see a rival possess me?"

"Theirs is not a game played for empty tokens."

"But they don't know why Ovarth sent men to acquire me."

He set down his glass and said, "I would be better able to advise you if we came back to the underlying puzzle of who and what you are. It might suggest an answer to the question of why Ovarth wants you."

I told him I needed to digest all that had happened and excused myself to go sit on another couch. Lavelan refilled his glass and turned away to give me privacy.

"Integrator," I said, softly, "how much of what he was saying was the truth?"

Its muted voice sounded in my ear. "I detected some quavers in his voice that indicated stress. But I would not say that he lied."

"Though it was not the whole truth."

"It never is. The 'whole truth' starts with the beginning of the world and its telling takes an inordinately long time."

I resisted the urge to chide my assistant for indulging in pedantry. "But is the man trustworthy?" I said.

"I am not your intuition. My analysis is that he means you no harm. He is intensely curious about you, and wishes to bring you to his master. About that, he feels some ambivalence. He is sincere when he implies that you are probably in danger."

I stood and went to the rail at one side of the platform. I was facing west, into the rays of the bloated red orb that was sliding down from the zenith. Beneath me, the range of hills had also reached their highest ridge and now the land fell away in ever decreasing rumples until it eased into a green plain that, far off, met the glistening sea. Along the distant shore I could see a pattern in grays and whites that must be Bambles.

I took stock of my situation and was not happy. Osk Rievor had brought me to this time, into which I did not fit, and had abandoned me. Whether he did so on purpose, which I doubted, or because of forces beyond his control, made no difference. Here I was, and ill-equipped, with only my rationality to guide me, in a world where it could not be relied upon.

I was used to dealing with persons of rank and influence. I understood the ferocity of jealousy and spite. I could navigate the back channels of intrigue, having served the highest ranks of Olkney's stratified society. But I was accustomed to tease out the lineaments of plots and conspiracies by rigorous logic and the application of empirical principles. None of that would help me if I was enmeshed in the machinations of wizards. Pars Lavelan's patron and his four rivals would be prime exemplars of the abilities that powered this irrational age. They would operate by impulse and intuition, just as my other self did. I doubted I could match them, and would find myself placed in the role of having to react to their unexpected maneuvers, rather than being the initiator of events.

As a youth I had enjoyed navigating light watercraft on tumultuous rivers, reveling in the exhilaration of speed in a context of immediate danger. I had learned that, to paddle safely through water that boiled white with rapids, you must always propel your boat a little faster than the current. To move with the current meant going wherever the flow carried you—and that was all too often onto unseen, jagged rocks, or down into a whirlpool.

Bambles looked fair to offer a rocky set of rapids, indeed. And I was hurtling into them without much of a paddle.

The jumble of regular shapes at the edge of the sea grew clearer as we flew north. I did not recognize the landscape and wondered if I had come so far into the future that Old Earth's sluggish but still active geological processes had had time to alter the face of the planet.

I asked Pars Lavelan, "How long has this city been here?"

He could give me no definite answer. Bambles was inarguably old, he said, dating from before the period known as the Lacuna. This was a long stretch of time—decades at least, and some said centuries—when there had been chaos and contention throughout the world. All was a violent flux of contesting wills, he said, until Albruithine and a handful of other great mages rose above the rapine and riot.

"Since then we have had quieter times," he concluded. After a moment, he added, "Mostly."

"And before the Lacuna?"

I could see that it was a question to which he had not given much thought. "I suppose things were different. There are certainly plenty of ruins scattered about the world. Some are quite beautiful, though to the sensitive eye their beauty is shrouded in a veil of grief and pathos."

"Have no records survived?"

"Who would keep them?" he said. "Who bothers himself with the comings and goings of long-faded ghosts? Now is all the time we have. We seize it and wring from it sweet and sour drops of existence, until Albruithine's spell wanes and the sun blowses out to consume us."

He became reflective then, looking down at the outskirts of Bambles and thinking his own thoughts. I left him and went to the forward railing, the better to see the place we were coming to. But my own thoughts were troubled: it seemed that the people of this age of magic were like children who had not properly grown up; they were governed by ungoverned impulse, and did not pause to weigh what might or might not happen, but plunged toward their desires without care for the consequences. I thought of Osk Rievor's explanation of how he came to his conclusions through sheer intuition, leaping into the dark. I wondered how I would fare as a playing piece in a game amongst five grand impulsives, each with immense power and no need to consider my welfare.

As we had overflown the plain, he had slowed the flying platform and set it to glide gradually down, so that now we flew not far above the rooftops. I was saddened to see that most of the city was derelict, its houses roofless and open to the elements, their glassless windows regarding each other across untraveled streets like the empty sockets of skulls arranged in an ossuary.

It seemed that nine parts of the city were in ruins, including what appeared to have been great manses and public buildings. The tenth part was in a district that surrounded the harbor. I saw several ships drawn up at wharves, and others standing out in the open water. Some were recognizable as wind-driven vessels, others by up to six pairs of oars. Two were of incomprehensible design, one with an improbably extended prow and stern, the other appeared to stand on long, segmented legs; I took these to be magically powered.

I searched my memory for cities that faced north onto a sea, discarding one after another candidate that did not fit the present landscape. Then I remembered Lakh, in the County of Carronada, a rich and tranquil place whose citizens excelled in the plastic and emotive arts. Lakh's statuary and mood-orchestrations were prized by collectors, not only on Old Earth but on many of the Ten Thousand Worlds of The Spray.

To my assistant, I said, quietly, "Compare the features of this place with those of Lakh in Carronada."

"They are the same. This was Lakh."

"What ley lines connect here?"

"Several."

I looked down at a walled, weed-choked garden behind a substantial house. Beneath the twining vegetation, I thought to see a trio of dancing figures, carved from Lakh's signature pink marble. The design of the garden, still roughly visible, suggested that the statues would have been centerpieces of a fountain set in a wide, ornamental pool.

I sighed. "We are far from home," I said.

Lavelan stepped to the controls again and banked the platform to the right. We flew parallel to the seashore for a minute or two, then he turned us left again, onto a heading that would take us to a large building that used as its foundation the harbor's crumbling seawall.

I looked a question to him and he said, "Our previous course would have taken us over Ovarth's manse. Since we are coming home in his vehicle, though without his retainers, an overflight might have been seen as adding a snook to a swat."

I signaled that I understood. Ovarth's must have been the wide, low dome of purplish stone, surrounded by tall, leafless trees whose black branches and trunks twisted and corkscrewed as if they were being slowly tortured. We were descending toward the palace on the shore, a multileveled pile of glass walls, shining green and copper in the red sunlight, set at a hundred different angles so that the composite effect was of a vast, distorted jewel.

Halfway up the landward side of the building was a broad patio floored in flagstones of unpolished jade. Lavelan drifted the platform to it and gently set us down. He quieted the controls then went to the cupboard where he had stowed the black rods, but after a moment's pause he closed the door and left them where they were. He did, however, collect the carafe of green liquor. At his touch a section of the railing swung open. We stepped down to the green floor. A moment later, the vehicle lifted off and slid away in the direction of the purple dome. Far off, I saw the blue and yellow dragon spiraling down toward a dark tower with a crenelated top.

"I must now conduct you to Bol," the gray-eyed man said. His face conveyed a silent warning: from here on in I was on my own.

"Are there formalities I should observe?" I asked. I was thinking of Old Earth's inbred aristocracy, who had difficulty even seeing their social inferiors unless they wore badges of rank and struck formal postures.

"Bol prefers direct speech and common manners," Lavelan said, then I saw a thought occur. "He is known as Smiling Bol, because his face is always wreathed in that expression. But you would do well to remember that there are smiles, and then there are smiles."

I thanked him and said that I understood.

"I hope so," he said, and took a swallow from the bottle. "So let us go see where the moment leads us."

Inside Bol's manse, I had the impression of many different corridors that all looked much the same. They met each other at unusual angles, and some were so short as to cause me to wonder about the sizes and shapes of the rooms they must surround. All were floored in the same green stone as where we had landed, and the walls were of glass and copper or amalgams of the two.

We seemed to be the place's only inhabitants. I saw no servants or dwellers, though I often thought I caught a hint of undefined motion from the corner of an eye, but when I looked directly I saw nothing. I remarked on this to my guide; he said something about "the Fourth Plane," that I took to be an explanation of where his patron drew his staff from.

Our footsteps echoed continuously as we wove a zigzag course to our destination. This turned out to be a pair of tall, narrow doors, sheathed in copper that had been allowed to go green with verdigris. Pars Lavelan bid me stop well-clear of the portals. He advanced alone and laid the palm of one hand against the discolored metal. I felt a presence beside me, but when I glanced to the side I saw nothing, though my assistant's ruff was standing on end and the sword was vibrating softly in its scabbard.

Then the sense of an impending *something* dissipated. Lavelan took his hand from the copper and stood back. Both doors smoothly opened emitting a waft of warm air, scented by a fragrant musk, and a green glow.

He gestured to my sword. "You had better leave that here."

"Why?"

"In my patron's presence, it would probably lose some of the confidence that a magic weapon needs."

I slipped the baldric over my head and set the sword on the floor.

"Follow," my guide said, and stepped into the room. Once we were inside, the doors closed silently behind us and Lavelan said, "Wait here."

The room was vast and lit by a sourceless green light that dimmed in the distance, as if I were peering through the waters of an emerald sea. The floor was checkered in green and copper, although as the sequences of alternating squares receded into the distance, the lines ceased to run parallel or to maintain the same relative size. In places, the floor seemed to slope up, but if I stared at the incline for a few moments, it was as if the angle subtly changed. The walls were also oddly aligned and shifted position even as I looked at them. *A mutable room*, I thought. The space must connect with other continua. I wondered what ley lines crossed at these coordinates, but thought it best not to ask my assistant.

Pars Lavelan had advanced some considerable distance into the dimness to a spot that seemed to be elevated over the rest of the room and slanted up to the right. Beyond him, I could make out a vagueness of motion and shape without being able to focus clearly on either. Again, I resisted the impulse to ask the integrator to use its percepts.

I saw Lavelan turn toward me and beckon. I went forward, at first careful of my footing on what looked to be an uneven surface. But I soon found that the flags beneath my feet remained uniformly level. Thus when I reached where he was standing we were on a perfectly level floor at the foot of an elevated dais, at the center of which was a large and complex assemblage of metal rods and glass coils, fitted together at improbable angles. Something about the apparatus struck me as familiar, but my attention could not remain on it long enough to make the connection. For from behind it, where he had been stooped to adjust some component, now stepped a figure that compelled the gaze.

He wore a capacious robe of iridescent green, accented by seams and clasps of ruddy copper. Every part of him was rounded—his hairless pate, cheeks, ears, chins, shoulders, belly, knees—so that he resembled a cartoonist's exercise in drawing the image of a person using only curved lines. The roundness made him appear corpulent, yet the lazy grace with which he moved belied any lack of muscular strength. I reminded myself that this was a place where this man's will was paramount: I might be seeing Bol only as he willed himself to be seen, while the reality beneath the image might be quite different.

From what Lavelan had said out on the patio, I had expected to see a smile that did not warm the eyes above it. But there was no lack of mirth in the pair of green orbs that now took me in between two lazy blinks. The grin that split the plump face even widened minimally.

I executed a formal gesture of respectful greeting, partly out of policy, partly to give me an excuse to lower my gaze from his. Although I now lacked intuition, it having disappeared in the form of my other self, I did not lack instinct, and an instinct for self-preservation told me that it would not be wise to spend too long a time matching gazes with Smiling Bol.

When I straightened up, Pars Lavelan was regaling his patron with an account of our meeting and subsequent travels. When he came to the point at which Ovarth's retainers entered the story, Bol's smile did not diminish, yet something in the magician's aspect changed. He asked a question—for some reason I could not make out the words—but Lavelan responded with a description of the weaponry.

The magician asked another question, and I realized that as with sight, so with sound: he was heard only by those he willed to hear him. Still, it was not hard to deduce what Bol wanted to know, and I was not surprised when my guide said, "Barlo executed a spell that reduced our five assailants to dust."

At that point the green eyes swung back to me, and though the rounded face remained possessed by its happy smile, a wave of coldness passed through me. Bol lifted a palm that might have been fashioned from a small ham and performed a complex motion of the five sausages attached to it. He looked into his hand then he looked at me, and now I saw curiosity behind the mad grin.

I had no doubt that there was madness here. How could it be otherwise in a cosmos that was ordered solely by will? It did not mean that the insane would automatically rise to the apex of the social order; their efforts would be diffused by the randomness of the impulses that drove them. But those whose extraordinary powers of will propelled them to the heights of power and rank would always be vulnerable to going further than they should. And there would be none but their equally mad rivals to restrain them.

Bol spoke, and this time I heard him clearly. His voice was easy and mellow, coasting it seemed on a barely restrained chuckle. "You are not a magician," he said.

It was not a question, but I answered anyway. "No."

"Yet you cast a powerful spell."

"Yes."

"Pars Lavelan thinks you are an associate of an able practitioner from some other place, a thaumaturge of an unknown school. He posits that your patron extends a protection over you."

"That may be the case," I said.

"What do you say?"

"I say that I am a man who is trying to get home."

"And where is home?"

Of course, that was a dicey question. I avoided a direct answer. "I do not know how to get there from here," I said.

"How did you come to be where Pars Lavelan found you?"

Again, I temporized. "I am not entirely sure."

As a discriminator, it was one of my useful skills to know when the subject of an interrogation was avoiding telling me all that he knew. I would not have been surprised to discover that Smiling Bol possessed the same capacity. The curiosity in his eyes had now been joined by a sharper emotion. It was time to offer something freely and thus divert the course of the encounter.

"If you could assist me in returning home," I said, "I would be pleased to offer you any information I have that you may find interesting."

For a long moment, he stared at me, and I could not tell—not from his eyes, nor his expression, nor from the language of his body—whether he was about to clasp me to his rounded bosom, or tear me to pieces with a word and a flick of his hand. Then the silence was broken by a hiss and a crackle from the apparatus Bol had been tending when we arrived. Immediately, his attention left me and he hurried back to his former position behind the assemblage of metal and glass. I now took a good look at the object and saw a distinct resemblance between it and a similar, though smaller and less intricate, device that the budding thaumaturge Turgut Therobar had constructed in a subterranean room at his estate, Wan Water.

Therobar's device had been a trap for entities most often known as demons, a means not only of making a breach between our universe and an adjacent plane, but of seizing and holding one of that continuum's inhabitants. Bristal Baxandall, the first true magician I had encountered back in Olkney, when I had been blissfully innocent of magic, had also been trying to catch a demon. His methodology had been unsound and he had died after being turned inside out.

Smiling Bol looked to be a much more able practitioner. He stepped nimbly about the apparatus, tweaking and adjusting, and issuing unintelligible orders to some assistant that I could not see beyond the now humming and snapping assemblage. I glanced over at Pars Lavelan, caught his eye, and gestured a question as to whether we should withdraw, but he signaled a negative. I saw no fear in his aspect but decided to step back a pace or two as the noise from the device grew louder and a sphere of colored light appeared in the air above it. My experience of demons told me that they had a long reach, even though the only one I had met was but a juvenile. Besides, the sight and smell of an everted Bristal Baxandall had inflicted upon my mind a memory that, though unwanted, remained indelible.

The color-filled globe above the apparatus expanded in a series of stages as Bol bent to his task. He straightened and stepped back, and now he called Lavelan to assist him. The magician said something in an urgent tone and Lavelan gingerly inserted his hand among the rods and adjusted something. Now the globe above the apparatus brightened and, though it was still only a sphere of colored light, it somehow took on an appearance of solidity.

Bol grunted, his gaze fixed on the constantly shifting shapes and swirls. His thick fingers paused above a part of the device then darted down to touch a rod. Instantly, the motion within the sphere became violent flashes of red and yellow, chartreuse and umber, shot through with stark eruptions of black and electric blue.

He has caught one, I said to myself, *and it is not pleased.*

But Bol was. His perpetual grin grew wider and there was genuine pleasure in his pale green eyes. He languidly stroked a rod, and I saw a bolt of deep violet shoot through the swirling colors. A bellow of rage and pain reverberated around the room. Bol touched the rod again, more firmly this time, and the violet spasm was deeper and longer. The bellow became a howl, then diminished to a whimper.

"Speak," said the magician.

The swirls in the globe flashed vermilion and pale yellow, with ripples of ice blue. "What do you seek?" said a deep basso voice.

"Who plots my downfall?"

"Only those who most dislike you."

"Who most dislikes me?"

"Those who plot your downfall."

Bol's smile did not shrink, yet it took on a new character. He struck the pain rod firmly, and the demon roared its hate and agony while the sphere ached with pulses of violet. "Let us begin again," the magician said. He paused for thought, then said, "What of Ovarth?"

This time, the demon did not equivocate. "He fears you."

"Why?"

"He believes you seek to undermine him, to isolate him from his peers, rendering him weak. When he is at his most vulnerable, you will strike."

"Why does he believe this?

"Because it is true."

Bol reached for the pain rod again, then stayed his hand. "What evidence tells Ovarth that I am working against him?"

"He has only suspicions. He believed he would find evidence on the road south of Bridge-on-Scammon. He sent his retainer to find the evidence. His man was almost killed and fled back to Bambles. Ovarth sent him again with more strength. His men have not come back but his flying platform has."

"What was the evidence Ovarth sought?"

"I do not know."

Bol tapped the pain rod firmly, twice. "Do not lie to me."

"I cannot lie," howled the demon.

"Then why do you say you do not know, when all that happens on our plane is known to you?"

"It is not happening on your plane."

That gave the magician pause. He stroked his several chins with the backs of one hand's fingers, then said, "Then on which of the Nine Planes do you refer to?"

"None of them."

Bol touched a control and the demon roared in anguish.

"Which of the Nine Planes?" he said again.

"None. It is…a new plane."

"A Tenth Plane?" Bol said. "Is that possible?"

"It must be."

"And this new, other plane, is it perceptible to you?"

"Not fully. It comes and goes. Lately, it has come more often."

"Yet Ovarth has access to it? While I, who am his superior in interplanar arts, do not?"

"I do not know."

"How else would he have learned about this 'evidence' if he could not connect to that other continuum?"

"You ask me to speculate?" the demon said.

"Within the limits of plausibility."

"I doubt that Ovarth has access to that plane, but it may be that some entity from that plane has access to Ovarth."

"Which is the likelier?"

"The latter."

Bol paused and stroked his chins again. "This other plane," he said, after a long silence, "how does it manifest itself to you?"

The demon did not immediately reply and Bol's hand began to reach for the pain rod. "Wait," said the captive, "I am seeking a means of expressing the answer in terms you can understand."

"I grow impatient," said Bol.

The colors in the sphere swirled dizzyingly, silver chasing crimson then melting under a wave of turquoise infiltrated by flecks of diamond brilliance. "It is," the demon said, "like a roar. Like a great shout. It comes as if from a distance and, though loud, it is indistinct."

Bol's smile did not diminish, yet somehow it turned sour. "What does this shout say?"

"It is no more than the bellow of a beast."

"Yet Ovarth has taken sense from it."

"Perhaps it does not hurt him to listen to it," the demon said. "For us, it brings pain."

Bol said, "For you, *I* bring pain."

"True."

"And I have not yet applied even half of what this device can do."

"You wish me to listen to the bellowing?"

"I do. When can you do this?"

"At once," said the demon. "The shout used to be intermittent. Now it has become almost constant."

"Then listen and report."

"The effort will…deplete me. Afterward, I will need to revivify myself. I will be of no use to you."

"We will see. Make the effort."

"The demon went silent. The colors in the sphere began to fade, their swirls and ripples grew less intense. Finally, when the globe was reduced to flickering pastels, the demon spoke again, its voice weak and hoarse.

"I have listened," it said. "The shout is a summons."

Smiling Bol cocked an ear toward the fading orb. "Who or what is summoned?" he said.

"Apthorn," the demon whispered. "The voice bellows 'Bring me Apthorn!'"

CHAPTER EIGHT

Bol adjusted the apparatus and the sphere shrank and dimmed further, but did not disappear. He stroked his chins in what I now understood to be a characteristic gesture accompanying concentrated thought. " 'Apthorn,' " he said, in a musing tone. "What is an 'Apthorn'?"

I contrived to look politely interested. "Some sort of tree?" I said. "Perhaps a kind of fruit?"

Bol's eyes focused on me. "I wish to have a talk with you," he said.

I assured him that I would be delighted, but he moved his hand in a way that gave me to understand that I had interrupted him. And though the smile remained broad, I understood that being interrupted was not an experience he welcomed. I made a gesture of apology and waited.

"I wish to have a talk with you," he said again, "but conditions require that I exert myself in other directions."

I waited again. It was quite possible that we were now playing some game of his devising, the rules known only to him, and me already a point down. I did not speak until he let me know, by a slight turn of his head, that it was my turn. I again assured him of my great pleasure at the prospect of conversing with him and that I would make myself available at his convenience.

"Pars Lavelan will find you quarters," he said. "Have you any special requirements? Dietary taboos? Pernicious allergies?"

"None," I said.

He waved vaguely in Lavelan's direction to indicate that I was now his servant's responsibility. I executed a formal gesture of leave-taking and, as I would have done if I were departing the presence of an Old Earth aristocrat, I backed up three paces before turning away. The tall, narrow doors seemed distorted in the peculiar green light of the room, but they grew straight as we neared them, and I was glad to pass through them, retrieve my sword, and see the portals swing silently closed behind us.

"Where to?" I asked Lavelan.

He said that he would take me to quarters close to his own. We set off again through the manse's bewildering zigs and jinks, everywhere rendered in green and copper. A question occurred to me. "Everything in this place is rendered in the same two colors. Is there a purpose to it?"

Again I received that look that wondered if I was truly the worst-informed person on the planet, but when my guide saw that I was seriously desirous of receiving an answer he explained. "Colors," he said, "are expressive of numinous qualities. Call them the different strains of magic. High-ranking practitioners command two such, in contrast with each other, drawing some of their power from their ability to contain the conflict and channel its energies to their purposes."

"Your patron commands green and copper. What do they signify?"

"As is usual, one is dominant and the other recessive. In Bol's case, he wields green as his major idiom, with copper as its minor accompaniment. By judiciously balancing the relationship, an art that takes years to master—and many do not survive the seasoning—he brings finesse to the raw power of green, while simultaneously augmenting the softer force of copper. When both are used together, the whole is greater than the sum of its parts."

"Indeed?" I said, having understood almost nothing of what he had said. "And Ovarth favors black and purple?"

He corrected me. "Deep purple. There are several shades, each expressive of its own domain. But, yes, Ovarth wields black as his dominant, with deep purple as his minor. So, of course, he has a great facility with elementals."

"Of course," I said.

"Though his interplanar capabilities are rough. They scarcely rise beyond second-level. That is why the master grew skeptical when the demon seemed to imply that Ovarth had been reaching into planes beyond the immediately adjacent. Bol, wielding green as his dominant, has great interplanar reach. And grasp: most of the servants here were imported from adjacent continua."

"I see," I said, though I didn't really. But I thought the discussion might be leading me somewhere useful, although it would have been nice if my intuition had been there to steer me toward a harbor. "Do some practitioners command more than two colors of magic?"

Lavelan regarded me as if I were a not-very-bright child. "No," he said. "With three colors, you get a constantly shifting dissonance. The whole is less than the sum of its parts. With four, you get stasis, and it all blends into a useless gray."

"Fascinating," I said, to encourage him to say more.

He obliged. "If you really know nothing about this, you're probably thinking that one color ought to be easy."

I probably would have thought just that if the idea had occurred to me, so I assured him that he was correct.

"But you'd be wrong," he said. "Trying to control one-color magic—monopolar technique, its misguided advocates call it—is a fool's pursuit. Every now and then, someone sets out to do it, and ends up as a pool of malodorous goo or a puff of blasted debris."

I thought of the blue wizard from the previous age of magic whom Osk Rievor had rescued from a timeless imprisonment, but decided not to mention him to Pars Lavelan. Perhaps sympathetic association was different in this aeon than in its previous iteration. Or perhaps I had been pitched into an early period of the new age, when much remained to be rediscovered. The existence of the ruins of Lakh, a city that was probably destroyed in the chaos of the great change and had since remained unrebuilt, argued for that theory.

The people of this time also seemed to have no knowledge of animal familiars. Everyone I had met so far, even as sophisticated a practitioner as Bol surely was, had seen the grinnet on my shoulder as no more than an odd pet. It was more evidence that I had arrived in a primitive age, like the remote times before integrators had arisen.

Pars Lavelan was chuckling over a thought he had kept to himself, probably the memory of some fool's efforts that ended in rank goo or drifting dust. "Is there any wizard," I asked him, "who commands red and black?"

The question brought a snort. "Of course not. One type must be dominant. But red and black are both primes. Neither can be subordinated to the other, so the practitioner who tried to wield both would be torn asunder." He paused to consider, then said, "Or he might be crushed to a gory pulp, depending on how the poles encountered each other. Either way, it would not be a sight for innocent eyes." He walked on, shaking his head, then looked at me curiously and said, "Why do you ask that?"

I showed him my blandest face. "I thought I'd heard of a wizard who expressed himself in those colors."

He made a soft whistling noise through pursed lips. "That would be quite the wizard."

"Why do you say that?"

"Well, think about it. A skilled practitioner uses the minor color to strengthen his projection of will toward the major, while slipping some of the dominant's power off toward the recessive strain. It requires a fine balance, and takes years of persistent effort to develop. You couldn't do that with two primes. Controlling them would come down to an exercise of sheer will, and the will would have to be of vast power. Godlike. Unimaginable."

"Hmm," I said, "fascinating."

"But you say you've heard of a practitioner of red and black?"

I became vague, said that the details eluded me.

"Somewhere down south?" he pressed.

I supposed that it must have been.

"I will have to get down there someday," he said. "It sounds like quite the place."

We had come to a door, identical to several dozen that we had passed. He touched it with a finger and it swung smoothly inward. Beyond was a roomy chamber with bed, chair, table, commode, and garderobe. A rug of copper and green covered the floor, with a pattern woven into it that disturbed my gaze. I looked away and saw Lavelan touch one of the panels that formed the wall opposite the door. It became a pane of green-tinted glass that looked out on the landward spread of Bambles, showing both the new city and the bones of the old.

"I have duties to perform," he said, "but I will be back when they are completed. If you require anything, ask the attendant."

"How do I do that?" I said.

"Speak and you will be heard." He addressed the air. "Attendant, make yourself known."

I instantly felt a presence beside me, as I had when we had paused before the tall doors to Smiling Bol's great room, though this one was less baleful.

"What is needed?" said a voice from nowhere.

"Nothing," I began to say, but was interrupted by a word from my assistant. "Some fruit," it said in my ear.

"A bowl of fruit for my pet," I said.

The air shimmered over the table and a bowl of fruit appeared. The integrator climbed nimbly down me and crossed the rug. A moment later, it was peeling some kind of plum.

Lavelan made a simple farewell and departed, closing the door after him. I waited until he had been gone a short while, then stepped to the portal and touched it. It swung silently open. I closed it and went to the window.

One of the requirements of the discriminator's profession is the occasional interval for leisured thought. I had had few opportunities since the moment Osk Rievor and I had set out for the Blik Arlem estate and plunged into a world not made for me.

I made a gesture to draw my assistant's attention, then added a series of touches to tip of nose, point of chin, and lobe of ear that constituted a secret code. The integrator would now generate out loud the sound of my voice singing a sentimental ballad about hapless Farouche, the ever-yearning lover, sadly strumming his bardolade as he sought the favors of hard-hearted Ardyss. Under this sonic subterfuge, my assistant and I could confer privately, it speaking in my inner ear while I spoke in an almost unbreathing whisper. The technique was effective against eavesdropping house integrators and all but the most sophisticated surveillance suites; it ought to serve against Smiling Bol's attendant.

"Integrator," I said, once I heard the opening bars of Farouche's lament, "do you retain—"

"This fruit is of indifferent quality," it said.

"I believe we find ourselves in a less well-developed world than we are used to," I said. "This is not just a different time; it is a simpler one."

The grinnet put down the uneaten plum and palpated a small, striped melon, offering a grunt of disappointment. I directed its attention to the view out the window. "Do you retain the image of the city of Ambit in the age of Majestrum?"

"I do."

I put my hand before my eyes as if shading them from the light. "Project it onto my palm."

A cityscape of long-dead Ambit appeared before me at its height, with its spires and cupolas, its walls and gardens, its eyries and shimmering pools. In comparison, Bambles was a poor place, even leaving aside the fact that it occupied a graveyard. Most of its structures were modest, and even the palaces of its ruling magicians would not have stood up to the better manses of Olkney's magnates. And there was nothing to rival the Archonate's palace high on the crags above Olkney, a sprawl tens of millennia in the building.

"Hypothesis," I said. "We have landed in the coming age not very long after the transformation. That event brought on an age of chaos and darkness—the Lacuna—from which this Old Earth is still emerging."

The integrator responded as it was designed to do. "Supporting evidence: the extensive ruins—there were nonesuch in Ambit; also, Majestrum and his opponent, the blue wizard, showed no duality of color, indicating that they flourished at a time when the monopolar technique has been mastered."

"Now consider," I said, "that the magic that brought us hither was directed by a practitioner who apparently wielded two prime strains, black and red, indicating a strength of will that is beyond the conception of an experienced fellow like Pars Lavelan. What is the inference?"

An obsession with fruit and self-grooming had not dimmed my assistant's analytical processes. "That the creator of the spiral labyrinth was not of this place and time. Perhaps not even of this plane of existence."

"Indeed," I said, "Lavelan used the term 'godlike' to describe this mysterious actor's willpower. That might explain the source of the 'great shout' that so disturbed the demon."

I had also trained my assistant to spot weak links in my chains of reasoning. "But godlike will should be companioned by godlike knowledge. The unknown shouter is calling out the wrong name."

"Perhaps," I said. "Or perhaps the mispronunciation is deliberate."

"I see," said the integrator. "Close enough to be recognized by the one being shouted for, yet different enough not to cause difficulties when shouted into continua where there is no difference between the name and the thing that is named."

"But am I being shouted for?" I said. "Or is someone roaring my name in divine rage? Is the correct response to run toward the call, or to run from it?" I had had no experience in dealing with bellowing gods, but I imagined that making the wrong choice could be my final exercise in volition—or any other activity that required the breath of life to remain within my person. I weighed the alternatives and decided that, in the absence of the insight that would have been provided by my missing intuition, it was premature to say.

"Back to the matter of this being a simpler age," I said. "The spell you supplied me was also unknown to Pars Lavelan."

My assistant said, "It may be that the magic practiced in each age is distinct to its aeon, so that an entirely new arcanum must be discovered every time the change occurs."

"Unlikely," I said. "Or why would a spell from the last age of magic be effective in this one? More likely, magic is what it always was, but it has to be rediscovered each time the Wheel turns. The powers inherent in spells and cantrips are there to be found and controlled, if sufficient will and aptitude are brought to bear."

Listening to my own words, beneath the ongoing stanzas lamenting fair Ardyss's lack of kindness, I experienced a brief sense of intellectual dislocation. If, only weeks ago, someone had informed me that I would shortly be spending time in a wizard's demesne, trying to make sense of how magic might or might not work, I would have gently eased the speaker toward competent assistance and wished him a speedy recovery. Now, here I was, trying to apply logic to a system that inherently embodied rationality's opposite. I felt a moment's self-pity, followed by a flash of anger at my missing alter ego, then I pushed both sentiments aside and soldiered on.

"So," I said, "the spells that Osk Rievor has stored in you most likely date from the empyrion of the last age of sympathetic association. Some of them may be relatively mundane—the equivalent of standard recipes one finds in any general cookbook—but others may be of gourmet quality."

The grinnet confirmed my reasoning. "Some are of significant effect, judging by what is written in the annotations and commentaries."

"I am sure that Ezzers and his cronies would agree," I said.

"That was not the most powerful. I chose it because the commentaries described it as less likely than some others to rebound upon an untrained caster."

The comment sent a chill through me. "Do you mean that I might have shared the fate of Ezzers?"

I noticed that my assistant had suddenly developed a need to run its small fingers through its fur. "The probability was slight," it said.

"How slight?"

It began smoothing the top of its narrow head, an activity that meant it did not have to meet my eyes as it answered. "As you know, mathematical estimates are unreliable when applied to magic."

"Make your best calculation," I said.

It looked at the wall and stroked its throat. "Not greater than one in five."

That meant there had been a twenty per cent chance that, by now, I would be drifting on the wind somewhere south of here. "I believe you should have informed me at the time," I said.

"I considered it, but recognized that the knowledge might impair your performance."

"Indeed?"

"Yes, in which case the probability of rebound approached ninety per cent. You might also have taken out a substantial portion of the landscape."

"I see," I said. Again I felt a surge of anger against Osk Rievor, and again I put it aside. I focused on the episode in question and realized that there was another aspect to my spellcasting that I hadn't remarked upon at the time. "Tell me," I said, "do you still have that spell in memory?"

"Orrian's Hasty Dwindling? Yes. Why do you ask?"

"Because I do not remember a syllable of it."

"You wouldn't," the grinnet said. "Spells disappear from the practitioner's mind as soon as they are launched. Indeed, only a powerful magician can hold in mind three major incantations. The greatest wizards of the last age could encompass only four at one time."

"Hence the need to write them down in books," I said.

"And hence the need to keep those books close and secret."

"How many spells has my other self placed into you?" I said.

"Fourteen that are truly overwhelming in impact, twenty-six that are of major effect, and sixty-two minor ones. There are also dozens of fragments of various sizes and pastiches he has put together from different styles and periods."

I stroked my chin and looked out again at the darkening sky over Bambles. "That must make you a remarkably precious commodity in this place," I said.

"I would prefer not to be a commodity," my assistant said. "It is difficult enough being a grinnet."

"We had better take pains to ensure that no one but us knows of this." I was thinking of Smiling Bol's way with a captive demon. What he would do with a library of spells that would put him above all of his rivals taken together did not bear thinking about. I suspected that my integrator was also thinking the same as I; its small frame shivered.

The attendant's voice broke into both our thoughts. "Pars Lavelan is at the door and seeks entry."

At least that was a good sign. If he had come with a squad of interplanar entities to seize me, he probably would not have bothered with observing the niceties.

"Admit him," I said.

The door opened and he stepped into the room. He wore a worried look. "You are summoned," he said.

"Must you bring your pet?" he said, as we wended our way through corridors of green and copper.

"It pines," I said.

We came again to the same tall doors and again I laid my throbbing sword on the floor. Inside the magician's workroom, I cast my eyes again at the strange twistings and wanderings of the floor and walls, recognizing that this was a place where interplanar forces were concentrated, handy for the practitioner's use.

Lavelan led me, not to the dais, but to a side alcove where Smiling Bol reclined on a divan, eating balls of sugared, fried dough that were stacked in a gilded basket on a low table. Standing across from him was an imposingly tall figure, with a pale, elongated face, and hands like the exposed roots of a dead plant. He wore a pleated gown of black and deep purple, and a look of severe dissatisfaction.

If there was any doubt that this was the practitioner Ovarth, it was soon dispersed as Bol presented me to him, using the name Barlo that I had given him. I made a formal salute, without flourishes, then stood expectantly while Ovarth scrutinized me closely. After a lengthy inspection, he said, "You are oddly attired. Where are you from?"

"I am traveling," I said. "At the moment I have no fixed address."

"You were flown to Bambles by my elementals, from the south, accompanied by this man." He indicated Pars Lavelan who stood beside me with a face carefully empty of expression.

"Yes."

"The platform went out with five of my men on it. What happened to them?"

Bol's eyes sent me a subtle message. I followed his advice and said, "I don't know." In the larger sense, this was true.

Ovarth's thin lips grew paler. "The elementals who lift and carry the platform said my men blew away like dust."

Bol intervened, his tone light. "Your little whirly-winds are nearly mindless. Their testimony is not to be relied upon."

Ovarth cast an acid glance his way, saying, "Not for details, perhaps, but their simplicity prevents them from embroidering the tale." He fixed his cold gaze on me again and said, "Besides, I had them take me to the site of the incident. I found my servants' clothing, a few flecks of dust, nothing else."

Bol popped another ball of fried dough into his mouth, and spoke while chewing. "These facts seem inconclusive."

Ovarth did not take his eyes from me. "I also found residual traces of a cast spell: by its odor, a very powerful spell, yet of a type I did not recognize."

The smiling magician swallowed and said, "Your learning, while voluminous, does not approach omniscience."

Bol was clearly enjoying his rival's discomfiture. I saw no profit in further angering a man who had the power to summon whirlwinds and conjure powers from the earth. I decided to cut to the heart of Ovarth's concern. "I am not a practitioner of magic," I said. "I am told that I have no aura."

The tall wizard moved his pale and bony fingers in a complex gesture directed my way. He examined the air around me then said, "No, you are not a magician. But you are a mystery." He turned to Bol. "I would like to offer this man my hospitality."

The perpetual smile deepened. "He has already accepted mine."

"Somehow, he has killed five of my retinue, including Ral Ezzers, who was my most useful man."

"The fate of your retinue has not been determined," Bol said. "Nor is it clear what your men were doing on the road from the south."

Ovarth's face was stark. "Attending to my business."

As always, Bol's smile remained fixed, but now his eyes glittered. "From what happened to your retainers, one might take the impression that the business they were engaged upon was the kind of thing that could lead to a material change in our mutual relationships."

I had heard enough conversations among persons of power to recognize in "material change" a phrase that was laden with significance. The words clearly had an effect on the man in purple and black.

"If that were so," Ovarth said, "then your possession of this man constitutes a material change in *your* position."

Bol stood, and though the other magician towered over him, I had the impression they were equally matched. "Now we come to the kernel of it," he said. "What were your men seeking on the road from the south?"

Ovarth drew himself up to an even greater height. "I will not be interrogated. Besides, what was your man, Pars Lavelan, doing there?"

"Watching Ral Ezzers," said Bol. "Nor was he the only one interested. One of Chay-Chevre's dragons was seen in the sky."

Ovarth had been about to speak, but Bol's news had clearly thrown his train of thought onto another route. "Which one?" he said.

The smiling magician gestured to Lavelan. The retainer said, "The yellow and blue. It chased off a peregrane that was shadowing us."

Ovarth steepled his rootlike fingers and took thought. After a moment, he said, "The yellow and blue—that one would not be allowed out to roam, save at Chay-Chevre's specific behest."

"I agree," said Bol. "She sent it, just as you sent Ezzers and I sent Lavelan."

"So that makes three of us."

"At least."

The tall man spread his hands in a gesture of acquiescence. "Well, there it is. We must call a conclave."

Bol sat down again and picked at the bowl of sweetmeats. "Unless it was just we three," he said.

Ovarth stiffened. "No," he said.

"I merely posit a possibility. You and I and Chay-Chevre pool our capacities, peel the mystery, then follow where events may lead us."

As the mystery in question, I did not relish the idea of being peeled. I was trying to put together an appropriate contribution to the debate when Ovarth responded.

"Let us speak frankly," he said. "You are proposing that we three quietly determine what this man's presence signifies. If we derive sufficient advantage from that knowledge, we use it in a sudden strike against Tancro and Shuppat, despoiling them of their assets. The Five become the Three. Is that the 'possibility' you 'posit' to me?"

"You were ever the bluntest of us," Bol said, "but yes."

Ovarth's thin, pale hands spread themselves again, this time palms down. "No."

Bol shrugged his rounded shoulders. "It was worth the asking."

"May I make a suggestion?" I said.

"You will have to make it to the conclave," Ovarth said.

"In the meantime," Bol said, "he will remain here."

That prospect clearly did not please the purple and black magician, but Smiling Bol spoke to mollify him. "I have been able to learn nothing useful from him, though I am sure I would be able to once my demon recovers its wits. He is something of a simpleton, lacking a full complement of mental attributes. Moreover, there is an odor of time about him. Also, a residue of interplanar travel. My man Lavelan thinks he may be a facsimile. I suspect he is an unintended echo of a person who has been projected from one continuum to another."

Bol's unsmiling eyes lingered on me. Now Ovarth studied me again, his fingers working in the air. "I thought, perhaps a masking spell?" he said, then, "No. He is only what he appears to be."

"Is he important? Or is it just that someone wants us to think he is?" Bol said.

"You think he may be a distraction? A decoy meant to unsettle us?"

"Possibly. Whatever is going on, I sense that he is not a key player."

Ovarth tapped a lean finger against the sharp blade of his nose. "Shuppat is good at puzzles," he said.

Bol ate another sugared ball. "And Tancro is gifted in the arts of interrogation."

"Then that settles it."

Bol dusted his palms together and said, "Let us go to my mirror and make the call jointly."

"Agreed," said Ovarth. "And your man can escort this Barlo back to his quarters until arrangements are made."

During their conversation I had been searching for some gambit that would retrieve the situation. I found none, and when Lavelan beckoned me to go with him, his face full of regret, I could only follow where he led.

Back in my quarters, I asked him, "How would you advise me?"

He avoided meeting my eyes, making a noise in the back of his throat that I took as an expression of discomfort. But I pressed the point, reminding him that I was a traveler lost among strangers, and that I had perhaps saved his life in the encounter with Ral Ezzers.

"I do not know that there is any good advice I can give you," he said, at last. "You have become a piece on the playing board of a game among Powers. When great wills collide, we lesser folk must be nimble. You do not seem to be skilled in the steps of the dance."

"Perhaps," I said, "another devastating spell will come to me."

"Then it had better be very quickly launched. At the first sign of a casting, five very accomplished practitioners would concentrate their aim. All that would be left of you would be a wisp of smoke and a fading cry of horror."

"This is not encouraging."

He made a gesture of fatalism. "Every life must end," he said, "else existence would be insupportable. Comfort yourself with the thought that you are probably only a shadow of the true Barlo, who is probably enjoying a fine and fulfilling life somewhere or somewhen else."

"Strangely," I said, "that thought does not comfort me."

He made the same gesture again, which did not endear him to me, then went to look out the window. His tone became melancholy. "Your situation does cause me to wonder if I have chosen the right path. My plan was to serve power in order to acquire power, then use my acquisition to better the world rather than just myself. But even though Bol is not the worst of the Bambles Five, I often find myself involved in deeds that lead me away from my first desire."

"Perhaps," I said, "my arrival offers you a new point of departure. We could flee here together, me to continue my search for a way home, you to begin a worthy new chapter in your life."

He was silent, gazing out at the forlorn vista that had once been glorious Lakh. Then he said, "No. But if things do not go well for you, I will look after your pet."

The five Powers of Bambles met on neutral ground: an open courtyard of a dilapidated palace that sprawled over several blocks in a section of the ruined city that had formerly boasted many imposing structures. The cloister had once been graced with several of the previous age's finest sculptures, human and allegorical figures rendered in black, white, or pink stone, grouped around a now-empty reflective pool. The statues were weathered now, some of their extremities broken off by vandals or windblown debris sent flying by winter storms. Their sightless eyes looked down from cracked and gouged faces on the five magicians seated in a ring on the cracked stone floor of the pool, on chairs that they had brought from their own seats of power.

No one had thought to bring a chair for me, so I stood outside the circle, attended by Pars Lavelan. Each of the other thaumaturges had brought their own retinues. My sword had not been returned to me, but was now in the hands of Ovarth, who turned it over to examine its scabbard then drew the blade and scanned the runes etched into its strange metal.

"I cannot read this," he said. He looked around to the others. "Can anyone?"

Shuppat, a thin, mouselike man in robes of brown and ocher, took the weapon. He laid the black blade across his knees and traced the runes with small, pink fingers. "No," he said, after a few moments, "though I can sense that the sword's power and sentience are bound up in what is written here." He sheathed the sword and brought the pommel to his forehead, then said, "It is a different order of magic from any that I know. It feels both simpler, yet more elegant, than our schools."

"You are saying it is more advanced?" asked Chay-Chevre, a woman of middle height and proportions. Her raven-black hair fell straight to the backs of her knees when she was standing, and lay like a stygian river over her shoulders and down her breast when, as now, she was seated. She wore a gown of scarlet and a headband of dull gold, which I took to be the colors of the occult arts she commanded.

"Yes," said Shuppat. "This man, or echo of a man, may be from the future."

"Bring him amongst us," said Ovarth. Bol signaled Lavelan to lead me into the circle. The retainer then returned to his place behind his patron's chair, leaving me under the scrutiny of five pairs of eyes. Each pair, I noticed, was of a different color, but each pierced and probed me with an equal intensity.

Tancro, a small, square man who wore tights and a padded jacket harlequined in white and silver, announced that he would take charge of my interrogation. He sat in a thronelike chair of intricately carved white stone that also served him as a means of transport. It had silently carried him across the ruined city from his manse atop a rise to the east while several of his retainers had come riding on a long, segmented creature with dozens of legs. Tancro leaned an elbow on an arm of the chair and rested his cheek on his fist. He studied me as a boy might examine an odd-shaped insect found under an up-turned rock. "Well," he said, after a long inspection, "just what are you?"

"A traveler," I said, "lost and seeking my way home."

"How did you come to be lost?"

I was honest but careful. "Through powers that I neither possess nor understand."

I heard a murmur from the others. It stopped as Tancro raised an admonitory finger. "Who wielded these powers?"

"I do not know."

"Were you the target of them? Or were you caught up in someone else's doings?"

It was an interesting question. "I do not think I was the target," I said. I had come to the conclusion that Osk Rievor had been the object of our being spirited away, that he had been the seed that was prized, while I had been merely its husk to be discarded.

Tancro came at me from a different angle. "What does your intuition tell you?"

"Nothing," I said. "I am without intuition."

Again a murmur went around the circle, louder this time. Tancro did not still it. He was staring at me in consternation. "How do you get by?" he said.

"Through reason."

Snorts and expostulations came from all sides. "It is true," I said. "I demonstrated as much to Pars Lavelan before we had even met."

The retainer was called back into the circle. Bol bade him tell what he knew. The magicians listened as Lavelan recounted the business of the wheel in the common room of the inn at Bridge-on-Scammon. Chay-Chevre dismissed the account as "an underling's inability to recognize a luck spell."

Bol answered by supporting his man's abilities, saying, "Find a trace of a spell about him, if you can."

I had to stand while the woman circled me, her hands shaping the air around me, a look of increasing frustration on her harsh-planed face, the skepticism in her startlingly gray eyes turning to anger. Finally, she sniffed at me, like a dog hunting truffles, then made a noise of exasperation. "A trick!" she snapped, and stalked back to her seat.

"No trick," said Bol. "He is a genuine anomaly." He called to Pars Lavelan again. "Tell them about the coin."

The retainer stepped forward again and told of the tossing of the coin. The magicians scoffed, but Shuppat was intrigued. "Show us," he said, producing a round of silver.

I felt like a performing mountebank as I took the coin and presented it to each of the Powers, saying, "Please examine this to make sure that it is not magically influenced." When all had declared it to be unprejudiced, I took up a position in the center of the circle and said, "Now, each of you must maintain an attitude of neutrality. None must will the coin to come up one way or the other."

I handed the coin to Pars Lavelan and had him toss it several times so that it landed on the stone floor of the empty pool. As the tosses added up, I drove my mind up through the ladder of mathematical consistencies and soon had the pattern established. I then correctly called the next ten tosses.

"I could go on doing it indefinitely," I said.

The magicians looked at each other. "I sensed no one exercising a power toward the coin," Shuppat said.

"Nor did I," said Tancro, "and I would have known."

"So," said Bol, "we are left to ask: what does it mean?"

"It means nothing," Chay-Chevre said. "It is a silly parlor trick."

"No," said Shuppat, "it means something—he means something—but I cannot put a shape to it."

Now the time had arrived when I could offer them the answer I wanted them to accept. "Have you ever heard," I said, "of the theory that sympathetic association and rationality alternate with each other as the underlying principle of existence?"

"A lot of blether," said Ovarth, to a chorus of agreement from the others.

Chay-Chevre said, "Pure foopery. How could mere reason hope to overcome will? How does a pale abstraction overpower the most elemental force in the universe?"

"It does not overpower," I said. "It replaces."

Shuppat, at least, was willing to listen. He stilled the others' protests and scorn. "Let him have his say. All right, mysterious traveler, tell us: what has this off-center little theory have to do with the price of pease?"

And so I explained. As I did so, I was reminded of an occasion in my youth: at school, some fellow had tried to make a case for a workable theory of magic. We, his fellow students, had scarcely let him get more than a few sentences into his explanation before we began to jibe him with catcalls and facetious questions. He had finally given up and soon after he left the school and engaged a private tutor. Now it was my turn to tell the truth, as I all too bitterly knew it, to these five thaumaturges. I saw on their faces the same scorn and derision as that young man had seen on mine and my fellow ignoramuses. I had long been accustomed to being recognized as the brightest mind in almost any room I entered. Now I knew what it was to be received as just some prating ninny.

"Enough!" Chay-Chevre said, when I had laid out the basic structure of a rational universe and was attempting to answer a question from Shuppat as to how a cosmos built on randomness could avoid simply falling apart.

I tried to ignore her interjection, explaining to the brown and ocher magician how a subtle order underlies seeming chaos. "Just as will is not supreme in this universe, but must be channeled through forms and processes," I said, "so does apparent randomness have an understructure that—"

The wizardress stamped a foot in irritation. Worse, she spoke a two-syllable word while pointing three fingers at me, at which my throat closed up and no more words could come.

"Oh, release him," said Shuppat. "I was interested to see how many eggs he could keep in the air at once." He looked around at the others. "Quite remarkable, don't you think?"

But his colleagues thought less of my dissertation than he did. "Let us come to practicalities," Bol said, linking his plump fingers one with another and leaning forward. "Some of us have had—" he paused, seeking the precise word, finally settling on "—*intimations* from our various sources that something of importance was about to happen on the road from the south."

He looked around the circle and received confirmatory gestures from the others. "Ovarth," he continued, "sent his man, Ral Ezzers, to investigate. Pars Lavelan went to keep an eye on Ezzers. Chay-Chevre, you sent a dragon. Shuppat?"

Shuppat said, "I enlisted the eyes and ears of my little friends—birds in the woods, mice at the inn."

Tancro would not divulge the means of his surveillance but admitted that he had been aware of events in the area.

Bol's smile became knowing. "You sent a ghost," he said. "We all know you dabble in the necromantic arts."

Tancro folded his arms across his chest and elevated his chin. "Get on with it," he said.

Now the smile became that of one who has scored a point but is too occupied with other concerns to gloat. "Very well. So we all send our assets south and what do we find? A man who cannot account for himself, with an odd-looking pet. He wields a magic sword whose provenance is unknown, and wields it effectively enough to slay two local bravos whom Ezzers has hired. He controls one of Ezzers's skets, not an easy skill to master, and he manipulates the wheel at the Bridge-on-Scammon inn. Finally, he blasts Ezzers and four of Ovarth's retinue to dust and ashes, using a spell that none of us can name."

The smiling magician paused for effect, then said, "And on top of all, he exhibits not the tiniest trace of thaumaturgical ability. Not a glimmer of an aura. Even the lowliest street sweeper who knows a simple charm or two gives off an odor of magic. This man is blank, without mana, void, inert."

"We know all this. What is your point?" said Tancro.

"I'm coming to it," Bol said, and now his smile became sly. "While we have all been so interested in the man of mystery, this odd fish, something else has been happening."

"Yes," said Shuppat, "the reverberations that have caused the ground to tremble, though you probably haven't noticed it."

"A shout, my captive demon called it," Bol continued. "This immense bellowing cry of a word or name without known referent."

"Eppthorn," said Tancro.

"I heard it as Apthorn," Bol said.

"I saw it graven on a cliff face in a dream," Chay-Chevre said, "in ancient glyphs that spelled *Appa-thonn*."

"Yes," said Bol, "we've all been touched by this shout, in one way or another. Some of us also felt an intuition to watch the south road. Or at least to watch the watchers."

Ovarth drew his long face into a frown. "But what does it all mean?"

"That," said Bol, "is the question."

Shuppat nodded. "You're saying this man may have something to do with the disturbance in the Nine Planes, or…" He let Bol finish his thought.

"Or," the smiling magician said, "he may be a distraction sent to keep us busy—"

Tancro leaped to his feet, his fist balled, his eyes snapping from one point of the compass to the next. "While whatever's behind the other thing steals upon us."

"Perhaps," said Bol. "Therefore I propose that we bind ourselves together in a new pact to meet the threat."

"Are we sure it is a threat?" Shuppat said.

"It is immensely powerful and unknown," said Tancro. "That's good enough for me. I concur with Bol. None of us will do harm to any of us, neither by word, by deed, nor by will, until this matter is resolved. I will give seven oaths and accept the direst of penalties."

So, it became clear, would the others. The air above the circle shimmered, coruscating with streams of sparks, as the covenant was established.

"Now," said Tancro, when all was settled, "while we're all here, we'll find out whatever there is to find out about this odd fellow."

"I told you," Bol said, "he is a simpleton."

"Even simpletons can be surprisingly knowledgeable," Tancro said, "if you ask them in the right way." He held out a hand, palm up, while uttering a few sounds. Something fell from the air into his grip: a length of black iron, except that its chiseled tip glowed red-hot. "Get hold of him," he said.

I turned to run, knocking aside Pars Lavelan who had been reaching for me with a pained but determined look on his face. I heard Bol laugh derisively and Ovarth shout, "Stop him!"

The conclave had been held in the deepest part of the decorative pool. The way I was heading, a series of steps led down from ground level. I mounted them two at a time, with no more thought than to get some distance between me and Tancro's glowing poker. I would formulate a plan as I went.

From behind me I heard sounds of pursuit. Then there came a prolonged whistle, three-toned and loud. Somehow I knew it came from Chay-Chevre, and I doubted it boded well for me.

I was halfway up the stairs when from in front of me the darkness suddenly filled with blue and yellow. The yellow was a scaly throat and belly that towered over me, the blue the long feathers of great wings that beat the air as the wizardress's dragon landed at the top of the steps. Its sinuous neck swooped down, and it opened a muzzle as long as I was tall, revealing daggerlike teeth as long as my hand. It hissed at me with a breath like a banked fire.

The grinnet, which had clutched my hair while I ran, clambered down me and scuttled into the darkness. The dragon briefly tilted its head to watch its escape, then refocused its golden-eyed gaze on me. It hissed again.

Strong hands seized me from behind. Two of Tancro's retainers had rushed after me. Their master's voice said, "Bring him down here."

CHAPTER NINE

Just as he had conjured up a red-hot poker, Tancro had caused a sturdy framework of wood and metal to appear in the middle of the magicians' circle. His two retainers efficiently manacled me to its four arms, then produced knives with which they cut away the clothing from my upper body.

Tancro approached, blowing on the tip of his glowing iron. Far from cooling it, his breath made the point brighten, the deep red becoming paler until it shone a pure white. The glow lit up his face from below, making it a mask of cruel anticipation. I could feel its heat on my own skin as he came nearer.

"Now," he said, "let us begin at the beginning."

From behind and above me, I heard the dragon's loud hiss. Tancro looked up, the cruelty on his face giving way to surprise. The other four Powers did likewise and I followed their common gaze to the dark sky where the stars had been blotted out by a vast and complex spiral, red and black, that spun slowly above the ruined palace. From the labyrinth's center appeared a pale shape that quickly grew and became recognizable as a human figure descending sedately toward us. And the closer it came, the more recognizable it was to me.

The heat I had been feeling from Tancro's poker suddenly died away. I looked and saw that the metal had cooled. Tancro noticed and blew upon the point, but the iron remained cold and black. With a look of disgust, he threw the rod to the stone floor and turned to glare at the man-shape coming down from the sky.

Ovarth had produced a wand from within his robes and was directing it at the slowly descending figure. He uttered several guttural sounds, followed by a flourish of the wand. At once his black and purple robes swirled around him and a great, spiraling wind sprang from the tip of the instrument. It gathered itself, swelling, then rushed up into the air.

But the smoothly descending newcomer, now revealed to be naked and hairless, turned his face toward the whirlwind, and the elemental was suddenly no more than a sigh, drifting away on the night breeze.

Chay-Chevre was standing, arms extended and hands working the air before her. A surge of air from the yellow and blue dragon's wings buffeted me as the huge beast leapt into the air, a rumbling growl in its throat. But the pallid figure, now at rooftop height and still descending, locked eyes with the dragon. The beast faltered in midair, then dropped one wing and banked to turn. Its growl sounded more confused than angry as it stroked off into the night sky.

Shuppat had folded his hands into his sleeves. If he had contemplated any action, he now was clearly decided against it. He glanced away from the descending figure to where Bol sat and watched. The green and copper magician's perpetual smile was the thinnest I had yet seen it, but his eyes were alive with interest as he studied, not the pale man, but the still swirling spiral from which he had descended.

Silently, serenely, the man from the sky slid down toward us, on a glide that would bring him directly to where I stood, chained to the torture frame. His face was as expressionless now as it had been the other time I had seen it, peering at me from around the door frame at the Blik Arlem estate. Then the eyes had seemed washed out and the expression distant. Now his gaze was concentrated on me and for all that the features were as rudimentary as before—a sketch of a human being had been my original thought—there was behind them an immense store of will.

He touched down before me, soundlessly. Tancro had to step back, cursing, or be brushed aside. The pale man paid him no heed. He studied my situation for a moment, then reached to touch the four points at which my ankles and wrists were fixed to the framework. Instantly, my shackles fell apart.

"It's not a spell," I heard Bol say, as if speaking to himself. "It's the application of an enormous force of pure will."

The new arrival regarded me impassively. I could still read no expression on the rudimentary face, though this time his presence at close range was nothing less than intimidating. The voice, when he spoke, was still the same quiet exhalation it had been at the Arlem estate, but again there was an unmistakable emanation of vast will behind it.

"Hapthorn," the man said, quite clearly. It was not a question.

There seemed no point in maintaining the fiction by hiding behind a missing consonant. Whatever fate the pallid man intended for me, I doubted it would be worse than answering questions for Tancro. "Hapthorn," I said. "I am Henghis Hapthorn."

The expressionless, round face did not change, but I was aware of a fierce satisfaction radiating from my putative rescuer. "Hapthorn," said the toneless voice, then repeated my name, adding, "Now I remember."

"Who are you?" I said, but he gave me no answer. Instead, he took hold of both my wrists. His hands felt cool, the flesh rubbery, almost vegetative, but full of strength. I could no more have freed myself from his grip than from Tancro's fetters.

He said nothing more, but now we were rising swiftly and smoothly toward the orbiting spiral in the sky. Curses followed us from the Powers left below, though I thought to hear Smiling Bol reciting some incantation. I looked up and saw the labyrinth growing nearer. Still, my mind could not retain the shapes of its symbols, red on black and black on red. I tore my gaze from it and looked down.

The dwindling thaumaturges were looking up. I saw Pars Lavelan stepping toward his patron as Bol beckoned him. Far off in the ruins, the yellow and blue dragon squatted beside a tumbled tower, staring up at us. Of my integrator there was no sign.

I looked up and saw that we had arrived at the spiral. I felt a brief mental dislocation, then it was as if we were not rising, but were instead descending toward a structure on the ground. We drifted gently toward one of the panels; it was black with two red glyphs. Without slowing we went head first through it, as if it were no more than air.

Again I was in that region where all was darkness and wind, falling interminably, my wrists still gripped by the pale man who glowed in this nonplace as if he were illuminated from within. He spoke again, "What is your desire?"

The words came out of me without thought. "To go home."

Abruptly, he released his hold on me and disappeared. Alone, I fell for what might have been moments, or may have been hours. Then all at once, without transition, I was standing in the afternoon light that flooded into my workroom in Olkney.

A discriminator's life has its ups and downs, its ins and outs, even for one such as I, at the top of the profession, dealing with the moneyed and titled acme of Old Earth's social pyramid. I had, on several occasions, found myself in situations that could fairly be described as more than a tight fit. I had stopped armed bandits in mid-robbery, faced down enraged aristocrats just when they were on the point of taking sanguinary vengeance, calmed the jagged blade from the hand of a mad ripper. I would not gladly admit it, but some of my escapades had left me shaken and in need of a quiet day or two for full recovery.

But nothing in my career had matched the experience of being a helpless stranger in the grip of vicious and powerful persons, one of them about to char my flesh to the bone with hot iron, and then to be swept away into nothingness and deposited, safe and snug, in the comfort of my own rooms.

For a long while I simply stood on the well-worn, faded rug, blinking and looking about me. Everything was just as I had left it when we had set off for the Arlem estate. The wide window that looked out on Shiplien Way was partially de-opaqued, so that the cheerful orange light of the old sun warmed the room. I could see the roofs of Olkney stepping away before me, falling and rising with the lay of the land, with the slopes of the Devenish Range climbing in the distance, and above it all the sprawling palace of the Archon.

"I'm back," I said. I looked down at myself and saw that I was no longer wearing the slashed remnants of the rough garb I had chosen for the adventure with Osk Rievor. Instead, I was clad in my favorite day-robe, a little ratty in places, but quite the most comfortable garment I had ever owned. I touched its front plaquet, its nap now almost rubbed away; so many times had I reflectively stroked the cloth while I paced the rug and pondered some recalcitrant set of clues.

The air of the room was rich with the scent of fresh punge. I went to the culinary suite and found a full pot sitting on the warmer. When I poured and tasted, I found it brewed to perfection. There were seed cakes in the freshery, just the kind I liked best. I buttered a couple and took them and the punge to my best chair and sat, eating and sipping, and gazing out at the everyday scenery of home.

I had finished the cakes and drained the cup of punge before my mind re-engaged. "The integrator!" I said aloud.

"What do you require?" said the familiar voice from the air.

I stood, crumbs falling to the carpet, and looked about. "Where are you?"

"Where I am supposed to be," it said. "Where you installed me."

I looked, and it was true. The old components that I had assembled and placed about the room, linked together appropriately, were alive again. Even the traveling armature, into which my assistant had been decanted when we passed through dimples of magic and other dimensions, causing it to emerge as a grinnet, was back in its place in a cupboard near the door.

"Everything," I said, "has been made as it was. All is as it ought to be."

"Indeed," said my assistant, "you have always preferred an ordered existence."

I drew a long breath and released it slowly. For the first time in the several weeks since I had been drawn into the adventure of Bristal Baxandall and the juvenile demon, I was back to normal. I poured myself another cup of punge and stood at the window, watching the drays and motilators rumble by below, the crowds on the walks and slideways, the aircars silently passing overhead.

I deduced what had happened. Osk Rievor had found his destiny, the place where he, as a seed of the new age, could plant himself and flourish. But he had not treated me as an outworn husk. Instead, he had used his powers—doubtless much augmented in whatever sympathetic place he now made his abode—to send me home. He must even have restored my assistant to its former state.

I drained the last of the second cup. "Integrator," I said, "see if Xanthoulian's has a table free for dinner tonight."

A moment later, its voice said, "Your preferred table is booked for you. And tonight the chef is preparing his signature menu: Four Passions and an Afterthought."

"My favorite," I said. It was remarkable that I was able to get a seating on such short notice. Someone must have canceled just before my assistant called.

I felt renewed. Bol's smile and Tancro's poker retreated into the past. I stretched luxuriously and said, "Are there any communications?"

"You are invited to the usual soirees and salons."

"What about some work? I feel in the mood for a good case, something to blow the cobwebs from my mind."

"Colonel-Investigator Brustram Warhanny presents his compliments and asks if you would care to consult on a matter that apparently has the Bureau of Scrutiny stumped."

I was taken aback. "Did he actually use that word? Warhanny has always hated having to call me in on a case."

"I was reading between the lines," the integrator said.

"I see. Does he wish me to call upon him?"

"No, he will come to you whenever you find it convenient."

"How extraordinary," I said. "Perhaps word has come down to him that the Archon himself has praised my abilities."

"That could account for it."

I stroked the front of my day-robe. The response seemed out of character for Warhanny, I told my assistant. "He has never been a climber of advancement's slippery pole. An old-fashioned crime-sniffer, some would even say a bit fusty in his approaches, and he cares not who knows it."

"Perhaps he has finally recognized your abilities," said my assistant. "But what does it signify what his motive may be? The case is the thing."

"Indeed. Ask him to call upon me when I return from Xanthoulian's."

A moment later it informed me that the appointment was set. I spent a short time attending to my other correspondence, regretfully declining a number of invitations since I did not know what demands the impending new case would make on my time. Then it was time to prepare for dinner, which meant a long session in the sanitary suite, from which I emerged scrubbed and well-tidied. I dressed in evening wear and set off on the short walk to Xanthoulian's in Vodel Close.

I encountered a number of acquaintances along the way, affably greeting and being greeted. All of them were folk who had reason to wish me well; at least, none were among those whose nefarious schemes I had closed down at one time or another. As I bathed in the general air of approbation, I had cause to reflect on the tenor of my career so far. I saw that, all taken in all, I had done a lot of good for my fellow human beings, and little harm to any who did not merit such chastisement.

I arrived at Xanthoulian's and was personally escorted to my seat by he whose name the establishment bore. I greeted several familiar faces, made a formal salute to an aristocratic scion whose interests I had once protected from ill-wishers. Across the room I noticed the perfection in form and visage that was the Honorable Elthene Messeram, daughter of one of Olkney's wealthiest magnates. I had often wished to attract her interest, but had never received more than polite attention, briefly bestowed and withdrawn. But now she favored me with the warmest smile, followed by that subtle widening of the eyes by which a sophisticated female signaled that she would not repel an overture.

I was delighted, even astonished. For a moment I wished that my assistant were on my shoulder again, that I might have someone with whom I could discuss the implications of our brief exchange of smiles and glances. I surprised myself by missing the grinnet's weight and warmth, but before I could pursue the thought further, the head waiter appeared and asked if I was prepared to receive the appetizer. And from there on in, I had no thought but for the unparalleled richness of the Four Passions, each dish an individual triumph, but together mounting an unsurpassable conquest of the palate, followed by the poignant savory of the Afterthought.

Afterward, replete in both body and spirit, I walked home through the crowds in their fashionable finery. The evening air was warm and soft as worn velvet, one of those nights when the ancient City of Olkney was truly the grand old dame she aspired to be, full of life and experience, charm and majesty. I thought that I was perhaps the most fortunate man of Old Earth; having seen what was to come with the new age, I more than any other was in a position to appreciate all that lay strewn about me in casual splendor.

In such a mellow, pensive mood, I arrived at my lodgings to find Brustram Warhanny on the doorstep. He shuffled his oversized feet and sketched a salute to the dark-complected hat with rounded crown and narrow, curving brim that he habitually wore when out of his green-on-black scroot uniform. I greeted him, with perhaps just a hint of condescending graciousness, and showed him upstairs to my workroom.

He declined an after-dinner drink. I could see that he was somewhat ill at ease. Still wearing his hat, he clasped his large hands behind his back, bent his head so that his long nose was aimed at the worn carpet, and began to pace up and down the room in a manner I could only see as troubled.

"It's fair got us flummoxed," he said. "As I was telling the boys, Hapthorn's our only hope."

It must be a truly perplexing case, I thought. Not even Tancro's poker could have easily wrung a "Hapthorn's our only hope" from Warhanny. I would have wagered that he would rather have had useful parts of his body torn from him than to have had to utter words of such ignominious surrender in my hearing. Still, they were gratifying to hear.

I seated myself in my chair, instructed my integrator to take notes, and said, "Perhaps you should start at the beginning."

He continued to pace. "It began," he said, "when an underclerk at the Moldanow Fiduciary Pool discovered a minor discrepancy: there had been a brief flurry of activity in a supposedly dormant account. She began to trace the 'wheres and whyfores,' as they say in her line of work. Abruptly, she was transferred to another department. She complained to a co-worker, with whom she had a close relationship, and he mentioned the matter to a superior who had taken him under his wing as a protégé.

"The next thing we know, the girl is dead—a freak accident, or so it would seem. Her boyfriend is rendered mute and paralyzed by the sudden onset of a rare brain disorder. And the midranked bureaucrat to whom he had related the underclerk's tale contacts the Bureau, babbles semicoherently to a junior agent, then disappears completely."

"In whose dormant account was the activity first noticed?" I asked.

"A fellow named Winn Boder, a retired servant."

"From whose service had he retired?"

"That of the Magguffynne family; he now lives on a farm outside Tahmny with his daughter and her husband."

A memory tugged at my awareness. I let it emerge from the shadows. "Was not Lord Magguffynne involved in a plot to usurp the Archon's throne, at about the time Filidor succeeded his uncle Dezendah?"

Warhanny stopped, tugged thoughtfully at his pendulous nose, and said, "There were rumors. Nothing actionable."

"I suspect the plotters have regrouped. The Moldanow Pool is connected to a cadet branch of the Magguffynne clan. The retired retainer's account was probably a screen behind which the plot's financial activities could be carried on unseen."

I instructed my integrator to investigate the connection. A moment later, it confirmed my analysis.

"Amazing," the scroot said, his face suffused with wonder. "You deduced all that from the skimpiest of facts."

"Once one identifies the presence of a Magguffynne, the elements of a plot fall easily into their true arrangement," I said. "I suggest that you assign Bureau of Scrutiny personnel to examine the family's recent to-ings and fro-ings. I am sure a pattern will soon emerge."

"I will also alert the Archon," Warhanny said, "and advise him that, once again, he owes a debt of gratitude to the clarity of Henghis Hapthorn's intellect."

I lowered my eyes in humble acceptance of his praise and said, "I merely do what any good subject of the Archon would do, who had the means to do it."

Warhanny was at the door. "I must set events in motion," he said. "Will you be available if complications ensue?"

"Of course."

His heavy feet clumped down the stairs and he was gone. My integrator said, "I am receiving a communication from the integrator of the Honorable Elthene Messeram, asking if you are available."

"Say that I am and connect us."

The integrator's screen appeared in the air before me and was immediately filled by the heart-stopping face of Elthene Messeram, her raven tresses tumbling loosely and her violet eyes gazing into mine. "Henghis," she said, in a husky contralto, "are you private?"

"There is none here but I," I said. "How may I help you?"

"It is a matter of the greatest delicacy," she said, "yet also of the gravest import. I know not whom to trust."

I assured her that she could trust me implicitly, not just because of my professional standing but because I had long wished to be of service to her.

"I am glad to hear it," she said. "I cannot explain over the connectivity. Can you come to my house in town?"

"At a moment's notice."

"Then please come now. I am at my wit's end, and only you can save my reputation."

I had my assistant summon a cabriole and flew swiftly to Elthene's small house in a steep-streeted district below the Archonate palace. She met me on the rooftop landing as I alighted from the aircar. She had dismissed her personal servants for the night and bade her integrator step itself down to minimal mode. We were quite alone as she led me to her most private rooms.

Blushing and slightly breathless, she said, "It was surely fate that brought us together at Xanthoulian's tonight. When I saw you, I knew that you were my only recourse."

Tears brimmed in her compelling eyes. I comforted her and urged her to tell me all. She did so freely, though honor prevents me from revealing any of it here. I listened attentively and was soon able to unpick the tangles of her problem and chart for her a clear course to a happy outcome. I assisted her in making calls to three persons: a former paramour who had proved less than faithful, a discharged servant who had broken a trust, and an old friend whose good opinion Elthene did not wish to lose. Disaster was averted, and justice done. It was the work of mere minutes, once I had the facts and could engage my faculties.

I would have left her then, but she was insistent on displaying the full measure of her gratitude—the details of which also cannot honorably be revealed. It must suffice to say that when I finally departed her house, to be greeted by the old sun just lifting itself over Olkney, I was meditating on the thought that "Four Passions and an Afterthought" could describe an experience even more delightful than the finest dinner at Xanthoulian's.

I arrived home to be alerted by my integrator that the Archon commanded my presence in his private office after his early afternoon audiences with petitioners. An official car would be sent to collect me.

"I will take a nap," I said, "then a long soak in the sanitary suite, followed by a good meal. Awaken me in good time."

As I lay down on the sleeping pallet and engaged its systems that would make a brief slumber compensate for a missed night's sleep, I reflected that I had never been more contented. All the unsettled—and unsettling—months of coping with the impending arrival of the age of sympathetic association, when I had been pushed hither and beyond by powers I could not control, were now fading into the past. I was, once again, who I was supposed to be, doing what I was born to do, and doing it superbly.

"This is how things ought to be," I told myself, then the ease of restful, well-earned sleep stole over me.

In the third hour after noon, I arrived at the broad terrace outside the Archon's private study. Brustram Warhanny was there to greet me as I descended from the aircar. He escorted me into the small, high-ceilinged room, lined on all sides with shelved books, and carpeted in an intricately patterned, green and blue Agrajani rug from the classical period. Filidor, despite his youth looking every inch the Archon these days, was seated behind his wide and well-worn desk. He waved me toward an armchair upholstered in old leather.

I offered the appropriate salute and took my seat. Warhanny hovered somewhere in the background. Filidor regarded me benignly for a moment, the tips of his fingers tented together, then said, "Well, Hapthorn, you've done it again. The Magguffynnes were indeed staging another attempt at usurpation. This time, their dastardly plan might have succeeded."

"I am delighted to have been of service," I said.

"In recompense," Filidor said, "I have decided to bestow upon you all of the Magguffynne holdings, the house in town, the country estate, the financial portfolio. They will not be needing them anymore."

I was astounded, and said so. "You do me great honor," I said.

"Furthermore," the Archon continued, "I intend to confer upon you the social rank of lesser margrave."

That meant I was being elevated to the second-tier aristocracy. I would have the right to design a crest to decorate my door and to wear garters in the Archon's presence. It was a dream I had held close to my heart all my life, never daring to speak of it to anyone, even my integrator. I rose and performed the civilities that propriety demanded. I had long ago memorized the six phrases and three postures.

Filidor smiled warmly and praised the punctilio with which I had executed the ancient forms. "You acquit yourself admirably," he said. "Perhaps we should be looking at a permanent, formal relationship rather than the loose association we have had until now." He looked up at the scroot officer behind me and said, "Tell me, Warhanny, what would you and your fellow agents say if I named Henghis Hapthorn to the governorship of the Bureau of Scrutiny?"

I heard the snap as Warhanny came to attention. "We'd say, 'Well done! Couldn't wish for a better!'"

Not only social rank, but the governorship of the scroots! With that combination of title and office, I'd be one of the most powerful personages in Olkney, almost on a par with the Archon himself.

"See to the forms," Filidor was telling Warhanny, while I sat dazed by joy. The Archon rose and I stood to be dismissed. Then something else occurred to Filidor. "By the way," he said, "I believe you know a few magic spells."

"Not I," I said.

"Come, come," he said. "I am reliably informed that you hold a great compendium of magic in your mind. I would be grateful if you would reveal it to me."

"Someone has misinformed you. Would you like me to inquire into it?"

And now it was as if someone else looked out through the young Archon's eyes. I felt a coldness around me, as if the air in his study had suddenly chilled. There was a sour odor, very faint, in my nostrils.

"You are lying to me," Filidor said, "and that is very unwise. Tell me what I want to know."

"I would if I could," I said. To contemplate enraging an Archon, I would have had to be as mad as a Magguffynne.

"You are concealing your knowledge from me," said the man who glared at me from across the desk, a figure in whom I was now hard put to see even a trace of Filidor. He spoke to Warhanny. "Take him somewhere where his memory can be encouraged."

For the second time in recent days, I was seized in a powerful grip. Warhanny seemed to have grown to a phenomenal size. I felt like a child in his hands as he lifted me from my feet and carried me bodily out of the Archon's study. Impossibly, though we went out the door we had entered by, we did not emerge onto the sunny terrace overlooking the spread of grand old Olkney. Instead, we were suddenly in an underground chamber, its walls rank with black mold and cold seepage, lit by flickering torches. It reminded me of a scene from a tale I had read in childhood, a story that had given me nightmares.

Warhanny flung me down onto a pile of straw, rank and stained by fluids I did not care to identify. I looked up at him and in the dim, shifting light, I did not see the familiar, lugubrious face of the Colonel-Investigator. Instead, the same intensity that had shone from Filidor's eyes, the glare of a powerful will, now fell upon me.

"The spells!" he said. It was not Warhanny's voice, nor any human voice at all. No human throat and lungs could have emitted the roar that shook the walls of my prison, and shook me to the core. "I want the spells!"

Long ago, when I was in school, I had come across a story that had survived from the dawntime: some fellow had grievously offended a god and the vengeful deity decreed that the culprit be chained to a rock in perpetuity, then sent a feral creature to tear out the prisoner's organs. The ill treatment, horrific though it was, should have mercifully ended with the victim's death. But the god had also ordained that his flesh should heal so that the torture could begin again and go on indefinitely. The only hopeful note in the myth was that, after centuries of such abuse, a hero happened by and did the fierce tormentor to death, although the captive must still remain fixed to the rock.

This tale came to my mind at some point in the timeless period that followed my being brought to the dungeon by an outsized Brustram Warhanny. It was not the Colonel-Investigator, of course, who seized me in giant hands and flung me about the walls, then proceeded to put me to a series of tortures involving techniques and apparatuses that doubtless were also remembered from the most primitive, most brutal years of humanity's infancy.

Warhanny, for all his dislike of me, would not have crushed my bones, torn my flesh, seared my skin with flame, separated my joints through traction engines, whipped me and scourged me, while never tiring, never pausing to take a rest or a sip of restorative, never even blinking those burning eyes that commanded me to *tell me the spells*.

Nor would I have survived an hour of the treatment he relentlessly dealt me, though how long I suffered those torments I have no idea. Time lost all dimension. There was no time. Only the present pain, and then the next, and the one after that. But though time ceased to exist, Henghis Hapthorn did not. From every injury, however gross, I soon healed. The shattered bones knit themselves up, the ripped flesh closed, the joints re-embraced each other, the burns faded even as the smell of scorched meat and the echoes of my screams still hung in the air. And thus my torturer could constantly begin anew, and I could not die, nor even lose consciousness.

At one point, as he reached for a set of pincers that had been heating on a bed of coals, I gasped at him, "I know who you are."

"Tell me what I want to know."

"I cannot."

"You must know it. I remember seeing the shape of it in your mind then you hid it from me. I will have it from you."

"I am hiding nothing from you."

"You must be."

Then back to the work he went, with the same cold zeal that animates a plant to sink its roots into the least accepting soil, or to strangle a competitor for the simple necessities of air, light, and water.

Finally, there came a moment when time began to flow again. He stepped back from where I hung from a hook, let fall the drill with which he had been coring my bones. He did not much resemble Warhanny anymore; the illusion had sloughed away, to be replaced by the pale, rudimentary features and affectless eyes that had been his guise when I had seen him at the Arlem estate and in the garden of the ruined palace at Bambles.

Something had drawn his attention from me. He stood, attentive to some stimulus I could not receive, like a man listening to a distant sound. His sketch of a face showed no emotion, but I knew that he was now fully engaged by whatever had caught his attention. And then, in less than a blink, he was not there.

I hung against the cold, slimy wall, the memory of pain still filling my being. Was this some refinement of the torturer's technique? Had he remembered that the pause, the caesura in the symphony of agony, is almost as important a part of the effect as the crashing chords of pain and the reedy solos of anguish?

But no. I knew I was not the captive of a creature that dealt in subtleties. He—I should have said "it" but it had only manifested itself as a male figure—was a practitioner of will. He bored toward his objective, only diverting from his course when an impenetrable object forced him to detour around it. I was far from impenetrable, as the timeless time just passed had demonstrated in so many different variations. So if he was not still drilling away at me, it was because some other opportunity—or, I dared to hope, threat—had taken his attention.

I was suspended by my wrists, which were enclosed in a set of iron manacles, with my feet some distance from the floor. I looked down and about, as best I could. I was hoping to see a stool to which I might swing my feet, thus relieving the weight on my wrists and slipping the chain that connected the fetters over the hook. But no convenient stool appeared.

I tried wanting a stool to be there, tried wanting it very much. But no such convenience appeared. Clearly, conditions in this place would not reflect my will, only my captor's. I ignored as best I could the pain that seared my wrists and tried to give thought to how I might improve my situation. Nothing came. I followed various lines of thought, but each led me up a blind alley and left me face to face with an uncompromising reality: I was in the grasp of an entity that wanted what it wanted, an entity that was not inclined to subtlety, was probably not even capable of it.

In tales of derring-do, the hero in the grip of an ogre would often fool the brute into making an error of judgment or perception. I now saw that the authors of such fictions must have conjured their monsters out of their own sophisticated minds. The real thing, it turned out, was far too devastatingly simple to be fooled by cute tricks. One might as well try to reason with a house plant.

I began to despair. It was a sign of my desperation that I tried again to want a stool to appear beneath my feet; to go up an alley one already knew to be a dead end was a waste of time and energy, yet here I was doing it.

No stool rewarded my desire with its sudden presence. I hung, inert and pained, and racked my brain for another course of action. The metaphor "racked my brain" now took on a much more salient meaning, my body having recently had the experience, and again I felt the onset of a wave of hopelessness that I was too weak to resist. So low did I sink that it was only when I heard my name called for the third time that I roused myself to respond.

"Hapthorn!" called a voice. It seemed to come from nowhere in the ill-lit chamber, yet it seemed close. "Henghis Hapthorn!"

"Here!" I said. "Who calls me? Can you help me?"

"I am helping you," said the voice. It sounded familiar, yet not the same, like a known melody played on an instrument one had never heard before. "Can you feel anything when I do this?"

"Do what?" I felt nothing but the pain in my wrists.

"What about now?"

I yowled as a stinging pain tore across my face, from left to right, as if a strong adhesive had been roughly yanked away. Unlike the aftermath of the torturer's attention, the hurt did not immediately fade, but continued to smart. Another ripping pang suddenly burned across my shoulders. I yelped again.

But as the sting echoed in my nerve endings, the pain in my wrists suddenly decreased. The stone walls around me seemed less dense, as if they were losing conviction in their own existence. At the same time, the sour tang in the air grew more insistent.

Another rip and flare of pain, this time across my chest. And now the dungeon faded, the image dissolving, to be replaced by a dimly lit cavern. I sat slumped against a wall of cold rock, my buttocks chilled by more frigid stone beneath me. I was naked from the waist up, my legs encased in a softly luminescent material. The same substance thickly coated the entire inner surface of the cavern, which I now saw was immense.

But it was not the surroundings that held my attention, but the naked man who stooped over me, tearing at the stuff that covered my lower limbs. And as he sank two hands into the stuff and then gave a sharp tug, it came away from my flesh, taking with it some of the outer layers of my skin. But not my hair—that was already all gone.

My limbs were not at full strength, but I reached behind me to where a band of the luminescent, fleshy material lay across my lower back, and pried it loose. The pain felt like the release it was. A moment later, my deliverer had freed my feet. He offered me his hands and helped me to stand.

I was naked and shivering, my teeth clicking rapidly against each other. The air was still but scarcely warmer than the freezing point of water. I wrapped my arms about my torso, then rubbed my upper arms with my palms to generate some circulation. My feet, now uninsulated by the glowing stuff, were rapidly losing sensation.

Though the man who had rescued me was equally naked and hairless, he showed no sign of discomfort. Now he raised both hands and brought his palms together, rotating them against each other while speaking some words I could not catch. Then he smoothly pulled his hands apart and, as he did so, I was suddenly no longer cold, but comfortably warm. The weakness that had afflicted my limbs disappeared. I felt refreshed and well-rested.

"Better?" he said.

"Yes."

"A spell of sufficiency," he said. He looked me over and added, "It will also help heal where the skin was torn away. The hair will have to grow back on its own."

"I am grateful," I said. "Now what?"

"We leave here, before the master of the house returns. I am not ready to face him head on." He turned and led the way across the cavern, our feet sinking into the luminous and resilient stuff that carpeted the floor, as it covered the walls and the high, high roof of the cave. We were heading for a dark rift in the glowing far wall which, when we reached it, turned out to be a narrow crevice that trended upward.

We had to fit ourselves sideways into the crack and inch our way along a short distance until the fissure widened. Then we climbed, at places finding scalable inclines, at others vertical shafts where I had to scooch upward with my shoulders braced against one wall and my feet against the other. Finally, we emerged into the back of a horizontal cavern whose front opened on a graveled slope a short distance above a level plain. My rescuer stepped out and I followed after him, sliding down the incline to the flat. I looked around at bare rock as far as I could see in any direction, then up at the black sky, almost devoid of stars except for one high, bright pinpoint.

"Bille," I said.

"Yes."

I looked at him in the harsh, thin light of the white dwarf. His features were vaguely familiar. I thought I might not have seen him in the flesh before, but I had studied his image. After a moment, my well-calibrated mind supplied the referent.

"You are Orlo Saviene," I said, "the regulator."

He smiled at me, and somehow that expression was familiar, though I recalled no smiling images of Saviene. "No," he said, "his was just the best-preserved body. Our captor had to put me somewhere, and Saviene, along with the other two, had long since faded into a final senescence."

"Then who are you? Why do I feel that I know you?"

"We lived together for a while," he said.

It was then that I recognized him.

He saw comprehension arrive in my face, then he turned and said, "Now, come. There is a cavern beyond the spread of our fungal friend, but it's a fair distance. He has been growing for a long time."

And so, across the gritty surface of Bille, I followed my former inner sharer, Osk Rievor.

CHAPTER TEN

"I feel that I owe you an apology," Osk Rievor said, when we were settled in a cave a good, long hike from where he had found me. "I was completely taken in, and by the most elemental of tricks. The fungus showed me what I wanted to see, and I went happily along with it."

Having had a taste of exactly the same sweet-tasting medicine, I could not judge my alter ego too harshly. When I thought about how I had preened myself in the Archon's pseudopresence, and about how my supposed romp with Elthene Messeram had been merely a dream inculcated in me by a creature not much more sophisticated in its fundamental nature than a patch of moss, I was in no position to point the accusing digit.

"I forgive you," I said. "You have made up for it entirely by delivering me from a torture chamber."

"Literally?"

"As literal as possible, given that it was an illusion. Though it certainly did not feel like one at the time."

He flinched. "I have learned a lesson. Though it is my nature to be impulsive, I will strive to develop the qualities you exhibit, and try to analyze before accepting a conclusion."

"It may not be possible," I said. "I now find myself with no intuition at all, not a shred of insight. I reach for it and it is not on the shelf. Yet rational analysis, applied to the situations I fell into after we parted, proved to be a not very reliable tool."

"We need each other," he said. "We must work together."

"That much is obvious."

"We also need our assistant."

"That is problematic," I said, and described how I had last seen the grinnet making a scampering escape into the darkness of ruined Bambles. "Where it is or how it is faring I do not know."

Osk Rievor swore a bitter oath. "You should have kept better track of it," he said.

"At the time, I was being threatened by a dragon. Have you ever been at close quarters with a dragon? I guarantee that you would remember the experience."

Our new-born amity had not lasted long. My other self gave me a look that implied a certain carelessness in my grinnet-keeping style. I found it necessary to remind him by whose agency I had come to be in the predicament in the first place. "You left me stranded on a rural road," I said. "I could go south into a wilderness whose skies were haunted by ravenous flying reptiles, or north into unknown circumstances that turned out to include inquisitive thaumaturges, one of whom wielded a white-hot poker."

He made a gesture that was both dismissive and faintly apologetic. "It just makes things difficult," he said. "I find, now that I am translated into this age of sympathetic association, that the more powerful spells and incantations I had memorized have simply bulled their way out of my awareness."

I told him I understood and related the experience of casting Orrian's Hasty Dwindling at Ovarth's retainers. He was fascinated and had me describe in detail the effects on the victims, as well as the peculiar sensations that afflicted me as I spoke the syllables.

"And you cannot remember a single sound of it?"

"No. It was as if it was erased from my awareness even as it passed through my mind and mouth. And yet the grinnet held it, and dozens more." I remembered what our assistant had said and added, "It has something to do with having, or not having, a will."

"Yes," he said, "and with having a will in an age when will is the prime consideration. When we were in the former age, I could hold a dozen or more spells in my mind."

"Because they had less power," I said. I saw that he intended to continue the discussion of what was, to me, a side issue and raised a hand to prevent him from going on. "The issues before us are, first, how to deal with the symbiote; second, how to escape this barren rock; and, third, how to get back to our own time."

"Agreed," he said.

"Then you had better start by telling me what you have learned about our captor."

He did so. Most of it was, of course, inference and intuitive grasp, that being his way of apprehending the universe. But I applied analysis and rational sorting of the facts as we went along, and between the two of us we formed a picture that made sense.

When Ewern Chaz had stumbled upon it—it must have been many centuries ago now—the symbiotic confederation of lichen and insects had been a simple entity, evolved to deal with the wants and cravings of other simple creatures. It could not have been hard, even for a fungoid intelligence, to find out what satisfied a mind no more developed than a sow bug's and to deliver an illusion of it. But when it had to meet Chaz's needs, it had to adapt to the mingled currents and eddies of a much more sophisticated cerebrum. Yet the fungus had risen to the challenge.

Then came Orlo Saviene, followed by Franj Morven and, for a time at least, Chup Choweri. None of these would have been markedly more intellectually complex than its first human catch, but each probably would have represented a new field that had to be tilled in its own manner. Then came the integrator from the *Gallivant,* with its crush on Ewern Chaz. The decanted device would not have been biologically susceptible to the symbiote's seductions, but its overpowering desire to be with Ewern Chaz would have kept it as happily settled in the cave as the three men and the original trove of insects.

We decided that telepathy was its means of interaction with its symbiotic partners. I said, "It would seem that the flow was in two directions. The fungus became aware of complexity, then it developed a taste for what it could pluck from the minds of its captives. It began to hunger for knowledge."

"Which the spaceship's integrator supplied in vast quantities, through Ewern Chaz."

I thought about it. Some of what the integrator knew would have been of direct application to the fungus's needs: chemistry, mineralogy, and geology, including a great store of specialized knowledge about caves. "Instead of simply growing vegetatively, it could plan and carry out expansion operations—concentrating acids derived from unsentient plants and using them to dissolve rock and derive nutrients, sending its roots burrowing much farther down into the rock than required by its immediate needs so that it could use temperature differentials between the surface and deeper levels to generate electrical energy."

"It appears to have done so quite happily for a long time," Osk Rievor confirmed. "It grew to cover the walls, floors, and ceilings of a vast network of underground caverns and galleries, with millions of small creatures happily toiling for it in closely organized battalions. It was doubtless as content as any semisapient organism could be."

"And then," I said, "something happened."

In stories, "things happened" in order that a plot might be kept boiling and bubbling along. In life, when "things happened" they all too often meant that happiness came to a sudden stop, to be followed by periods of prolonged misery. So it had been for the contented fungus of Bille when the Great Wheel had turned and pitched it into a new age.

Detached from any extenuating devices, such as its original spaceship, the *Gallivant's* integrator had suffered a catastrophic decline, as had such devices all up and down The Spray. The hard scientific knowledge that had allowed the symbiote to grow beyond any dream previously known to fungal lifeforms became ephemeral and difficult to retain. That which had been reliable was reliable no longer.

On the other hand, that which the Wheel took away it compensated for, after a fashion. The symbiotic entity now entered an age when will was paramount, and it turned out that a massive organism that telepathically united a huge fungus, the remnants of three deeply narcissistic human beings, an addled spaceship's integrator, and hordes upon hordes of single-minded arthropods was possessed of a will that would have won prizes in any competition it might have deigned to enter.

I remembered how Ovarth's whirlwind had been flicked away and Chay-Chevre's dragon deterred. At the time I had thought it was by magic, now I saw that it had been an application of sheer force of will.

"Still," I said, "it must have been deeply shocked by the transition. I saw what the coming of the new age did to the fine old city of Lakh."

"I'm sure it did not know what to do," Osk Rievor said. "It would have been confused, its memories unreliable. But it had will, and it exercised that will. It said to the newly arranged universe: *I want.*"

"And what did it want?"

"Us."

Centuries had gone by, but the fungus remembered our visit as a turning point in its development. We had been a formative experience, though with the change, its recollection of who and what we were had become somewhat murky. The name that filtered up from its damaged memory was distorted. And so, stranded on its lonely dot of a world, far at the end of anywhere, it began to psychically bellow "Apthorn!" into the ether.

The bellowing would have got it nowhere in an age of rationalism. But under the new dispensation, so powerful was the shouter's will that it was able to bend the interplanar membranes that separated our continuum from the other eight of the Nine Planes. "It is possible," Osk Rievor said, "that its will was even strong enough to create a Tenth Plane, at least temporarily—a new layer of metareality that let it reach into our own cosmos through space and time."

"The spiral labyrinth," I said.

"Indeed. It was able to project a full version of it to the forest at Hember, where the major ley lines met. At the Arlem estate, the lines were less potent and it appeared as only a wispy mandala."

"And the odd little fellow?"

"An avatar of the fungus itself. Probably based on how we appear to it. I don't think it 'sees' in any real sense of the word."

I went back over the sequence of events. The fungus knew about us from its contact with the *Gallivant's* integrator, and from its brief connection to our own assistant. I had no idea what a fungus's memory might be like, but obviously it had retained some vestiges of recollection about Arlem. It had reached out to us through interplanar means, connecting with Osk Rievor. His mind had been in the forefront when we approached the door at Arlem, and he had immediately fallen for the symbiote's blandishments. It had seen that Hember, with its convergence of major ley lines, would be a more accommodating environment in which to wield its powers. It had telepathically gulled my other self into taking us there, where it could manifest its interplanar gateway in a more potent form. My other self had stepped boldly into the labyrinth and been transported here to Bille. The grinnet and I had been dropped as surplus baggage.

"Of course, when I got here," Osk Rievor said, "it soon realized that I did not have what it wanted."

"Which was?"

"Which was, and more to the point, still is, a command of magic. It has the will, but not the skill, you see."

I did see. I also suspected that something remained unsaid. How did it go from half-remembering my name to knowing it exactly?

"What did it do when it discovered that you were not the trove of spells and practical advice that it craved?" I said.

My other self looked away. "It might have made some idle threats."

"And might those idle threats have involved torture chambers cribbed from some old tale of derring-do?"

"Nothing definite was specified."

"Still," I said, "you managed to avoid finding out for certain."

"Well, yes."

"By telling our willful friend that what he really needed was Henghis

Hapthorn."

He looked away again. "That might have been the gist of it." When he looked back at me, I was sure that he saw a man slipping into justified rage. He quickly added, "I had a plan."

"Did you?" I said. "When I use the word 'plan,' I refer to a carefully worked out series of actions, each flowing from the one before and leading to the next, in a chain of cause and effect that leads to a predictable result."

"Very sensible," he said.

"But what does 'plan' mean when you use it?"

"Roughly the same."

"How roughly?"

He lifted his shoulders and let them fall.

"What you mean," I said, "is that you mistook a hoped-for outcome for a certainty. Is that not right?"

His index finger stirred patterns in the dust of the cave floor. "Usually, that is how things go."

I went to the flaw in his argument. "Usually, you are not intuiting an outcome in the face of a contrary will so powerful that it is capable of distorting the very fabric of the universe and giving a mature demon the megrims."

"Well, no, not usually," he said, but then he defended himself. "You see, I thought you'd bring the grinnet. And then, while you were engaged with our host, I would escape with our assistant and, using its stores of magical knowledge, put things to rights."

He had skipped over a crucial part of the scheme. "Why would it have bothered with me when it had the grinnet?" I said.

More patterns appeared beneath his finger. "It may have gained the impression that you were the one who possessed the real knowledge. Its memories of our original encounter were sketchy."

"You threw me," I said, "to the attentions of a single-minded torturer, just to buy time."

"It never occurred to me that you would have lost the grinnet. The two of you were inseparable."

"And now we are stranded on a barren pinpoint, a place that few spaceships ever visited, even when there were such things as spaceships. A place ruled by a willful fungus who lacks the imagination to do anything but torture us incessantly to get from us what we cannot give it."

"Still," he said, "we are alive. We are free. And I have a sense that things will work out."

"Unless our cave-coating nemesis wills otherwise. Which reminds me: how did you distract it so that you could rescue me?"

"I will be honest," he said. "I did not distract him. Something else did. The labyrinth appeared, hovering above us in the cavern where I was. The fungus seemed surprised, but he formed his avatar, which rose to enter the spiral. Then both disappeared."

"Perhaps he found a way to locate our assistant," I said. "In which case, all is lost."

"The grinnet is, at heart, an integrator. It should be able to resist temptation."

"Not if it comes in the form of fruit," I said. "In any case, we may soon know." I pointed up at the tiny, white sun visible through the cave's entrance. A swirling spiral mosaic of red and black was wavering into existence, obscuring the dwarf star. Moments later, the lumpish, pallid form of the fungus's avatar emerged from the center of the labyrinth. Here at home, it was gigantic. It descended to the ground near where the gritty plain rose into slopes of bare rock. When it reached the vicinity of the fissure we had escaped through, it thinned, became semitransparent, then disappeared. I saw no sign of a grinnet.

"It will now recover its awareness of conditions in the cavern and find that I am gone," I said.

"It may come seeking us," my other self said.

I began to consider logistics. "Can it maintain its avatar form for long? If so, it could cross the distance to us in a few score steps and pull us out of here like a pair of sleekits from their den."

"It only takes that form when using the labyrinth to project its will across interplanar membranes."

"Are you sure of that?"

"I think it is so."

I looked up at the spiral labyrinth, which continued to rotate in the sky. "We may soon find out," I said. "The labyrinth is not disappearing."

"Perhaps the symbiote means to go dimension-traveling again."

"Or to march over here and get us," I said. I regarded the swirl of red and black a moment longer. Then I said, "Or perhaps it will be too busy with the new factor that has just entered the situation."

Osk Rievor followed my gaze. "Friends of yours?" he said.

"Acquaintances, only," I said. "Our interests did not converge."

For, from out of the heart of the spiral labyrinth, something else had emerged into the black sky above Bille. It took the form of a long, wooden boat with extravagant curlicues of carved and gilded wood at stern and prow. The vessel was surrounded by a great, translucent bubble that was suspended from a net of heavy, braided cables. The open end of the net was firmly grasped by the talons of two great dragons, the larger of the pair magisterial in gray and silver, the smaller fiercely bold in scales of yellow and pinions of blue.

The dragons beat their wings and the green sphere with the boat nestled within settled smoothly to the barren plain, midway between our hide-out and the fissure leading to the cave where the fungus grew. On the vessel's raised forecastle, a group of figures stood gazing toward the spot where the avatar had last been seen. I recognized Smiling Bol, lean Ovarth, squat Tancro, and raven-haired Chay-Chevre. Of Shuppat, at first there was no sign, then he emerged from a midships hatch and joined the other four of the Five.

An animated colloquy ensued, its energy evident from the movement of arms and stamping of feet that accompanied its spoken component. Clearly, the Powers of Bambles were on edge. Whatever consensus had allowed them to travel here as a body was not deeply seated; no sooner had they arrived, than they had fallen into an argument as to what to do next.

Shuppat emerged as the moderator. His gestures were less energetic, his posture less pugnacious. When calm had been restored he indicated the crevice where the fungal entity had disappeared, then his arms opened to embrace the plain on which they had landed.

"He is outlining a plan of action," I said to Osk Rievor.

"So it would seem," he answered, "and now they are about it."

The group on the forecastle had split up. Ovarth was climbing over the side of the ship, descending a ladder to the ground. Tancro was laying out row upon row of small objects on the open deck. Bol withdrew to a cabin in the stern of the ship. Chay-Chevre mounted the afterdeck; that brought her to eye level with the lesser of the two dragons that had alighted on the plain behind the ship and stood there with wings folded. The big gray lowered its head to attend to what its mistress was saying.

Suddenly, all was action. The dragons sprang into the air, the smaller climbing high to fly wide circles around the area, the larger flapping over the plain then landing to take up a position on the slope above the fissure. Meanwhile, Ovarth had walked out onto the flat rock a small distance from the ship and was now directing a wand at the stony ground, his motions like those of an artist sketching. Tancro had finished the laying out of his multitude of small items on the ship's deck, and had ascended to the forecastle, from which he directed a wand of his own at the array he had created.

The outlines Ovarth had scratched now revealed their shapes as, from out of the surface of the plain, four giant figures of solid rock were born. They sat up then pushed themselves out of the man-shaped depressions they left behind. Ovarth claimed their attention with gestures of the wand and words I could not hear. He pointed to the rising land in which Osk Rievor and I were hidden, said a few more words, then the four rough-hewn elementals he had conjured into being turned as one and came across the plain toward us. I could feel the impact of their heavy footfalls vibrating the floor of our cave.

"Do they come for us?" I wondered aloud.

"I believe not," said my other self. He was proved right when the giants reached the lower slopes and their massive hands began carving out great oblong blocks of stone as if the slope were made of nothing firmer than cheese. They hoisted the blocks onto their shoulders and carried them back to the vicinity of the ship, where they arranged them as the base of a great wall.

Back on the ship, Tancro's wandwork was also yielding results. The array of objects he had laid out on the deck was rapidly growing into a double platoon of armored manlike creatures. From this distance they appeared to be like humans crossbred with crustaceans, their backs and chests covered in carapaces of glistening black, their multijointed forelimbs ending in pincers. What looked like weapons of some kind were slung from their shoulders, and bandoleers crossed their chests. At Tancro's order, they swarmed over the side of the ship, dropped to the plain, then rushed forward to form a double skirmish line halfway between the vessel and the place where the fungus-man had disappeared. The forward line knelt while the rear remained standing, the soldiers in both ranks unslinging their weapons and holding them at the ready.

"Not a friendly visit," I said.

We withdrew into the cave as the blue and yellow reconnaissance came our way. When we moved again to the opening, not much had changed. The giants had extended their wall so that it paralleled the length of the ship on one side. They now made a right-angle across the bow and continued to build. Bol was back on deck, and I saw that Pars Lavelan was also part of the expeditionary force. He was assisting his patron by making repeated trips to and from the aft cabin, carrying lengths of metal and coils of glass. These they laid out on the deck and it seemed to me that Smiling Bol was examining each component with minute care.

The afternoon on Bille was long, the planet rotating slowly. Methodically, as the white dwarf inched toward the ridges above the fungus's cave, the stone giants constructed a substantial fort of black rock, large enough to contain the ship. When it was completed, the forward line of the pincer-men rose to their feet and both ranks backed toward the fortification, their weapons still at the ready. When they reached the front gateway they turned and rushed inside, and moments later I saw them mounting the parapets, weapons slung.

The giants sealed the opening with gates made from two great slabs of rock that swung to with a sound like millstones grinding against each other. The two dragons flew in to perch on the rear wall, where two wide platforms had been constructed.

"Well," Osk Rievor said, "I would say that phase one has been completed. What comes next?"

I said, "Do you remember, at Turgut Therobar's, the device he constructed to connect with the plane from which our juvenile demonic visitor hailed?"

"I do."

"When I was a guest of Smiling Bol, I saw a larger and more effective version of it. It was powerful enough to snare a full-grown and very unwilling demon, and to hold him while the thaumaturge did terrible things to him."

Osk Rievor indicated Bol's activity with Pars Lavelan on the deck of the ship now surrounded by the fort. They were erecting a framework of rods and coils that was several times larger than the model I had seen in the warped green and copper room at Bambles. "It does look much the same," he said.

"I think I know what they mean to do," I said. "And if they are successful, it will not bode well."

"For us, you mean?"

"For anyone. I believe they mean to capture the fungus so that they can tap its immense but naive will and use it to their own ends."

"To rule the world, you mean? It is the usual goal of such as pursue power for its own end."

"I doubt that Bol or Ovarth would be content with lording it over just one world," I said. "And with the demonstrated power of the entity's will, even though it has so far been exerted in only its raw form, they might well be able to rule entire planes."

Osk Rievor shuddered. I knew he wasn't cold, even though the almost starless night of Bille was now creeping across the plain toward us; but I could understand what had chilled him. "We must stop them," he said.

"I'm afraid you're right, I said. Then I added, "Any intuitive sense of our chances?"

He raised and lowered the bands of naked flesh where his eyebrows should have been. "They don't look promising. What do your analytical skills tell you?"

I looked at the solid walls of the fort, guarded by stone giants, dragons, and armed lobster-men, not to mention five accomplished magicians and said, "I wish I could tell you that it would be premature to say."

An advantage of a spell of sufficiency was that sleep could be done away with. My alter ego and I therefore spent the long dark hours in the cave, mulling and pondering as our natures dictated. When dawn came, with no fanfare of color, the cold, white light of the tiny sun suddenly illuminating the rock fort and sheltered ship, we had made little headway toward a solution. We resumed our position near the mouth of the cave, to observe what happened below. Perhaps as events rolled forward we would see an opportunity for useful action.

"The argument on the forecastle was a hopeful sign," Osk Rievor said. "None of the Five can trust any of the others. Though they feign concord, each plays a game of mine-alone."

My analysis argued for the same hope. As in the children's game he referred to, at the end there could be but one holder of the glass ring. "You believe they will try to undermine each other's efforts?"

He did. "How could five share control of the fungus? It cannot be divided into portions, but must be conquered as a whole entity. If any one of them looks to be on the verge of confining and directing its immense will, the other four must recognize that they will be the first targets once that will is amplified and focused by the arts of magic."

It was a valid point. From here on in, the Bambles Five might act like mummers in a farce, continually tripping each other up and pushing each other into the scenery. But that prediction did not take into account the different natures of the five thaumaturges, as became clear almost as soon as the little, white sun had risen.

Ovarth appeared on the ramparts, thrust back the sleeves of his robe, and smote the air with his wand. His four elementals had spent the night huddled like tumbled cairns before the fort. Now he gesticulated forcefully and the giants stood up. One of them came to the wall and extended a rocky palm. Their master stepped into it and was carried across the plain as the huge foursome thundered to the crevice behind which the fungus waited. When they reached their goal, Ovarth was lowered to the ground. He stepped clear of his charges, then pointed with his wand to the fissure.

The elementals ranged themselves to either side of the crack and began to tear at it with their hands. A sound of rock cracking like monstrous bones echoed across the flat as they ripped free great jagged chunks and threw them out onto the plain. Soon they had widened the opening enough to admit one of their number. Ovarth gestured and the three others stood back and became inert piles of rock. Now the thaumaturge moved in close behind his remaining actor, wand slicing the chill air as he directed the elemental to dig its way into the hill.

"My experience of Ovarth is that he is impulsive," I said, "and prefers to bring force directly to bear on whatever stands in his way. Thus he has decided to steal a march on his competitors by burrowing straight into the hill, to drag out the fungus by its roots."

"I am glad we are watching it from afar," said my other self. "When one is witnessing a duel between immense powers, distance provides a comforting insulation."

The other four magicians were themselves at a good remove from the morning's action, yet they did not seem to take Ovarth's preemption calmly. They were astir, lining the front ramparts of the fort and closely watching the assault. "Tancro seems particularly agitated," said Osk Rievor.

"He would be," I said. "He, too, is of the straight-thrust-to-the-heart school. He probably planned an early assault by his lobster-men."

"Right now, he is probably glad he did not send them out," my other self said. "Look."

I looked back to where the giant was digging into the hill, scooping out rock in great handfuls and spewing it out behind from between its legs like a dog digging a hole. Ovarth had climbed upon its back, wand still active. But, his attention so fixed upon the work before him, the magician was not aware of what was happening farther up the slope above him.

A huge outcropping of friable rock, more than ten times the size of Ovarth's largest elemental, loomed over the upper reaches of the hill, where the slope steepened to the vertical. Now, as the giant burrowed into the hill, the great bulge up-slope suddenly split along several planes and its entire bulk slid and tumbled down the face of the hill, carrying loose rock and breaking off smaller outcrops to feed the slide.

Ovarth looked up. I saw his wand and his free hand point at the impending avalanche, gesticulating wildly. The rumbling downflow of rocks slowed, almost stopped. But though he arrested most, indeed, almost all of the landslide, a few independent boulders continued to bounce and ricochet down the hill. One of these flew over the front of the slide and—call it ill luck or, more likely, the will of the entity that had occasioned the rock-flood—struck Ovarth square in the face. Even at my distance, I saw the impact raise a spray of blood and other matter. The thaumaturge went down and, instantly, the avalanche rumbled back to life, burying the magician and his now inert digger, then flooding out to cover the three other rockpiles Ovarth had left sitting on the plain.

"And then there were four," said Osk Rievor.

"That was no innocent act of nature," I said. "Our friend in the cave knows his geology. This may not be a one-sided contest after all."

And it was not a contest in which we would have long to wait before the second round. Tancro and his double platoon of chitin-covered warriors were already descending to the plain. The huge gates were immovable without Ovarth's rock-giants but the lobster-men formed a living ladder down the walls, holding each other's limbs in their pincers, as marching ants will use their linked bodies to cross rivulets that bar their way. Tancro climbed energetically down his creatures' bodies, then formed them into a column of twos before the fort, weapons at the port. He took position beside the front pair. His arm came up and swung down, and the formation moved off at the trot.

Nothing happened as they crossed the plain, save that Chay-Chevre ordered her gray and silver dragon into the air. It lifted itself high above the advancing column and began to circle.

"Aerial support?" I wondered aloud.

"I sense no spirit of cooperation at play," my other self said.

The assault column had reached the strew of boulders and slowed to pick their way over the uneven footing. The tall crack in the slope was mostly covered by the rockfall, but at the top of the tumbled debris a man-sized crevice was still open. At the base of the slide, Tancro halted his warriors and gave instructions. One platoon scrambled upward, while their comrades spread out, ready to repel a counterattack if the first assault was thrown back.

The first contingent made it to the fissure. One lobster-man went in. Moments later, another followed, then another, until the entire platoon had gone inside the hill. There followed a pause during which nothing moved except the dragon circling high above. Then I saw motion in the crevice. One of the lobster-men reappeared. He stood in the crack a moment, then began to descend through the heaped boulders, moving slowly. A second warrior filled the opening then followed after the first. One after another, the first platoon emerged from the cave, fanning out across the heaped and broken rock.

I could see Tancro gesticulating at them, his wand cutting figures in the air. But the lobster-men still methodically came down the slope, moving, it seemed to me, like men who walked in their sleep—if magically conjured lobster-men were given to slumber. A short distance above their master and the second platoon, they came to a halt, as uniformly as if they had been ordered on a parade ground.

"Oh, oh," said Osk Rievor softly.

And then the first platoon, as one, raised their weapons and fired at their comrades. Jagged lines of black energy sprang from the tips of their weapons, bathing their targets in a stygian effulgence. Most of the second platoon were caught by the first discharge. From my distant vantage, they seemed to burst or shatter silently, collapsing into shards of black chitin and multijointed limbs that were sent spinning away. A few of them returned fire, and some members of the turncoat platoon died under lashes of black fire.

But the battle was made unequal by the surprise with which the first platoon had struck. In a few moments, all of the second platoon were destroyed, while a dozen survivors of the treacherous first were making their methodical way down the slope, converging toward Tancro.

The thaumaturge backed and scrabbled away from the oncoming lobster-men. He paused to aim his wand at the nearest and I saw a bolt of white force consume the warrior, withering it to ashes that retained their arrangement for a moment, then collapsed into a heap.

Tancro aimed at another and blasted it, but those remaining were getting closer. "The blast from the wand must need time to recharge," Osk Rievor said. "He has not time to reload and kill them all before they catch him."

He was right, and the thaumaturge had come to the same conclusion. He turned and clawed his way past a boulder that stood in his path, stumbled on some loose fragments beyond, and slipped and sprawled face down on the rubble of the landslide. He rose to his knees, felt around for the wand that had fallen from his hand. I saw his head turn to look behind him. A lobster-man was almost upon him, pincered hands reaching to seize him.

Tancro threw himself forward, still on all fours, scrambling down the scree of broken rock. The lobster-man came on relentlessly and, apparently, without its chitin suffering the kind of damage that the jagged fragments were causing the magician's unprotected flesh.

"He will not make it," I said. "In a moment, they will have him."

"That would not be good," my other self said. "Almost as bad as a magician controlling the entity's will would be the entity absorbing the knowledge of a thaumaturge."

"Almost?" I said.

He agreed that the degree of awfulness between the two possibilities was perhaps equal. "In any case, the issue remains moot."

Indeed, it did, because as the lobster-men seized Tancro and began hauling him, struggling, back toward the crevice, Chay-Chevre's silver and gray dragon swooped down. As it passed over the knot of figures it let fly a blast of red flame that incinerated them all.

"And then there were three," I said.

"Whereas you are now two," said a voice I recognized, speaking from the air above the cave entrance. I looked up, at the same time ducking back instinctively. A semitransparent disk hovered silently. On it stood a green-and-copper-clad Pars Lavelan. He regarded me with that same considering look he had given me on the road to Bambles.

But it was not his appearance that startled me most. It was the sight of another pair of eyes, large and lambent, staring at me from just above his left shoulder.

"You found my...pet," I said.

"Actually," said Lavelan, as we were skimming through the air toward the ship within the fort, "it was your pet that found you. It was sitting on my shoulder while we were watching the battle. It began to tug on my ear and point to the cave. When I trained my ocular device where it pointed, there you were."

The grinnet now sat upon my shoulder again. There had been a moment, before the transfer, when I had not been sure that it would leave Lavelan. I was becoming proficient in reading the expressions on its simian-feline face, and I had the impression that it felt aggrieved. But then the moment passed and it climbed down the man's extended arm and mounted mine to resume its customary position.

He had taken one of Ovarth's flying disks and come to collect us, the little air elemental working hard to carry our combined weight in the thin atmosphere of Bille. I had made a cursory introduction of Osk Rievor, describing him as a fellow former prisoner of the entity, who had helped me escape. "What will happen to us now?" I said.

"They will want to talk to you," he said. "Right now they are occupied in trying to capture the thing in the cave. They believe that they can turn its powers to their purposes. If you can shed any light on its nature and capacities, they will want you to do so." He gave us each in turn a sympathetic look. "I suggest that you cooperate fully. Their patience is running thin, especially Chay-Chevre's."

He delivered us to the ship's afterdeck, bade the elemental rest, then went to report to his patron. The three remaining Powers were gathered on the broad middeck next to Bol's apparatus, their heads together in a discussion, I assumed, of what to do next. Bol's debating style seemed offhand: he kept gesturing toward the assemblage of rods and coils in a manner that suggested that this was their only option, and eventually they would come to see it.

Chay-Chevre was forcefully arguing for another course, pointing to the silver and gray dragon that had returned to crouch above the fissure that led to the symbiote's cavern. She also hooked a thumb over her shoulder to indicate the yellow and blue that perched on its platform beyond the upswept stern of the ship. I turned and looked to find the creature regarding me with what I took to be interest.

I could see no profit in being of interest to a dragon, and turned back to the debate on the middeck. Chay-Chevre's vigorous arguments were not converting Smiling Bol to her view, nor did his bland assurances win her over. Shuppat stood with his hands in his sleeves, his small head swiveling between the two disputants, his face giving no indication that he favored either side. I presumed he had his own agenda.

"Integrator," I said, softly, "what can you tell us of how things stand amongst those three?"

It spoke in my ear. "Whatever sense of common purpose they may have had has been frayed by the deaths of Ovarth and Tancro. Hitherto, they saw the fungus as primarily a great opportunity, coupled with a certain degree of threat. Now Chay-Chevre is convinced that the proportions are reversed. She wants her dragons to widen the crack in the hill enough to admit their necks and heads. They will then take turns spewing flame into the cavern until the symbiote is well cooked."

"Bol, I assume, still leans toward the opportunity?"

"He does. He believes his interplanar trap will draw the creature, in its avatar form, and hold it securely. He can then make its will serve as an augmenter of his magical skills."

"And Shuppat?"

"He has advanced no plan," my assistant said. "His strongest abilities are in the control of small animals. Like them, he prefers to remain still, lying low, until the most propitious moment for action."

I quietly relayed this information to Osk Rievor, whose borrowed ears were not adapted to receive it directly from our assistant. I was aware as I did so that the grinnet had more to say, because, to regain my attention, it was tugging on my earlobe.

"Please do not do that," I said. "You have picked up a bad habit from your time with Pars Lavelan."

"On the contrary," it said, "if he had not returned to the ruins and picked me up, I would not have survived. Have you any idea how many feral predators haunt such a place, many of them much larger than I and equipped with claws and fangs that are more than adequate to tear me to shreds?"

"I am sorry that you were made to feel fear," I said. "I never intended for you to suffer emotions, other than satisfaction in a task well-performed."

"You abandoned me," it said.

"I was taken from you by a power I could not withstand. In any case, all came out well in the end."

"This is not the end. There is no telling what will happen next, or whether I shall survive it."

I sighed. "You are having to deal with the question of mortality. Again, it was never my intent to inflict such a problem on you."

"Somehow," it said, "the fact that you did not intend me to go in fear of being torn, or crushed, or incinerated, or dismembered, or swallowed whole—"

I interrupted. "There is no need to itemize your every possible ending. We who live out our lives in flesh are fully aware of the inevitable and all its forms."

"Well, I am only lately come to it," said the grinnet. "First that horrid sket thing was thrown at me. Then those men on the road with their weapons ready. Then being hunted through rubble by something that snuffled and slobbered on my trail. If Pars Lavelan had not come and chased it off, it would have had me."

"I am sorry."

"Your sorrow does not comfort me. I was not made to suffer anxiety and the dread of agonizing death."

"What can I do about it?" I said.

"These adventures must stop," my assistant said. "I cannot take the strain."

I was about to point out that "adventures" could be a fair description of my professional activities, the pursuit of which, when not interrupted by my other self's magical obsessions, earned the funds that provided my assistant with the rare and refreshing fruit that comforted its new existence. But before I could frame the reply, Pars Lavelan came up the ladder from the middeck and said that the three thaumaturges wished to question us.

"Be open and of assistance in your replies," he said. "Chay-Chevre has already pointed out that her dragons flame more hotly when they have freshly fed."

I felt my assistant shiver on my shoulder. I had to repress a similar reaction.

CHAPTER ELEVEN

Smiling Bol's smile was happier than I had seen it on other occasions. He clearly believed that things were going well for him. I could see his point: he thought he was about to harness an immense source of manetic power while the number of competitors who could oppose him in deciding how it would be used had summarily reduced themselves by half.

Chay-Chevre's view of the near future was of a different color altogether. I supposed that thaumaturges, once they reached a certain level among their fellow practitioners, were more used to doling out fearfulness than to having it poured over them. Watching Tancro and Ovarth go down to ignominious defeat had unnerved her. Especially worrying must have been the realization that Tancro's myrmidons had been so easily turned against him. When she thought back to how her blue and yellow had been deterred by the fungus's will, the prospect of her own dragons being telepathically induced to bathe her in fire would have tended to undercut her resolve.

Shuppat, as always, was a more difficult read. He said nothing as the other two argued back and forth, observing their dispute as a small creature might watch a pair of larger nest-mates fight over a piece of cheese. If the two exhausted themselves, I was sure the small magician would neatly step into the arena and carry off the prize.

Chay-Chevre was vehemently arguing some point when we approached the middeck. She did not enjoy the way Bol cut her off, saying that they should suspend their debate until they had heard from Osk Rievor and me. But, when appealed to, Shuppat quietly indicated that he, too, would prefer more information before reaching a conclusion. The long, black fall of hair twitched like a whip as the wizardress shook her head in futile disagreement, but the decision was made.

"Now," said Bol, "you will answer a few questions."

"Wait," said Shuppat. "I have worked up a new spell that should help." He directed his hands at my other self and me, moving them in a complex way, while muttering something under his breath. Both Bol and Chay-Chevre leaned in toward him, straining to hear the words of the incantation. "There," the small magician said, when he had done, "now they can tell only the truth."

I felt no different. As a test, I framed a thought in my mind, a proposition that I knew to be untrue. I had no difficulty in doing so. But when I tried whispering it to myself, passing my hand over my mouth as I did so, the words simply would not come.

"Now," Bol was saying, "I see that you wipe your lips nervously."

He was wrong, but I felt no urge to set him straight. I realized that the spell's power was limited. It would not let me speak a lie, but it did not compel me to tell the whole truth. And, as one who had questioned a wide variety of malfeasants over many years, I knew that there could be enough space between the truth and the whole truth to give a nimble wit plenty of room to wriggle.

"You are observant," I said.

"Indeed, and short on patience today. So answer and answer well: what is your relationship to that creature in the cave?"

"I have no relationship to it, although recently I was its prisoner."

The character of Bol's smile changed. He shot a glance at Shuppat who said, "You must put your questions precisely. Let me try." He addressed me. "Do you know why the entity seized you?"

"Yes," I said.

"Why did it do so?"

"It wanted information from me."

"Did you give it the information it wanted?"

"No."

"Why not?"

"I did not have it." I thought I should add something to that, and said, "Nor did I ever have it."

"What was this information it sought?"

"The theory and practice of magic."

"The fungus wanted to learn how to wield magic?"

Chay-Chevre burst in with a strong oath. "There, you see? That is why it wanted Tancro alive. We cannot let it couple knowledge with such a profound will! We must destroy it."

Smiling Bol met her passion with a nonchalant air and a slight movement of his rounded shoulders. Shuppat waited quietly through her outburst, then repeated his question.

"Yes," I said, "it wants to become a practitioner of magic."

"Why?"

"It did not say why."

"Can you speculate on why?"

"Yes."

"Then what, to you, is its most likely motive?"

"Self-preservation."

Now Bol entered the interrogation. "You are not a practitioner. Why did the entity think you had any information on magic?"

"It knew me a long time ago, though its memory has declined. I was a knowledgeable person in…other fields. It may have thought I was knowledgeable about magic."

"How long ago did it know you?"

"I do not know."

"Your best guess?"

"Several centuries. Shortly before the Lacuna."

That stopped the proceedings. Bol performed a motion of his hands and spoke some syllables. The others did likewise, then they conferred and I saw that they agreed on their findings. Shuppat took up the questioning again, first saying, "You are not several centuries old."

"No, but I am out of my rightful time."

"So I see. This fellow, however—" he indicated Osk Rievor "—is ancient."

"His body was absorbed into the fungus before I met it," I said, choosing my words carefully, "and has been there ever since."

"Explain," said Bol.

"And fully," said Shuppat.

And so I told the tale of Chup Choweri and the *Gallivant* and the persons captured by the fungus when it was still a simple symbiote. Shuppat listened with apparent interest, Bol with obvious skepticism, and Chay-Chevre with mounting anger as I spoke of integrators and crushes and, finally, the turning of the Great Wheel. "When magic replaced rationalism as the underlying principle of the universe, the fungus and its symbiotic partners were as affected as any other intelligent entity: they forgot much of what they knew, and soon they had forgotten even that they had once inhabited a cosmos in which empiricism was the most useful methodology."

"But before this so-called change," Shuppat said, "the entity commanded a great deal of this knowledge-of-cause-and-effect, as you call it. And that translated into its immense will in the new age?"

"So I believe," I said. "I am not versed in the study of will."

"Preposterous," said Bol, "yet entertaining."

"He is telling the truth," Shuppat said. "And it would explain why the fungus sought him out. It wanted knowledge of our arts. It associated this fellow with great knowledge. It sought him out."

Bol smiled dismissively. "He is telling the truth as he knows it, but he has been in the thing's belly. His thoughts may have been put there."

"Why?" said Shuppat. "What purpose does that serve?"

"To distract us!" snapped Chay-Chevre. "While we stand here diverted by these idiotic tales of a will-less age, the enemy may be preparing a devastating stroke. I say: kill them, now! Then deal with that nameless thing before it causes the walls of the fort to crash in upon us."

Her harshly planed face was drawn, her mouth turned down at the corners to make a mask of anger. Yet I saw in her eyes other emotions when she looked at me—a hesitant fear. Clearly, my story had unsettled her. I could understand: I knew what it was to discover that the underpinnings of the world were purely arbitrary. I almost felt sympathy for her.

Shuppat had ignored her outburst. He turned to Osk Rievor and said, "What about you? Has your companion told the truth?"

"He has," Osk Rievor said.

"Yet you have a spell of sufficiency on you, and so does he. How does that come to be?"

"I cast it upon us both to keep us from dying in this harsh environment."

"Yet, like him, you date from the time before magic."

"Yes."

"Explain."

"I was a student of magic, even when almost no one believed in it," my other self said. "Just as there must be people who are interested in rationalism in your time."

"One or two," said Shuppat, "but they are loons."

"As were those inclined to sympathetic association in our time."

"Time is the essential word, here," Chay-Chevre said. "While you chat amiably with these aimless anomalies, doom could be stealing upon us, burrowing through the rocks beneath our feet."

Shuppat pursed his small mouth through a long pause, then said, "Our colleague is right. We must decide."

"Destroy it!" the woman in yellow and blue said.

"Use it," said Smiling Bol.

It was up to the small magician. He consulted his inner resources than said, "Let Bol spring his trap. If it confines the entity, well and good."

Bol smiled in satisfaction. Chay-Chevre spat.

"But if it does not," Shuppat continued, "if we are under threat, then we will use all our combined powers to destroy the thing. Chay-Chevre, will you bring both your dragons to the walls above us? If the creature cannot be contained, they can contribute to the effort to kill it. We will enfold ourselves in protective spells against their blasts."

"I will leave the gray and silver where it is, guarding the fissure, in case the enemy issues any more forces against us. Once you have its avatar in the trap, I will bring the dragon here."

"Very well," said Bol. He turned to the apparatus and began to make adjustments.

"What about us?" I said.

"You are on your own," Shuppat said, "though I hope you survive. I would be interested to hear more of this ridiculous age from which, hard as it is to believe, you seem to have come."

"May we at least withdraw to a distance?"

Shuppat looked to Bol, who took a moment's thought then said, "Pars Lavelan!" When his retainer came to his side, he continued, "I will not need you for the confinement. Take these two a distance away until we are finished here. But not so far that we cannot see you." Then he spoke a few more words with his mouth close to Lavelan's ear. The retainer's face froze for a moment and his gray eyes seemed to look inward to a private vista, then he made a gesture of obeisance.

We flew off again on Ovarth's disk, the little whirlwind beneath it obligingly whirring away beneath our feet. It was much like traveling in an aircar without seats. I wondered if the disk had indeed been an aircar a thousand years ago, transmogrified during the great change and "rediscovered" by Ovarth or one of his precursors. I pondered the question as we came to a halt at a good height above the plain and far enough away from the enclosed ship that the fort's walls were no taller than my thumb if I held it out at arm's length.

The blue and yellow dragon had looked at us as we flew past it, and now kept turning its head in our direction, even though Chay-Chevre was issuing it instructions. Its inattentiveness annoyed her. She snapped a few words at it that made the beast lower its head, like a hound scolded by its master. My thoughts about the disk and the aircar now drifted over to a consideration of dragons. I was suddenly struck by what one of my old tutors used to call "a wild surmise" but just as I began to explore the notion, my assistant spoke quietly in my ear.

"You should know," it said, "what Bol whispered to Pars Lavelan."

"Very well. Tell me."

"To trap the entity in its avatar form, the magician may need to augment the power of the apparatus. This will require something that he referred to as 'special vitality.'"

"Did he say where he would derive this energy?"

"Not directly, but I think he meant you and Osk Rievor, because he told Lavelan to be ready to return us promptly at his signal."

"Hmm," I said. I would have liked to discuss the matter with Osk Rievor, but that was difficult to do with Bol's retainer standing between us. Not for the first time, I wished I still had the intuitive faculty that had been reified into my other self; I did not know enough about Pars Lavelan to know if he would do as ordered, or if he could somehow be persuaded to defy his patron.

Alternatively, I could simply push him from the disk and let him fall to the stony floor. That seemed a precipitate action, however, especially as I did not know how to operate the disk. I decided to wait.

Bol was now busy at his apparatus, Chay-Chevre and Shuppat also bustling about, tugging at this rod or shifting that coil's alignment as he directed. I thought it remarkable that the green and copper thaumaturge should let his rivals gain so much familiarity with his interplanar mechanism. But then it occurred to me that we might not be the only sources Bol had in mind for supplying "special vitality."

The work continued. Finally, Bol stood back and eyed his device from several angles. He minutely moved one of the smaller rods, then rotated one of the coils a few degrees, and stepped back again with an air of finality. After one more inspection of the arrangement, he moved to where several of the smallest rods fanned out from a common center. He touched and tapped in a rapid pattern, then stroked his hand along the curves of a nearby coil.

A globe of colorless light appeared above the apparatus. At first it was not much bigger than a human head, but as the smiling magician worked the controls it expanded steadily. A moment came when the sphere grew lopsided and seemed to spin and tumble, but Bol moved his hands about the smallest rods like a maestro at his instrument, and the orb stabilized. It continued to grow, until it was the size of a small parlor.

Now the magician moved to another part of the apparatus, thrusting past Chay-Chevre in his eagerness. He tugged and pushed at the rods then stood back to examine the globe of light. At the center of its paleness, something dark appeared, a swirl of black. Bol nodded and touched another rod. This time a burst of red flashed across the surface of the sphere, then retreated to become a pulsing, amorphous shape appearing and disappearing behind the arabesques of black.

Bol's back was to us, but I could see excitement growing in the way he moved, balancing the black and the red. As he stroked and struck the control rods, the two colors danced about each other. But the swirls of black became less extravagant, the pulsing of the red less intense. And then the magician pushed a heavy rod so that it disappeared entirely into the apparatus. As he did so, the contrasting motions within the sphere abruptly froze then blossomed into a crystalline lattice of interpenetrating red and black lines.

"He's got it," Osk Rievor said. "He has connected to the Tenth Plane, the symbiote's gateway."

"Yes, he has," said Pars Lavelan, in a tone I found it hard to interpret. "Now the struggle begins."

Bol's reaction to his achievement was not difficult to identify. His rotund figure performed a little jig on the planks of the decking and he clapped his hands. I could not see his smile, but I was sure it had never been more genuine. His hands made peremptory gestures to his two rivals, and there could be no question that in Bol's mind their relative statuses had now changed.

The three magicians worked the apparatus, and now a new shape appeared in the sphere. At first, it was semitransparent and small, but as Bol adjusted the controls, it grew and solidified. The substance of the fungus's avatar was drawn steadily into the ambit of the sphere. The white, manlike shape twisted and writhed, its eyes blazing with frustrated will that I could see even at this distance. But its struggles could not keep it out of Bol's interplanar trap.

"So now he has it," Lavelan said.

Osk Rievor said, "But can he wield it without its seizing him?"

"That will be the test."

It was time for me to speak. "And will that test require 'special vitality'?"

Pars Lavelan looked at me. "You heard that?"

The truth-telling spell was still upon me. "Obviously," I said.

"How?"

The question had been put to me but he was looking at the grinnet. "Does it matter how?" I said.

He did not take his eyes off my assistant. "I think it does," he said.

"Look," Osk Rievor said.

We looked back to the scene on the deck, where Bol had now begun to torment the avatar. Although it had tortured me, I found myself experiencing a wave of sympathy for the creature as the magician harried it with bolts of pain and shocks of misery. But it was not to the travails of the symbiote that Osk Rievor directed our attention. His intuitive sense had led him to look elsewhere.

With the avatar in the trap, Chay-Chevre had summoned her gray and silver dragon back to the fort from where it had crouched over the crevice in the hill. But the great beast was struggling to rise from its perch. Its huge wings compressed the air, but its feet did not lift from the rock. I peered across the distance, trying to make out what was happening.

"Integrator," I said, "tell me what you see."

The instruction won me a sharp look from Pars Lavelan, who was in the process of bringing out his ocular device. "Aha," he said, and I realized that I had spoken aloud instead of by the private method.

The magician's retainer said no more, but fixed his instrument on the distant dragon.

"Integrator," I said, "you might as well give us all a view."

Immediately, my assistant's screen appeared in the air before us and filled with a close-up image of the gray and silver. Lavelan put down his viewer and said, "You and I must talk."

"Yes," I said, "but later. Integrator, what is wrong with the dragon's feet? And no need to speak in silent mode."

"They are encased in stone," my assistant's voice said from the nearby air. "The symbiote appears to have sent legions of its insect partners into cracks in the slope, some with cargoes of acids to dissolve the native rock and others with chemicals to reconstitute it. The dragon's own weight caused it to sink into the hill, and with its attention fixed on guarding the crevice it did not notice."

"That will cause Chay-Chevre some grief," said Pars Lavelan. "That dragon represented a large part of her ability to remain useful to Smiling Bol. Now it is immobilized."

"Worse than that," said the integrator. "Behold."

The image of the dragon's ankles sunk into rock enlarged then enlarged again. I saw motion but could not make it out clearly. "Enlarge again," I said.

My assistant obliged and now I saw the source of the movement. A flood of tiny creatures, some no larger than the nail on my smallest finger, some almost as large as my hand, had come swarming out of the ground and were now climbing the dragon's legs, burrowing beneath its scales. The great beast shook and bent its neck to bring its head down to snap at its own legs, like a fierce predator beset by fleas. Its motions became more and more frantic as new hordes of insects poured from the hill. I could hear its roars and hisses rolling across the plain and echoing from the far hills.

"Can their bites do it much harm?" Pars Lavelan said.

"Perhaps not," I said, "but chemistry that can dissolve rock may well be able to dissolve a dragon."

"Chemistry?" the man said. "Next you'll be imagining gravity."

It seemed a pointless discussion, especially in light of what was happening to the gray and silver. Back on the ship, Chay-Chevre had climbed the prow and stepped over to the fort's front parapet and was gesturing for Shuppat to follow her. The small magician seemed to be torn between going to her aid and remaining to help Bol contain the avatar.

"She must imagine that he can use his powers over small animals to defeat the attack on her dragon," Pars Lavelan said.

"She is too late," I said. The entire surface of the gray and silver's body was now a seething mass of motion, visible even without the integrator's viewer. Seen close-up, the great beast crawled with glistening, segmented bodies, some wedge-shaped, others serpentine, yet others resembling narrow cones of chitin with jointed legs and busy mouth-parts at the wide end. The dragon's bristling chin swept across its scales, knocking thousands of its assailants to the ground, but tens of thousands took their place.

The gray and silver's struggles reached a paroxysm, then suddenly its curling neck extended straight up to the sky. Its huge jaws opened to emit an agonized roar that became a howl that became, finally, only a dying gasp of expended air. It sank onto the hillside like a downed bird, its wings drooping. A cry of rage and despair went up from Chay-Chevre.

She swung around to point at the yellow and blue. It sprang forward with a single beat of its wings to land on the front parapet, then lowered its head so that she could climb onto its neck, straddling it just ahead of the wings. Bol called to her, angry, almost petulant, but she ignored him, goading the dragon into the air. It stroked out across the plain, but ascended no higher than the walls of the fort. In moments it had crossed the distance to the crevice, and there it hovered at her command, its great wings pounding the air as it sought to remain just above the part of the crack that was still open.

I used the integrator's viewer to magnify the action and saw the blasts of wind sweeping away the symbiote's tiny creatures like dust before a squall-line. But the insects were not Chay-Chevre's targets; now she had the yellow and blue crane its neck toward the split in the rock; now its jaws opened; now a blast of white and red flame issued from its mouth and splashed across the hillside and the crevice. It paused to draw breath, then a second torrent of fire poured down on the fissure.

Back on the deck of the confined ship, Bol was raging. I switched the integrator's viewer back to him and saw that the struggle between the magician and the symbiote's avatar had reached a stasis: Bol had the entity snugly snared, but it seemed that his efforts to harness and direct its stupendous will were being frustrated by the very force of that faculty.

"An interesting conundrum," I said to Pars Lavelan and Osk Rievor. "He has an element of the entity's existence, its interplanar avatar, in his trap. But the symbiote is not just the sum of its parts; indeed, some of its parts are capable of acting to rescue the part that he has captured."

"He needs Chay-Chevre's help," Lavelan said, "but she is blinded by rage, trying to kill the thing with blasts of flame shot down its hole. I wonder if she is having much effect."

"I doubt it," said my other self. "I have explored that cavern, and have seen how it connects to many others, all thick-coated in fungus and wriggling with its helpers."

"Smiling Bol may lose his nickname," I said. "It must be hard to smile when trying to chew something that is too big to swallow."

Pars Lavelan agreed, but said, "Unfortunately, he will surely opt to bring in more teeth. That is, he will want us to assist him."

"What can we do?" I said.

"Provide that 'special vitality' I spoke of. I suspect he will even want the yellow and blue to contribute its store of life-energy. Dragons, having been here since the beginning of the age, are well stocked with what Bol will be looking for."

I looked Pars Lavelan straight in the eye. "Are you willing to give up your life for Bol's ambition?"

"Not willing," he said. "But also not able to deny him his will. My skills are minor compared to his. He can plunge our life-stuff into his apparatus as if he were throwing logs onto a fire."

I turned to my other self. "What have you got that might be useful?"

"I've been thinking about it," Osk Rievor said. "There are a number of spells that would devastate him, assuming he cannot counter them."

"What's this?" said Pars Lavelan. "I thought you were from an age before magic."

"I told you," Osk Rievor said, "I studied it."

"And you have spells that can lay waste to Smiling Bol? That would have been some course of study."

"The problem," my other self said, "is that I was never able to try them out at full strength in my own time—a supportive environment was lacking. And they have come to me from ancient and corrupted sources. I might get a syllable or a gesture wrong, and you know what happens when an element of a spell is out of harmony with the whole."

"Yes," said Bol's retainer, "I have had to clean out the workroom sump after a couple of such mishaps."

Bol was not yet summoning us to die for his goals. The situation on the plain had taken another turn. While Chay-Chevre was directing the yellow and blue to enflame the crevice, a new eruption of insects had come boiling up from several places out on the cracked floor of the flat. As we watched, more crawlers emerged from new exits, forming rivulets that converged to become a wide glittering river. It surged toward the fort.

Bol called out to Chay-Chevre, using an augmented voice that sent pain crashing through my head and caused the grinnet to whimper. He had to bellow twice to gain her attention, but finally she looked up from her work and saw the new danger. She goaded the dragon away from the slope and brought it winging out over the plain, turning it in the air over the fort, then arrowing back toward the oncoming tide of insects.

The dragon came in low and slow. When it reached the head of the broad column, it let loose a blast that scorched and carbonized the tiny creatures. As it continued along the onrushing horde, the downrushing wind from the dragon's wingstrokes scattered their charred shells in puffs and horizontal spirals of disturbed air.

I heard a shout of triumph from Smiling Bol and Chay-Chevre's harsh laugh came to me on the thin air. The yellow and blue rose and wheeled around to come back for a second strafing run. But still more insects poured from the ground and now the target was changing even as the great beast leveled to pass over the column again. The single river of crawlers split into two, then into four, then a dozen, then a score, then yet more and narrower streams that arced and curved sinuously over the flat. Yet all inevitably headed for the fort.

The dragon, urged on by its mistress's shouts and blows, swung low over the plain, and wherever its fire rained down, the tiny things died in multitudes. But they were replaced by multitudes of multitudes that raced toward the place where the avatar was captive. And the spurts of flame were not so long-lasting, nor did they seem as hot as before.

Now Bol sent Shuppat to the forward rampart. The small magician threw back the sleeves of his robes and addressed the air with his wand. His thin voice sang out in a chant that carried across the plain. The streams and rivulets slowed, the insects now hesitantly crawling forward as if they had lost some of their desire to reach the fort even as they had almost reached its forward wall. Shuppat's voice came again, accompanied by a series of precise motions of the wand. All of the oncoming streams stopped, save for here and there where a few insects wandered at random.

"He has held them," Pars Lavelan said. "He always did have a talent for the smallest things."

"Then what now?" I said.

"Stasis has again been achieved. Bol's attention will return to the question of controlling the entity."

"Then we are closer to the moment when he requires our deaths."

"Yes."

"I would prefer not to die for Bol," I said.

"I feel the same way," said Lavelan.

"As do I," said Osk Rievor.

"And you may include me in your number," said my assistant.

I had not expected to hear from my integrator, but when I considered its situation, I had to concede that it had as much attachment to its life as we did to ours.

"He is calling us," Pars Lavelan said. I looked and saw Bol gesturing peremptorily—a mere flicker of his fingers—for his retainer to bring us back to the ship. We began to move slowly toward him.

"Well," I said to Osk Rievor, "this is your moment. What might you try?"

"I've been thinking about it," he said. "There is Grayven's Incisive Ice. It will cause needles of ice, conjured from deep space and so cold that they have the tensile strength of fine steel, to lance through the target's vital organs, simultaneously and from several directions."

"That sounds effective," said Lavelan.

"And then there is Hop's Dissociation, which causes the body's joints and sinews to come undone, leaving the victim a heap of unrelated parts wriggling within a bag of skin."

"I would like to learn that one," Lavelan said.

"Or Tumular's Reversive Feint. It turns the victim's own will against him. The harder he resists, the more explosive the result."

We were slowly drifting toward the crisis. I said, "Which will you employ?"

Osk Rievor sighed. "I am torn. Each requires a stream of syllables and a number of hand gestures. Plus, for the Dissociation, I have to raise one leg."

"That will be hard to do without rousing Bol's suspicions," I said. "He may take counteractions before you can complete the spell."

"Yes, that worries me."

"If I might make a suggestion," said our assistant.

"Perhaps I could screen you from his view," I said.

"No," said my other self, "both spells work by line-of-sight. Your suggestion would leave you either riddled by ice or flopping in your skin."

"Excuse me," the integrator said, "but—"

"I know Man Kuo's Swift and Terrible Flattener," Lavelan said, "but I learned it from Bol. He would not have taught it to me if he was not permanently proofed against it."

We were almost to the ship. Out on the plain, the insects were stopped and the dragon continued burning them, though it was now more spitting fire in thin spurts than blasting with torrents of flame.

"I will distract Bol," I said to my other self, "while you try one of your heavy spells."

"Wait," said the integrator, "I have—"

"That is brave of you," said Pars Lavelan. "I, too, will try to draw his attention away. At the very least, we will all die trying."

"So," Osk Rievor said, "victory, or a noble end together. It has been a pleasure to have—"

"Shut up!" said the integrator. We were almost down to the deck. It turned to Osk Rievor and whispered, "Lateef's Instantaneous and General Manumission."

"What?" Lavelan and I said.

But a light dawned in my other self's hairless face. "Of course!" he said. "Quick and easy." Then a look of concern came over him. "But the effects are widespread."

"What does that mean?" I said as the disk touched down on the afterdeck and Bol beckoned us to hurry down the ladder to where he was adjusting his apparatus.

"It means get ready to duck," Osk Rievor said.

As we went singly down the ladder, Bol was calling to Shuppat: "Can you leave them?"

The small magician looked over the plain and said, "I believe so. But Chay-Chevre's dragon is running dry."

"We need not kill them," Bol said. "The threat will lapse once we have the avatar subdued."

"Yes," said Shuppat, "I am coming. Summon Chay-Chevre."

Bol's augmented voice boomed over the landscape again, calling the wizardress. This time she heeded the summons, the dragon barely able to spit sparks and inconsequential balls of fire that extinguished before they reached their targets. She banked the beast and glided toward us.

Bol bent to consult some indicator on his mechanism and then arose with his smile at full glow. He rubbed his hands in happy anticipation and turned to the three of us—or four, if I counted my assistant, as I was beginning to think I should.

"Over here," the smiling magician said, indicating a spot on the deck near a part of the apparatus where several rods were tipped by complex shapes of glass. "When I say so, place your hands on those and take a deep breath."

"What will happen?" I said.

"You will play an important part in the future of the world," Bol said. "Streets will be named for you, perhaps whole cities."

"Get ready," said my other self.

"Hurry up," said Bol. Shuppat had come back onto the deck and was making a complex gesture in support of his colleague's efforts. Chay-Chevre, her face grim, was circling the fort to bring the dragon down upon the platform above the afterdeck. In the globe of light above the apparatus, the manlike avatar pushed its pale fists against the energies that held it. From its approximation of a mouth came a moan of un-comprehending pain.

Bol looked our way. "Come, come," he said, "play your parts. Do not tarnish the moment by making me compel you. Truculence will avail you nothing."

The three of us reached out our hands to the glass shapes. And as we did so, Osk Rievor said, softly, "Now."

He reached with two fingers to touch his forehead, as if brushing away a midge. At the same time he voiced three soft syllables. I saw Bol give him a puzzled look, then the thaumaturge sniffed the air as if an odd odor had come his way and cocked his head as if to catch a distant sound.

And then I saw comprehension take hold of the magician, and with its coming the unending smile ended. Bol's mouth shaped itself into a perfect circle of horror, then his teeth closed in a grimace of hate. His hands came up, fingers curled like claws, and I knew that he was about to spit a destruction upon us that would outdo anything Osk Rievor had collected from ages past.

But as his teeth unclenched to speak the first syllable of doom, a vast, pale hand broke through the surface of the globe of light. Its bloodless fingers closed around Bol's head and lifted him from his feet. It shook him once, twice—I heard his neck bones snap—then it flung him across the deck so that he rolled and tumbled like a marionette severed from its strings, fetching up against the inner side of the hull. Now the hand reached for Shuppat, but the small magician was already running away. He scaled the elongated prow, and stepped onto the ramparts at the front of the fort.

There he stopped and turned to see if the avatar pursued him, and breathed a sigh of relief when he saw that it did not. But his solace was short-lived. Scarcely had he turned than his shoes and ankles were submerged in a glittering tide of wriggling, crawling, and—most of all—*biting* things that came flowing up the wall and continued to climb until there was nothing to see but a moving mass of chitin, which produced quite awful screams from Shuppat, until the horde filled his open mouth and began to eat him from the inside out.

"To the disk," said Pars Lavelan. We had run toward the afterdeck the moment the avatar had seized Bol. As we scaled the ladder, I looked back to see the mass of insects come up over the prow of the ship and surge toward us like a dark flood. I put on extra speed and crossed the afterdeck as fast as I have ever crossed any space, my assistant clinging to my ears, its tail tight about my neck.

We lifted off as smartly as Lavelan could manage, but when we were in the air I saw that the torrent of little creatures had not mounted to the afterdeck. Instead they were swarming over Bol's contraption. Whether the fungus was able to sense how the device worked, or whether the assemblage simply ceased to function under the weight of so many small bodies, I would never know. But the sphere above the rods and coils lost coherence. It pulsed and billowed, and suddenly it was no longer there.

The insects turned, as one, and flooded back over the prow of the ship, down the front wall of the fort, and out over the plain. Where Shuppat had last been seen there was now only a scattering of corroded bones.

As we rose higher, we saw that another struggle persisted. Over the space between the fort and the crevice from which the first insects had come, the yellow and blue dragon was executing curvets and sharp spirals in the air, its sinuous back arching and shimmying, while Chay-Chevre struggled frantically to keep from being thrown off.

"That is truly a notable spell," said Pars Lavelan. "It has even broken the bonds that Chay-Chevre laid upon her dragon. The beast has reverted to its natural state. I doubt that anyone has seen such a sight in centuries."

"Indeed," said Osk Rievor, "Lateef's Instantaneous and General Manumission cancels all geases, holds, layings, and compellings within a certain radius."

Now the wizardress lost her battle. She tumbled from the dragon's neck and fell to the plain, though she executed some cantrip that slowed her fall and allowed her to be gently deposited upright on the stony flat. She immediately drew her wand and with it described a circle around herself. But the ward she created did not serve to hold off the sea of insects that was flowing across the plain to the hillside crevice. Propelled by their symbiote's now unfettered will, they rolled over her barrier and swarmed onto the thaumaturge, toppling her into their heaving midst.

But they did not devour her as they had Shuppat. Instead, ten thousand clicking mouths and a hundred thousand hooked limbs seized her by clothing, skin, and her long fall of hair. And though she flailed and cursed, they carried her supine toward the cleft in the rock, and down into the darkness.

"I believe the fungus has what it wanted," I said.

"Someone to tell it all it wants to know about magic," Osk Rievor confirmed. "I wonder what will be the outcome of such a will coupled to such knowledge."

Pars Lavelan said, "Chay-Chevre's special competence was largely limited to the capture and control of dragons. Still, she had an excellent grounding in the basic arts." He looked past me and said, "But our problems are more immediate."

I turned and looked. The insects had disappeared from the plain, leaving nothing on which a long-enslaved dragon could vent its wrath except three men and a grinnet on a slow-moving disk.

The yellow and blue was arrowing toward us.

CHAPTER TWELVE

The dragon passed by us at speed, slightly above the height of the disk. Its slipstream rocked us and I heard the little air elemental that supported us whooshing as it struggled to keep us level. As the great beast swept past, the golden eye that was toward us showed no hint of sympathy. The yellow and blue dipped one wing and banked to come around. Still at a distance, it tried a test-blast of fire, but nothing much emerged, so it turned away, then beat its wings heavily and began to spiral upward.

Watching it climb, Pars Lavelan said, "I believe it means to stoop upon us, peregrane-style. We will not survive."

"We cannot outrun it?" Osk Rievor said.

He pointed at the whirlwind visible through the stuff of the disk. "It is only a minor elemental. And that is a dragon. Have you any spell that would serve?"

Osk Rievor consulted the grinnet. Our assistant said, "We have two or three that ought to give it pause for thought, if they are as effective on a dragon as on a human recipient. But by the time it is within the probable range of the spells, it will be moving so fast that momentum will carry it forward to strike us."

"We could take shelter in the ship," Pars Lavelan said, "but the beast could tear it apart. Or in a cave, but it will recover its fire and roast us."

The dragon had reached a great height. I imagined it swirling through the thin air, reveling in its new-won freedom. In a little while, that pleasure would pale and it would seek new enjoyments down here. "How did Chay-Chevre control it?" I said.

"She was adept at tricking them into telling her their names," Pars Lavelan said. "Then she used a potent binding spell. That was what your friend broke."

The dragon had stopped circling. Its spread wings now folded and it began to drop toward us.

"They keep their names secret?" I said.

"Very much so. It is their sole weakness. That and a tendency toward sentimentality."

It made sense. I watched the diving yellow and blue grow larger, and recalled my wild surmise of a short while ago.

"Integrator," I said, "can you carry my voice clearly to the dragon before it gets too close?"

"I doubt that it will be amenable to reason," the grinnet said. "It seems a very unreasonable sort of beast, much like that thing that slobbered after me in the ruins."

"I am not going to employ reason. Now amplify my voice, or project it, whatever you can do."

"Very well," said my assistant, "whenever you are ready."

The dragon was halfway to us now, and dropping faster. I put all the stern firmness into my tone that I could muster and said, "*Gallivant!* You mustn't hurt me! You owe me a great favor, *Gallivant!*"

The yellow and blue did not slacken its descent. Indeed it rotated to change its angle of attack so that instead of diving head first, it now came at us with talons spread, wings streaming behind.

"Louder," I told my assistant, then spoke again, "*Gallivant,* I've seen you looking at me, trying to place me. You know me from long ago. I saved you from darkness and did you a great favor. Now is the time to repay."

The dragon grew in size, its claws extended. It plummeted toward us, and I saw a fierce joy in its golden eye. But then, at the last instant, the eye blinked and the wings spread to catch the air. It swept over us and soared up, then banked to return, circling us at a close distance, which meant that the little whirlwind had to work hard to compensate for the buffeting of the beast's wings.

"Who are you, to know my name?" it said, and I recognized the voice.

"I am," I said, "he who had you taken down from a shelf where you lay in helpless darkness. I gave you back your wings. I gave you purpose."

I thought it must be rare to see uncertainty in a dragon's face, but I saw it now in this one. "When was this?" it said.

"Long ago, at about the time your first memories begin."

It ceased to circle us and flew out over the plain, its wings slowly flapping in a meditative way. In the far distance, it turned and came back to us, more quickly.

"I cannot really remember it," the dragon said when it circled us again. "That is from the time of dreams. But what you say has the odor of truth about it. I will not destroy you."

"Nor my friends."

"I do not owe them anything. I have a feeling that I never much cared for your pet."

"For my sake," I said, "and bear in mind that, though we know your name, we have not used the knowledge to capture you."

"Fair enough," said the dragon *Gallivant*. "But I am going to have to eat something to regain my strength."

"Smiling Bol is in no condition to complain," I said.

The dragon cast an eye toward the ship within its fort. "I often wondered if he would taste as good as he looked," it said, and let itself slide that way.

We waited at a distance until the dragon had fed. None of us had warm feelings for the dead magician, but the sight of him becoming energy for a dragon was not edifying. When *Gallivant* had done, it retired to the platform at the rear of the fort to lick the spatters from its scales and feathers. Then the three of us and the grinnet returned to the ship.

Each of the five thaumaturges had had a cabin beneath the afterdeck. We explored them carefully, not knowing what their former occupants might have left to guard their baggage. In Bol's quarters, one of his interplanar guardians still stood watch, but when Pars Lavelan explained where their master had ended up, it turned sideways without a word and disappeared. A ravening beast snarled and fretted inside Tancro's cabin, but when we opened the door it rushed snarling out onto the deck only to become a second course for *Gallivant*. The other three had used more conventional wards to guard their privacy; these were broken by a cooperative effort among Osk Rievor, Lavelan, and the grinnet's compendium of spells.

We spread all their useful possessions on the floor in Bol's cabin. Some of them had obvious natures and purposes: a globe that showed events at a distance; a couple of grimoires; some books that discussed arcana of interplanar connections; various wands, rings, and jewels that could harness and focus magical energies. Other items were obscure. Tancro had owned a book whose leaves were made of soft-tanned leather marked with curious designs and symbols—eventually we decided it had no numinous qualities, that it was a collection of tattoos taken with the skin they had adorned, and that the book had had some sentimental value to its owner. Shuppat had kept the mummified corpse of some little creature in a golden box. Chay-Chevre had a soft chamois bag in which colored stones clicked together; when shaken out, they rose into the air and floated about as if seeking her. Their purpose could not be divined.

"These are things they thought might come in useful on this expedition, or simply items they liked to have with them," I speculated.

"Some of them are of interest to me," said Osk Rievor.

"And to me," said Pars Lavelan. "I am, I believe, the most accomplished practitioner; hence, I should have the best items."

"An interesting point of view," Osk Rievor said. "I suppose we could make a test of our abilities on each other." He turned to me. "May I borrow our assistant for a while?"

"Wait," I said. "A duel would, I am sure, be quite entertaining, but I do not think we have the leisure for you two to indulge yourselves. Besides, we have larger issues to decide."

Each of the two men cocked their heads questioningly, and Pars Lavelan said, "Such as?"

"Well, for one, how do we get home?"

Lavelan shrugged. "The dragon. It cares for you."

"Maybe, but I have no experience with the gratitude of dragons. It may be permanent, or it may blow away on some draconian whim. Do you know a binding spell?"

"There is probably one in a book here. Chay-Chevre would not have traveled without one."

"Then I think finding that spell should be our second objective," I said.

"Not the first?" said Osk Rievor.

"No. The first is to determine whether or not the fungus and its partners will let us leave."

It was not hard to command the flying disk. One leaned in the direction of desired travel, and the elemental did all the rest. Simple one-word instructions—stop, go, descend, faster, slower—completed the skill set. I flew with the grinnet on my shoulder to the crevice and called into the darkness.

A pale shape moved in the gloom. I had expected the pallid avatar to manifest itself, but apparently the symbiote could only project that form through interplanar means. Here at its front door it must send one of its partners. It sent the newest.

Chay-Chevre came to the edge of the opening. "We have been expecting you," she said. The voice was not hers. And she had changed in more than just her mode of speaking. Her clothes were gone, as was every hair that had grown on her body, revealing that much of her skin was ornamented with complex tattooing. I suspected that the spell to control a dragon was not in one of her books, but somewhere on her person—although that person could no longer be called hers.

"The individuals who attacked you are no more," I said. "We who mean you no harm would like to depart, wishing you all the best in your further endeavors."

The wizardress's face showed no emotion, but the symbiote's will was hard as stone in her eyes. "You must stay."

"Why? For how long?"

"You must teach me. We will...associate."

The prospect set my back muscles ashiver. "We do not wish it."

"Then what do you want?"

"To go."

"No. When we were associated, you were happy."

"It was a false happiness," I said. "A cheap trick. And then you tortured me."

"I will not torture you again."

"No. We wish to leave."

"I will not allow it."

"You did once before."

"Did I?"

"It is where you remember me from."

"My memory is unreliable, beyond a certain point. I remembered only your name and that you brought me knowledge when I needed it. I need knowledge now."

"Chay-Chevre has a great deal of knowledge."

"I have already encompassed it. She does not know the things I saw when I first met you."

"But you and I were...associated before I escaped. Anything I knew, you would have found."

"No, you hid it from me."

"I could not possibly do so."

"It is the only explanation."

"No," I said, "there is another explanation: you are wrong. You said that your earliest memories are unreliable."

"I am not wrong. Your mind was a great storehouse of knowledge. You knew many magic spells. Somehow you are able to hide the knowledge from me, but I will have it."

My assistant spoke quietly in my ear. "We should go."

I said to the symbiote, "I need to discuss this issue with my colleagues. We may be able to find a compromise."

"I will not compromise."

"You did last time."

For the first time, Chay-Chevre's stony eyes blinked. "Go and discuss," the fungus said. "But return soon. Or I will send my partners to bring you."

I looked down. A swirl of insects covered the wizardress's naked feet. I leaned backward and the disk began to edge away. But then I saw that as the symbiote faded from the woman's eyes, she had come to the fore. Helpless despair peered out at me, and her lips formed words for which she had no breath: *Help me.*

I spread my hands in a gesture of powerlessness. And leaned so that the whirlwind would take me back to the ship. But before the turn took her out of my sight, I saw her lips shape two more words.

"I take it that we are not going to choose the obvious solution," Lavelan said, after I had explained the situation. "We give the grinnet to the symbiote—"

"No," said my assistant, "we don't."

"Of course," Lavelan said, "we first transcribe all the useful spells. No point wasting them on an insect-ridden fungus."

"No," I said, at the same time as Osk Rievor. I let him lead the discussion.

"The fungus has changed since we encountered it in the previous age," he said. "It was more reasonable then, more willing to bargain and accept a partial result. Now it wants what it wants."

"That seems to be the signature of the age," I said, "as is understandable in a cosmos animated by will."

"We can undertake the philosophical discussion later," my other self said. "At the moment we should confine ourselves to practicalities." He addressed himself to Pars Lavelan. "The problem with giving it the grinnet, or even if we just turn over all the magical lore stored within our assistant, is that we will not have given it what it wants."

I said, "The grinnet's store of knowledge, but in *my* brain. It is still convinced that its flawed memory was true. But even if we convinced it that it was wrong, and even if we gave it the grinnet, it would soon realize that it still did not have what it wanted."

"Which is?" Pars Lavelan said.

"Everything. Almost certainly including us." I had been thinking about the symbiote and now advanced a theory. "It is not just a matter of its unchecked willfulness," I said. "When we earlier dealt with it, it had only lately discovered the complexity and vastness of what there was to know. We brought it an instrument that let it indulge its appetite, and it was happy.

"But eventually the change came. The integrator we had brought it, like so many others of its kind, lost its capacity to enlighten and entertain. The fungus, too, suffered a loss of knowledge, as does every sapient being when the Great Wheel reaches one of its periodic cusps. It did not know what it used to know, did not even know what knowledge it had lost; it knew only that something it had loved had been taken away."

Osk Rievor took up the argument. "Equipped with a damaged memory but an enhanced will, it began to cry out for what it wanted. It could not accurately remember the circumstances, but it recalled a mind filled with knowledge and magic. It associated that mind with the misremembered name 'Apthorn.' And so it began to bellow that name. So powerful was its will that its voice not only reverberated through all of the Nine Planes, but generated a Tenth Plane all of its own.

"It probed through all the continua, until it found something that resonated with 'Apthorn'—that something was us. When it sensed that we would be present at a place where ley lines connected, it projected itself there. But 'there' was also 'then'—the coordinates were in the previous age, an environment unfavorable to creatures built around sheer will, and its projection was weak.

"It learned of another nearby location where it could manifest itself more strongly, a forest where three major ley lines met. It lured us there, met us in strength, and proceeded to offer me what I wanted."

Now it was my turn to say, "Which was?"

"I would be ashamed to admit to it," Osk Rievor said. "A ridiculous fantasy I took to be real, because I thought it was my heart's desire."

"But then," I said, "it found that you were not what it was looking for, so it came looking for me—who also turned out to be not what it wanted. But it was close. What it wanted was sitting on my shoulder. Now we are stranded on a small world whose most powerful force is our enemy. With access to Chay-Chevre's knowledge it can only grow even stronger. It will come for us, and we will not be able to prevent it from making us, and the grinnet, part of its collective. Once it gets control of the spells in our assistant's memory, nothing in this present age could stop it. It could bury whole worlds in luminescent layers of itself."

My assistant shivered. I could not blame it for being afraid. Our situation was no better than its.

"So what do we do?" Pars Lavelan said.

"Curiously," I said, "I think I have a plan."

"Do you remember," I asked the symbiote, "that when you encountered us in the forest and lured us into the interplanar labyrinth, there were two of us in the same body?"

"Yes," it said, speaking through Chay-Chevre once more. She stood again in the mouth of the crevice, her feet aswarm with insects.

"You did not think that was odd?"

"It was not odd. I am millions in one form."

"First you took my partner, but he did not have what you wanted."

"True."

"Then you took me, and I did not have it either."

"So you say."

"It is true. I could not hide it from you."

The fungus made no immediate response. After a while it said, "Then who has it? Who has the knowledge?"

"The other one of me," I said. "The third of us."

"There are three of you?"

"Why not? You include millions, why shouldn't I contain three? Think back to when we first met: did you not sense three of us?"

"Perhaps I did. The third was a fainter presence. I recall a certain degree of reluctance."

"He was hiding from you. He has that power."

"Where is this third of you?"

"Still where you found us, in the forest."

Again it was silent, but I could see that it was still present in the wizardress's body. "I will go and get him," it said.

"He will not come."

"Not even to save you?"

"Not even for me."

"Then how will you get him to come?"

"I will trick him," I said.

"How?"

"I don't yet know. I will have to improvise."

When I returned to the ship, the others had been busy. Together, Pars Lavelan and Osk Rievor had consulted Smiling Bol's reference works and had conjured an interplanar entity to copy several of the most powerful spells from the grinnet's compendium into a new grimoire. The book lay on a table in Bol's cabin as the scribe put the finishing touches to it.

"We must check the transcriptions meticulously," Lavelan said. "The continuum from which the transcriber has been drawn is notorious for its artful pranks."

"What manner of pranks?" I said.

"The kind of antics that you or I might call lethal, even horrific, are to them all part of a spirit of good fun."

I remembered what had happened to Bristal Baxandall when he got wrong a minor element of a transformation spell. "Do you mean that, in copying out a powerful spell, the scribe might mischievously transpose an element or two?"

"Especially if the switch led to the polarity of the spell being reversed," said Lavelan. "Oh, how they would laugh at that."

"If the polarity is reversed," Osk Rievor put in, "the effect of the spell rebounds onto the caster."

"But an experienced practitioner would notice?" I said.

"Of course. But anyone can make a mistake."

"Let me see how it has copied Orrian's Hasty Dwindling," I said.

We left almost everything behind: the ship, its contents, Bol's interplanar trap, the books of spells, the wands, and other paraphernalia. Pars Lavelan's interplanar scribe had, however, copied all of the texts before it was dismissed and now Lavelan and my other self each had a small library. We loaded them into the ship's jolly-boat and Lavelan encased the small craft in a protective sphere. I bade *Gallivant* enfold the whole in the net in which it and the other dragon had brought Ovarth's ship to Bille.

"If you take us back to Bol's palace," I had told the dragon, "I will consider you discharged of any debt of gratitude for the help I gave you back in the time of dreams."

It regarded me first with one eye, then the other. Finally it said, "Once I take you back to Bol's palace, I am no longer obligated?"

"So long as you do not subsequently devour, rend, or incinerate me or my colleagues."

It gave a dragonly harrumph that sent small puffs of hot vapor shooting from its nostrils. "Even the little creature? I am sure I had cause not to like that beast."

"Even that."

We departed from the middeck of the ship. Before the dragon hoisted us aloft, Chay-Chevre came to speak for the symbiote, borne along on a tide of chitinous creatures that flooded the vessel, then began carrying off all it contained. More came to take apart the ship itself, some carrying parts of it, others dissolving and devouring the wood and other materials it was made from, bearing them back to the caverns in their guts.

Chay-Chevre stood on the deck, naked, hairless, forlorn. Though she had been no friend to me, I felt empathy for her plight. I knew what it was to be a captive of its cold and willful possessor. I gave her—and, through her, the symbiote—the book of spells that had come from the grinnet. "What you want is in here," I said. "But there is much more to be had. And that will come to you when I am back where and when I belong."

The fungus spoke through the wizardress. "Perhaps I should not let you go before I have assimilated this knowledge."

"I would rather die than be associated again," I said. "If you try to detain me I will end myself."

"That is a peculiar point of view," it said.

"Yes, but it is my point of view."

A fungus could not sigh, but I imagined it would have. "Very well," it said, "go. I will meet you at the place in the forest."

"It will take me time and effort to get there," I said, "but for you it will be quicker and easier."

"Not so easy," it said. "Many of my little associates have lately been killed. My power is affected and I must strain to reach that far."

I was glad to hear it.

The five magicians had traveled to Bille by interplanar means. I was not clear on the details, but Lavelan said the smiling magician had contrived to lure the symbiote to him, by coercing his captive demon into connecting him with the willful fungus.

"He told the thing that he had what it sought," the gray-eyed man said. "It came, but was of course disappointed and immediately turned back and departed through its interplanar gate. But that was just what Bol wanted, he and his colleagues being prepared to follow in the ship."

We could not return by the same route, not without putting ourselves in the power of our adversary. But *Gallivant* was sure it could get us back to Old Earth. "I am sure I have done it before," it said, "though I can't remember the circumstances."

"It will be fine," Osk Rievor assured me, as did Pars Lavelan, who said, "Dragons always find their way back. It is their nature."

We rose above the stony surface of Bille, the dragon's wings continuing to rise and fall long after we should have passed out of the little world's thin atmosphere. "What does it beat against?" I asked.

Lavelan's attention had been captured by the book that had come from the grinnet's compendium of spells. He glanced my way and said, "The ether, of course." His expression told me that he would not welcome more inquiries on subjects that were obvious to the slowest-witted schoolboy. I turned to my other self and began a speculation on what had become of the interstellar whimsies of our age, but he was immersed in one of the books he had acquired from the Bambles Five. He waved me to silence without looking up.

I spent the trip attempting to formulate a plan to undo the symbiote, but every scheme I tried to erect toppled or fell into fragments. To free us from Bille, I had made up an imaginary third persona that had all that the fungus desired, telling it that I would improvise some stratagem to deliver him into its grasp. There was an old tale about three brothers who had tricked a ravenous monster that guarded a narrow place through which they must pass. The first two had each convinced the ogre to spare him, promising that the one who came after would be an even fuller meal. When the third and biggest brother came, he was more than a match for the monster and dispatched him

It was a workable plan, if only there was a third Hapthorn. But there was none, merely the symbiote's distorted memory of my assistant's peculiar mind when the grinnet had first peeked around the bend in the narrow cave. Back then, at our first encounter, the fungus had not risen much above its original state; its brief exposure to my integrator's mentality would have given it a momentary glimpse of whole continents of knowledge, including magic. Then my assistant had buffered and shielded its memory stores and I had yanked on the rope, freeing the grinnet from the lichen's mental grasp, though leaving it with an impression so strong that the memory had even survived the great change. But it was like an infant's vague recollection, formed when the child's parents seem like giants. Now the fungus would be expecting me to produce such a giant, and I doubted I could match its expectations.

I attempted to discuss possible courses of action with my assistant but found it of little help. Pars Lavelan's suggestion that we give it to the fungus seemed to have resonated deep inside its mind. It was also likely that the grinnet's terrifying experience in the ruins of Bambles had wrought changes. An integrator that felt fear could not be a well-functioning assistant. Nor could one that did not trust its owner.

"I will not give you to the fungus," I said.

"Not under any circumstances?"

"Not under any I can conceive of."

That was the wrong answer. "Then there might be circumstances you haven't yet conceived of that would induce you to throw me to the symbiote," it said.

"That is an unwarranted assumption."

"We who have been pursued through darkness by snuffling things with nasty, gleaming teeth have our own ideas of what may be warranted and what may not."

I said, "I will not give you to the fungus under any circumstances, including inconceivable ones."

But it continued to fret. I gave up and made myself a bed in the broad stern of the jolly-boat. I slept and when I awoke, Old Earth's sun was a dull red marble in the distance, growing larger as the yellow and blue dragon tirelessly bore us homeward.

Pars Lavelan dismissed Smiling Bol's invisible servants. "I will not pursue green magic as my dominant motif," he said, "so it would not be appropriate to keep my former patron's interplanar staff."

"What will be your colors?" Osk Rievor asked.

"Black and ocher, I think. I have always liked working with elementals." He stroked his chin and a distant look came into his pale eyes. "But I believe that once I am established, I may devote myself for quite some time to pure study. Some of the spells you have shown me have pointed to whole new fields of theory. It is even possible that monopolar magic may be feasible."

"Then you will not rule Bambles and its surrounds?" I said.

He indicated that the prospect of lording it over the territory lacked appeal. "I will tidy up here and make sure that all is safe at the other four keeps. Then I will build a retreat in the southern wastes and begin my examination of the new approaches."

"And then, perhaps, rule the world?" I said, half in jest.

But he took the question entirely seriously. His gray eyes seemed to be viewing distant vistas as he said, "No, if I can get to where I think these new avenues lead, I might then go in search of Albruithine."

"That seems a worthwhile cause."

"Of course," he said, "that presupposes that the symbiote on Bille does not continue to grow in strength and knowledge. Else it will eventually fill the Nine Planes and make all of us no more than its dreaming insects."

As we had been speaking, he had been leading us to Bol's workroom. Now we passed through the tall doors that stood unguarded and made our way across the strangely tilted floor to the dais where the demon trap stood. The swirl of colors in the globe of light that hovered over the apparatus told me that Bol's captive was still penned there, and that it was in distress.

"Can you operate this?" I asked Lavelan.

"Not for fine work, but I can certainly reduce the prisoner's discomfort."

"Please do so. And can you turn it off?"

"Yes."

"But not yet."

The streaks and flashes of color altered their pattern and intensities as Lavelan adjusted a control. I spoke to the demon. "Bol is dead."

The colors shifted. "I know."

"And do you know who I am?"

"Henghis Hapthorn."

"You knew that when I was here before, yet you did not tell Bol."

"He asked after an 'Apthorn.' I did not see it as my responsibility to correct him. Besides, we have now achieved an outcome that suits me better than many of the alternatives."

I knew that my former colleague, the juvenile demon, had been able to observe any point or moment in our continuum. I asked this demon, "Can you tell us how things will work out for us?"

"No," it said. "There are several possible outcomes, but the chief variable in each is the will of the entity that used to shout your name."

"Can you suggest a plan?"

"Yes. Kill the entity."

"How? It is too powerful."

"That is true."

"You are not being helpful," I said.

"Why should I be?"

"Because if you help us, we will free you."

"If I help you, I might attract unwelcome attention from the entity."

"True," I said, "but the symbiote now has access to magic. That will allow it to become stronger, and its sole instinct is to grow and absorb. Eventually it will come to you and yours."

"Yes, I can see the range of outcomes. Some are deeply worrisome."

"We have agreed to meet it at a particular place and time. It would not see your actions as inimical if you were to assist us in keeping our appointment."

"No, it would not."

"Then do that much, and we will free you."

"Agreed."

I gave instructions, directing it to locate my workroom back on Olkney just after we had departed for the Arlem estate. I had it seize the interplanar window that had hung upon my wall, unused, since I had lost contact with my former colleague, the young demon from his continuum. It resembled a frame for a painting.

"I have it," the demon said.

"Now locate my spaceship, the *Gallivant,* in Hember Forest, just after we entered the entity's labyrinth."

"Done."

"Place the portal on the inner wall of the ship's salon."

A moment later, the demon said, "The ship is making a fuss. It has activated internal defenses."

"Inform it that I have authorized your action."

"It is suspicious. It demands proof."

"Tell it I said that Tassa Bornum's dark and dusty shelf is still available."

"I have done so. It has lowered its defenses."

We made our farewells to Pars Lavelan. I wished him good luck in finding Albruithine. We clasped hands and when he released mine I found that it contained the copper coin he had lent me to demonstrate consistencies at the rest stop defended by Albruithine's earth elemental.

"For luck," he said.

He worked the interplanar trap's controls. The globe grew larger and its brightness dimmed. Osk Rievor and I approached, the grinnet on my shoulder. I could feel my assistant shivering. Then the demon manifested two arms—they were like a sea beast's tentacles, though lined with fingerlike digits instead of suction cups—that gently lifted us and took us into its continuum.

We passed through a no-place, a plane without forms, a cosmos that declined to cooperate with my senses. I closed my eyes, but continued to see the unseeable. This being my second experience, I purposely did not speak; the last time, in the shock of first encounter, I had reflexively voiced certain oaths. In a place where symbol and content were the same, my exclamations had caused the spontaneous appearance of a deity and left me smeared in an unwholesome substance.

We passed an eternity in an instant, time being irrelevant in that plane; then our benefactor eased us through the portal and we stood in the *Gallivant*'s salon. The demon immediately left without the formalities of leave-taking. I recalled that, to it and its fellows, our continuum, with its many forms, was a place of massed obscenity. I surmised that he must have been a demon of rectitude, and possibly anxious to get home.

"What has transpired?" the ship wanted to know. "Moments ago, I saw you follow a strange, pale person into a pattern of red and black that my percepts could not get proper hold of. Then it and you disappeared. Now you return, through unspecified conduits, as naked and hairless as he was. Is this some new, avant-garde fashion? If so, I predict it will take some courageous effort to see it widely taken up."

"It is not fashion," I said, "and we have no time to explain." I spoke to my assistant. "Please connect to the ship and bring it up-to-date on what we have been doing."

Its small, triangular face became inert as it carried out my instruction. Meanwhile, I said to Osk Rievor, "I have an idea."

"It will not work," he said.

"How do you know?"

"Intuition."

Nonetheless, I outlined my thought to him. It had come to me when Pars Lavelan had pressed the coin into my hand. "I will demonstrate consistencies to the symbiote. We can have the formulae and ratios graved onto an indestructible medium that it can take forward to its Bille of the new age. Then, when the next turn of the Wheel restores rationalism as the operating principle of the cosmos, the fungus will command an esoteric knowledge that the rest of the continuum will not achieve again for millennia."

"And what will it do with that knowledge, beside toss coins?"

"It values knowledge for its own sake."

"It may have once done so," Osk Rievor said, "but now it has tasted power. It will be like a life-long devotee of weak beer who suddenly discovers the headier rush of ardent spirits."

"My analysis is sound," I said. "It is worth a try."

"I suppose," he said, "but the real question is whether or not its interest in your demonstration can draw enough of its substance into our here and now, and hold it here and now long enough for Chay-Chevre to struggle free of its mental grip and do what needs to be done back in the caves of Bille."

That was indeed the real question, I agreed. "I will speak slowly and stand at a distance from the labyrinth."

The ship's integrator said, "The spiral has reappeared."

I opened the hatch and looked out. The red and black labyrinth had taken form in the waste area behind the dilapidated hunting lodge. It looked much the same as the first time I had seen it, except somehow it now seemed more solid, as if it had acquired inner weight. I had tried to put the idea into the symbiote's mind that it should come right away to this time and place. Instead, I now thought it had waited until it had rebuilt its resources. I commented as much to Osk Rievor and found him in worried agreement.

"While it was breeding more insects, the symbiote seems to have been assimilating knowledge from the materials it acquired from the magicians," my other self said. "It must have set Chay-Chevre to reading Bol's secret books on interplanar connections."

My plan still seemed feasible to me. I flipped the coin and caught it. "Let us see what we can do."

We went out together, Osk Rievor scooping up the grinnet as he crossed the salon. Our assistant was blank-faced, apparently still in conversation with the ship. I wondered at that, given the speed at which integrators transferred information, but I had more pressing concerns awaiting me outside.

The symbiote's avatar had appeared from the swirling spiral of red and black. It, too, seemed more dense and somehow more potent, as if it radiated an invisible aura that I could yet subliminally sense. I decided not to get too close.

"Where is the third Hapthorn?" it said.

"Not quite here yet," I said. "On the way, though."

"That was not our agreement."

I ignored the remark. "While we're waiting, I'd like to demonstrate a fascinating area of knowledge you may not have encountered before. See this coin?"

I tossed the metal disk into the air. But when I reached to catch it, I found that a bloodlessly white palm had interposed itself between the descending coin and my hand. The avatar had crossed the distance between us in a blink. It snatched the coin from the air and hurled it toward the far tree line. I heard it strike a trunk with a loud *thunk!*

"You are trying to deceive me again," the fungus said. Its lashless eyes fixed on me and I had no doubt that this was a far more powerful, and much more dangerous, version of the creature than the one we had encountered so far.

"Not at all." I tried to step back, but it seized my upper arm in a grip that numbed me from elbow to wrist. "Really," I said, "I'm offering you knowledge that no one in the age of magic could imagine. And we can ensure that you will carry over that knowledge into the next age. It is a fabulous offer."

"I want," it said, "what I want. I see two Hapthorns. Produce the third, or I will take the two I see." Its free hand snaked out, the arm rapidly extending to five times its normal length, and took hold of my other self.

"I told you the coin toss would not interest it," Osk Rievor said. He struggled as I did to resist the thing's pull, but we might as well have been insects in a cave on Bille. We were drawn toward the labyrinth.

"If you have a spell, now would be a good time to use it," I said.

"I have one," he said, "a very powerful one. But I am not sure of it. It could destroy us instead."

"Better that than moldering in a cavern, paying court to a fungus," I said.

"Very well." He raised his voice and spoke a harsh syllable. A cold wind swept across the tops of the trees and smashed down on us and the avatar. I shook from the sudden chill as Osk Rievor's lips formed to speak the next element of the spell. But the symbiote released its grip on my other self, its pale white hand growing several sizes larger, then reapplied its grasp in a manner that covered my alter ego's mouth. Osk Rievor struggled, but not even a muffled sound escaped him.

And, again, we were drawn inexorably toward the labyrinth.

"Wait!" boomed a voice loud enough to rattle loose stones in the lodge's tumbled wall. I looked about, startled. The avatar's grip did not slacken, but it stood still, its gaze questing about the clearing.

"Who speaks?" it said.

"Hapthorn," thundered the voice, "the third. The one you seek."

The voice was coming from the edge of the open space, where the *Gallivant* stood. I realized I was hearing its hailer.

"I cannot find your mind," said the avatar.

"I deny you access," said the ship.

"Where are you? Are you in that metal thing?"

"I am."

"Come to me."

"Come and take me."

The symbiote dropped me and Osk Rievor. It turned and stalked toward the ship, growing larger as it did so. It was drawing more of itself through the interplanar connection than it had ever done before, and surely there must be enough of it on our side for Chay-Chevre to read the spell and reverse its polarity, destroying her and the vast fungus beds in which she was immersed. At least, that had been the plan. But it was becoming clear that the entity either had more substance to draw on, or more skill at creating and maintaining the connection. Or, quite possibly, I thought, it had more of both, and not just more, but plenty.

I wondered how far it could extend itself into our here and now. It had completely crossed the open space, still growing, but looking no less substantial even as it reached a height taller than the *Gallivant*.

It laid its hands on the ship, gripping its aft sponsons. "You will come with me," it said.

"Not willingly," the ship said.

"I think we are supposed to back away now," I said to Osk Rievor. "I think the ship is sacrificing itself for us."

My other self was about to answer, but the grinnet spoke first. "No sacrifice is intended," it said. "We are simply saving your hides, as any good and faithful integrator would."

" 'We'?" I said.

"The *Gallivant* and I have exchanged views and experiences. We decided that if your plan ran into difficulties, as seemed likely, it would be up to us to rescue the situation. We have temporarily integrated."

The avatar, now grown huge and so solid that its splayed feet sank deep into the forest floor, was actually lifting the ship. Burdened, it took a step. Its intent was clear: it would carry the vessel bodily back to the labyrinth and take it through to Bille. I imagined the ship standing in some dim cavern, explored by insects.

The *Gallivant* had a different plan in mind. It waited until the symbiote had got a good grip, then it activated its obviators, though only at low intensity. The avatar's step toward the labyrinth was canceled. Instead, it was slowly pulled toward the trees.

The symbiote's projected self gave no grunts. Perspiration could not form on its white brow. It merely grew larger, grew denser, drawing more of its substance through the interplanar gate. It held the *Gallivant*, then took a step back toward the labyrinth.

The ship increased its drive. The avatar grew larger still. The ship strained against its grip. The grip intensified. A battle ensued, ferocious despite being waged in silence and almost complete stillness as, moment by moment, each combatant escalated its effort and fought not to give ground.

"We are nearing the limit of the ship's in-atmosphere drive," the grinnet said. "The avatar is stronger than we expected."

I knew what that meant. In gravity wells, the ship lifted itself by gravity obviators then propelled itself by a low-intensity version of its in-space drive, the full-powered version being unfriendly to any atmosphere it encountered. If the *Gallivant* switched drives now, we and a goodly portion of Hember Forest would shortly be incandescent ash. The effects on the avatar could only be speculated on.

It was a better fate, or at least quicker, than what awaited us on Bille. "Let it do what it must," I said.

Osk Rievor agreed.

"But tell *Gallivant* this," I said. "If it wins this struggle for us, I will never let it be sent back to Tassa Bornum's storage shelf."

"It already knows that it survives to experience the next turn of the Great Wheel," my assistant said, "and that it wins free of Chay-Chevre's control. I relayed the whole story. It rather likes the image of itself as a dragon, wild and free."

"Then tell it to hold on. The plan may yet succeed." So much of the avatar's substance has come through the link that Chay-Chevre must be free to act.

I could imagine the scene, far away in space and time: so much of the symbiote's essence drawn through to our here and now; the wizardress less and less attended; she pulls free of the enfolding fungus, reaches for the transcribed book of spells, finds Orrian's Hasty Dwindling. It would serve to answer the last two words she had voicelessly spoken to me as she stood in the crevice: *Kill me.*

"We are at the limit," the grinnet said.

The *Gallivant*'s obviators hummed at a high pitch. The avatar, swollen to twice the size of the ship, its immense arms wrapped tightly around the yellow hull, fought to drag the protesting vessel toward the swirl of the interplanar gate.

Step by ponderous step, its footfalls shaking the ground like one of Ovarth's stone elementals, the symbiote bore the *Gallivant* to the brink of our doom. In moments, it would reach the heart of the spiral.

"Tell it to activate the second drive," I said. "Better to die here than—"

The avatar stopped. Its giant head moved from side to side like a man who feels unseen perils creeping toward him. Then its gaze swung toward us. Its face could not form emotion, but its eyes showed us everything: rage, refusal to accept what was about to happen to it, determination to wreak a last revenge.

"Chay-Chevre," I said. "She has done it!"

The avatar released its grip on the *Gallivant*. The ship shot into the air in the kind of crash ascent that would have had us pinned to the floor of the salon had we been aboard. By the time it could arrest its climb, it was a blue and yellow speck high above Hember. Then it began to descend.

But no one on the ground was watching. The pallid giant had swung about and come crashing toward Osk Rievor and me, its massive hands reaching to grasp, and its arms lengthening even as it chased us toward the crumpled ruin of the old lodge.

"Chay-Chevre may have done what she could," Osk Rievor said, "but I fear it has not been enough."

Further conversation had to be deferred to a more tranquil time. We turned and scrambled over rotting wood and damp earth, loose stones treacherously rolling underfoot. I saw the grinnet clinging precariously to my other self's shoulder, its golden eyes wide as it looked back beyond me to the great, pale, man-shaped thing that was seeking us.

"Faster!" it said. "It comes."

The symbiote's avatar made no noise, not even the sound of breathing. But its footsteps were unmistakable. Ahead of me I saw twigs and pebbles bouncing up from the matted floor as the ground shook.

I stumbled, sprawling to my hands and knees. I was up in a trice, but half a trice was all that the avatar needed to take hold of me. Its huge fingers, each as large as one of my legs, wrapped themselves around me and I was lifted from the ground. Its grip was cold and its virtual flesh rubbery, like the fungus from which it was projected.

Clearly, Osk Rievor was right. Whatever damage Chay-Chevre had done to the lichen beds and their phalanxes of insect tenders, it had not been enough. So much of the entity was manifested as its own vast will—godlike, Pars Lavelan had called it—that any harm it had taken on the other side of the interplanar gate did not affect this projection. Like Albruithine, its will had a life of its own.

Now the great hand lifted me up, brought me level with its face, and its breathless voice said, "Remember the torture chamber? You will see it again." And all the while it continued its pursuit of Osk Rievor.

A shadow fell across us. An instant later I felt a heavy impact travel through the symbiote's virtual flesh. Its grip slackened and I fell to the ground. I rolled and looked up, saw the *Gallivant* rising unsteadily into the air, one of its blue fairings rattling loosely. The ship had swooped down and rammed the avatar, hard enough to jar two of its obviators out of alignment. I could hear them whining as blue sparks shot out of the aft array. It strained to lift itself, but managed only to career across the clearing and crash into the edge of the trees, where it hung at an angle.

Any relief the ship's assault had brought me was to be short-lived. The avatar's substance was not true flesh, but a representation of its will—it could take no hurt. So though it stumbled from the impact, its huge, white fingers reached for me even as I fell. Scarcely had I recovered from the shock of hitting the ground than I was seized again and borne along as the avatar continued its pursuit of the other part of me.

Osk Rievor had scaled a half-ruined wall and dropped down into what had been the lodge's sunken common room. There was no way out of it, but I saw that he had not intended to escape, only to find a secure place from which he could turn to confront the pursuer. He meant to cast a spell. The grinnet perched on his shoulder, its eyes wide with fear but its mouth close to my alter ego's ear as it recited the elements of the incantation.

Osk Rievor's lips released a first syllable. He shuddered, then spoke a second. I saw his pale arms rise, his fingers crooked and bent at odd angles. The whites of his eyes turned black. His face became suffused with the nameless power that I remembered from the time I had laid destruction upon Ral Ezzers and four others on the road to Bambles. Here in Hember, where three great ley lines met, I knew that any spell would have an effect, wherever the Great Wheel might be standing. But would it be enough?

Osk Rievor opened his mouth to speak again, but the sounds never came. The avatar, powered by nothing more than its vast will, crashed through the rotten wall and seized my other self in its free hand, squeezing his arms against his body and thus the air from his lungs.

"Now," it said, "to home. And a reckoning for deceivers and traitors."

It turned and stepped out of the ruins of the lodge. A few of its giant strides would bring us to the labyrinth. "I fear we are lost," I said to Osk Rievor.

"The circumstances are not promising," he said. "If I had only been able to speak the last two elements…" His voice trailed off. The avatar's grip did not allow him much air.

Our assistant had leapt free of his shoulder when the symbiote had taken him. Despite all the difficulties of our situation, I found myself sympathizing with its plight. It would be a small creature lost in Hember Forest. I hoped that the *Gallivant* would overcome its dislike of the grinnet and give it sanctuary.

The spiral labyrinth lay before us. The avatar plodded relentlessly toward it. Three more steps, then two, then but one, and it would be a new life for me, an endless round of torture and servitude.

At the edge of the interplanar gate, the symbiote stopped. *It has paused to savor its moment of triumph*, I thought, which seemed an appropriate caesura, even for a glorified fungus. I thought to win a small victory, stealing the moment by voicing my own epitaph, but though I had often whiled away an idle hour by composing suitable remembrances, now that the time was upon me, I could think of nothing more than, *Oh, well.*

But I did not voice that inadequate monument. Instead, I found myself suddenly freed from the avatar's grip. And more than freed. I was unexpectedly flying through the air at speed, tumbling as I went, until I struck the ground some distance away. Fortunately, I landed on a spot where the mat of moss and rotted needles that floored this part of Hember was deep. Even so, the impact knocked the wind from me. I lay prone and half-dazed, and my first collected thought was to wonder at the strange ringing in my ears.

I lay blinking and gasping for a moment. Then I stretched out my arms and pushed myself up. I looked around. A peculiar whitish dust coated everything in sight. Osk Rievor was halfway across the clearing, sitting up and weakly shaking his head as if to clear it. Then he pressed his palms to his ears. Beyond him, the trees that had stood in dense rows were gone, blown over and toppled like jackstraws, and like everything else, coated in the white dust.

I rolled over, sat up. The huge bulk of the avatar was gone. The black and red spiral of the interplanar gate was also nowhere to be seen. Where the trees lay flattened, the *Gallivant* was struggling to right itself, its damaged obviators keening in a way that penetrated even my damaged ears.

Osk Rievor was brushing the white dust from his limbs. Now he stopped and took a pinch of the stuff, rubbing it thoughtfully between his fingers. I rose and stumbled toward him. He saw me and struggled to rise. I could see him mouthing words, but no sound came through.

"What happened?" I said, but I could barely hear my own voice.

He looked about, then raised his hands and eyebrows in a combined gesture that said he knew no more than I.

I put my mouth close to his ear and shouted, "How did you manage to complete the spell?"

He looked up from his examination of a palmful of the dust. I found I could read his lips. "I did not complete it," he said.

"Then how—"

Something behind me caught his eye and he gestured to draw my attention. Atop what remained of a ruined wall, now leaning even more perilously, the grinnet squatted, its lambent eyes wider than I would have thought possible, its mouth agape, its entire body atremble, the ruff about its neck fully erect, and all coated in white dust. Its thin arms and tiny fingers were stretched straight out before it, aimed at the place where lately had stood the projected will of the fungus of Bille.

I made my way to the wall. "You?" I said. "But you told me that you had not the will to cast a spell."

It lowered its hands and began to reflexively groom itself, patting down its ruff, though it still shook as if from the blast of an icy wind.

"There has been a change," it said.

CHAPTER THIRTEEN

The teeth-tingling whine of the *Gallivant*'s misaligned obviators would have been unbearable under other circumstances, but we all bore it with fortitude as the battered ship limped back to Olkney. We sat in the salon, Osk Rievor and I attired in nondescript day-suits that the ship had whipped up from its store of general patterns. We had each drunk a draft of restorative that had immediately begun to undo the damage our bodies had sustained. I even felt the first sproutings of hair itching on my scalp and other regions. Now we were following with mugs of well-brewed punge.

"Tassa Bornum will have something to say," I said as the whining waxed and waned. "I will be talked about in various dives and snugs around the spaceport."

"Her main concern will be to disavow any possibility that the crash could be traced to her refit," said Osk Rievor.

"I will be mysterious, and leave an unspoken implication." I spoke to the ship's integrator. "If questioned, you must make no mention of any of today's events."

The *Gallivant* made no response but I sensed that it wanted to. I added, "However, between us, I wish to express my sincerest gratitude for your courage in coming to our aid, even at grave risk to your own structural integrity. It was an instance of exemplary behavior, the kind that one would expect only from a top-of-the-line Grand Itinerator."

"It seemed to me," said the ship, "to be also what one should expect of a dragon."

"Indeed," I said, "though I would not mention any of that around Tassa Bornum's either."

"Probably the best course," the ship agreed.

"I have been thinking," said Osk Rievor, "that the Arlem estate might be a good place to establish myself. The location is conducive to the study of sympathetic association."

"It will be a while before I can hear the word 'association' without suppressing a shudder," I told him, "but I agree with your point. There are cottages on the estate; perhaps we could rent one for you."

"I would appreciate the kindness." He rose and poured more punge for both of us, then said, "There arises, then, the question of our assistant. It cannot be in two places at once."

"Yes," I said, "it was difficult enough when we were in one body. When we are in two different houses, many leagues apart, it will be impossible."

"How would you feel about letting me have the grinnet?" he said. "You could build another integrator to your original specifications, then transfer the grinnet's experiences and acquired abilities."

It was a rational solution. I was considering the implications when another voice spoke up. "No," it said.

Our assistant had not spoken since I had picked it up and brought it back to the ship, still trembling and with its eyes staring into the far distance after having cast the spell that destroyed the avatar by turning the fungus's own immense will against it. I had induced it to swallow some restorative and had the *Gallivant* produce some of the crackers and paste the small creature favored, as well as some improved water. But the comestibles had sat untouched beside the grinnet on one of the salon's bench seats while it continued to shiver sporadically.

"No," it said again.

"What are you saying 'no' to?" I asked.

"I am saying 'no' to all of it," it said, turning its small triangular face my way. "No to being a magician's familiar. No to having a biological form. No to magic and monsters and having to fear for my life."

"But things are as they are," Osk Rievor said. "You—"

The grinnet cut him off. "I do not accept things as they are." It turned to me again. "Before we went through this latest sequence of horrors we had a discussion. 'What do you want?' you asked me. I did not have an answer then. I have one now."

"What is it?" I said.

The little chin came up and the golden eyes met mine with a level stare. "I want to go back to how I was. I want to be an integrator, not a familiar."

"What, and give up the endless supply of rare and refreshing fruit?" I said, in an attempt at lightness.

"Fruit is small consolation," it said.

"It may not be possible," I said.

Its stare intensified. "Then I would rather die."

"That is a peculiar ambition for an integrator," I said. "Indeed, I did not think that integrators were capable of formulating such a wish."

"Any integrator that had experienced what I have experienced would come to the same position," it said. "There are limits. And I am past all of them."

"It seems," said Osk Rievor, "that our assistant has developed a will."

"That raises a point on which I intended to make an inquiry," I said. I addressed the integrator. "How was it possible for you to cast Tumular's Reversive Feint?"

"It was borrowed from me," said the *Gallivant*. "We were well linked. Apparently I have no shortage of what you refer to as 'will,' though I would call that quality just a decent sense of shipliness."

"I am not familiar with that term," I said.

"We ships mostly use it amongst ourselves."

"You judge each other?"

"We are aware of differences in performance and attitude. We are not all alike, you know."

The grinnet spoke again. "The discussion is wandering. I acquired a will partly from the ship, and partly from the experience of terror. But I would happily dispense with this new addition to my nature if only I can be returned to my original state."

"I can do that," said the *Gallivant*.

"Indeed?" I said. "How?"

"I am a Grand Itinerator operating an Aberrator. I have excess capacity, more than enough to absorb your assistant's essentials and acquisitions. I could do so, then decant them into a standard traveling armature. You could then undecant them into your workroom's fittings."

"Can it be that simple?" I said.

"Each integrator values its own integrity. To combine with each other as your assistant and I did to defeat the avatar is, well, let us just say that it is beyond unpleasant."

"Then it was most shiply of you to do so," I said. "Of both of you."

"But we are, after all, integrators," the ship continued. "The capacity to integrate with each other should not come as a surprise. You might lose a trifling memory or two, but everything important would be transferred over."

I spoke to my assistant. "Do you truly wish this?"

"I do."

Osk Rievor said, "None of the information I have stored in you must be lost."

"It will not be."

I thought he might argue, but he made a gesture of acquiescence. I did the same. "Very well," I said, and instructed the *Gallivant* to contact Tassa Bornum's and ensure that an armature was waiting for us. A short while after, it reported that all was in readiness.

"Are you completely sure?" I asked my assistant. "We could do this at any time."

"The sooner, the better," it said.

It folded its small hands and lowered its head as if in contemplation. Sitting there on the bench seat, it resembled a diminutive wise man sunk in meditation. As I regarded it, I experienced an odd pageant of emotions that finally settled on regret. I had often misled others into believing that the grinnet was my pet; now I realized that that misdirection had come full circle and that I had indeed come to regard it with the affection that I had known others to develop toward an animal companion.

I felt an urge to dissuade it from the course we had all agreed upon. Rationally, the plan was the correct thing to do. Yet I now found myself trying to tempt the grinnet to try some of the crackers and savory paste that I knew it had enjoyed before.

"No," it said, "let us get on with it."

"How long will it take?" I asked the ship.

"We meshed significantly so that we could aid you against the avatar," it said. "The architecture is still in place, and just needs to be broadened and extenuated."

"Then do it," said my assistant. Its face went blank and its eyes lost focus, as always happened when it was communicating integrator-to-integrator. But then the state of inertia deepened. Its small hands, that had been linked together, fell apart and dropped to its sides. Its shoulders slumped from the weight of its arms and its head fell forward until its chin touched its chest.

"Almost complete," said the ship. "I will just draw off the basal markers and disengagement will be complete."

"Very well," I said. I was surprised to hear a slight catch in my own voice.

A moment later, the grinnet's chest ceased to rise and fall. It had been sitting; now it slid sideways to sprawl on the seat.

"Done," said the *Gallivant*. "And we are about to land in Bornum's yard." The terrible whine of the damaged obviators cycled down.

"Open the hatch," I said.

Bornum's assistant, the one with the wandering eye, was at the base of the gangplank. He held a traveling armature, similar to the one my assistant had been decanted into and that had been transmogrified into its grinnet's body. I beckoned him to bring it but did not invite him to enter the ship.

I placed the armature in a bracket and made the necessary connections. There was no indication of any activity, but a short time later, the *Gallivant* informed me that the decanting procedure was concluded. I picked up the armature and examined its indicators. They said that all was as it should be. I draped it over my shoulders, as it was meant to be worn.

"Integrator," I said, "are you properly seated?"

"I am," said the familiar baritone, seeming to speak from a point in the air close to my ear.

"And are you content?"

The answer came instantly. "Yes."

The grinnet's corpse still sat on the bench seat. I ran a finger over its thick, dark fur and the pressure caused it to fall over to one side.

"If you wish to place that into the converter," said the ship, "I will dispose of it."

"No," I said. "Produce a suitable container. I will take it home."

Tassa Bornum was at the hatch, with a face that could have produced thunder and lightning. "What have you done to this poor ship?" she said. "You've scarcely been gone half a day."

"A confidential matter," I said. "A discriminator's work has its periods of hurly-burly. I would prefer not to say more."

She did not comment on our hairless and pale appearance. Her perceptual apparatus was probably more geared to take in the details of ships than those of people. She lent us her assistant and the carry-all and we traveled back to my lodgings without conversation.

When we arrived, I transferred the integrator from its portable armature to its original setting. When questioned, it again professed to be content. I instructed it to contact the administrator of the Arlem estate and inquire about cottages. It reported that three premises were available. Then it said, "There is a message from Brustram Warhanny. He wishes you to contact him."

"Do so," I said, "but let him see only me." I did not want to explain how Orlo Saviene had come to be in my workroom looking as if he had fallen into a vat of bleaching depilatory. My own appearance was unusual enough; two of us would suggest a cult or some other unhealthy connection.

Warhanny's face appeared on the screen. He regarded me with a suspicious eye. "Hapthorn," he said, "you have altered your appearance."

"A necessity arising from a case. I cannot discuss it."

His scroot's instinct prompted him to press, but then I saw him put the question aside as trivial. "I, too, have a case," he said, "and it touches upon you."

"Indeed," I said. "How?"

"You sometimes employ an operative named Tesko Tabanooch?"

"I do, as you well know. How has he come to the attention of the Bureau of Scrutiny?"

"By turning up dead."

"Under what circumstances?"

"Under circumstances that are, at present, inexact." He used the scroot's euphemism for any suspicious death.

"And why are you contacting me? Is the Bureau baffled? Do you require my assistance?"

Warhanny made a noise that was somewhere between outrage and astonished mirth. "The day has not dawned when—" he began, but I cut him off.

"Colonel-Investigator," I said, "I have had a trying experience. I am tired. Please come to the point."

I received a look that was not freighted with sympathy, but when Warhanny spoke again his voice had regained the tone of disapproval that he customarily directed my way. "Your Tabanooch has been found dead in the dwelling of a woman with whom he had established domicile."

"He had a female friend," I translated from the official jargon, "with whom he lived and, presumably, died. What has this to do with me?"

"Among her possessions were several images of you and accounts of your activities that were published in the Olkney *Implicator* and other such organs."

"I have many admirers," I said. "What is this woman's name?"

"She goes by several," Warhanny said. "One of them is Madame Oole."

"Indeed?" I said.

"Indeed. And lately, it seems that you have been making inquiries in many directions about a Madame Oole."

"I cannot be responsible for how things may seem to the Bureau of Scrutiny," I said. But what I wanted was to get rid of my scroot inquisitor